glas

NEW
RUSSIAN
WRITING

4

Editor: **Natasha Perova**
UK editor: **Dr. Arch Tait**
US editor: **Ed Hogan**

Literary Consultants:
Sally Laird, Andrew Bromfield, Yuri Sorokin, Tom Birchenough

Designed by **Emma Ippolitova**
Cover illustration: **Elena Mukhanova**

Photographs: Vladimir Shishov, Eduard Nikiforov, Alexander Karzanov, Nikolai Kochnev, R. Netelev, Eduard Kudryavitsky, Oleg Smirnov

GLAS Publishers, Moscow 119517, P.O.Box 47, Russia
UK address for enquiries, subscriptions and payments:
GLAS, c/o Dept. of Russian Literature,
University of Birmingham, B15 2TT
Tel.: 021-414 6044, Fax: 021-414 5966
North America Sales and Editorial office, GLAS
c/o Zephyr Press, 13 Robinson Street, Somerville MA 02145
Tel: (617) 628-9726, Fax: (617) 776-8246

ISBN 5-7172-0002-1
ISBN 0-939010-35-6 (US)
U.S. Price $9.95
U.K. Price £6.45

©Translation copyright, 1993 by GLAS

Издание этого номера осуществлено за счет средств русских и иностранных редакторов.

Contents

Victor PELEVIN. The Blue Lantern 14
Mid-game 25
The View from the Window 44
Zufar GAREYEV. Facsimile Summer 52
Yevgeny KHARITONOV. Teardrops on the Flowers 66
Vladimir MAKANIN. Klyucharyov And Alimushkin 88
Friedrich GORENSTEIN. Bag in Hand 116
Zinovy ZINIK. Mea Culpa 138
Yuri MILOSLAVSKY. The Death of Manon 154
On Exile 163
Lev RAZGON. The President's Wife 170

Communal Living

Boris YAMPOLSKY. A Crowded Place 182
Ksenia KLIMOVA, Elena SALINA. A Marriage of Convenience 185
Alexander TEREKHOV. Communal Living 188
Pitch Black Void 191

Poetry:

Marina TSVETAEVA 205
Gleb ARSENYEV 211
Olga SEDAKOVA 221
Alla LATYNINA. The Literary Prize and the Literary Process 228

About the Authors 236

> "Stay, fleeting moment!..."
> Goethe, Faust

Just as love is very much part of any human life, for the soviet citizen it was often accompanied by another equally powerful emotion — fear. For various reasons, as this collection shows, the two have always gone hand in hand in Russia. Here love is seen from various angles: the imprisonment of the first Soviet president's wife under Stalin (Razgon), homosexual love punishable by Soviet law (Kharitonov), unrequited love driving man to disaster (Makanin), adolescent longing for love and the fear of rejection (Gareyev), an old granny's love for the shopping bag which is her provider (Gorenstein), love as adventure and misunderstanding (Zinik), anti-love among the dregs of society (Miloslavsky), trans-sexuals' surreal experiences (Pelevin), and love in that typically Soviet institution, the communal flat.

Each person models his or her own world to live in, alone with oneself. Only writing gives us a chance to discover these innumerable unique worlds — from cancer wards to prison camps, those hells on earth to which we are drawn by a strange fascination. Literature has been written for centuries, yet each generation's authors still manage to find new angles of vision and new literary idioms. This has been amply demonstrated by the recent awarding of the first Russian Booker Prize. Two short listed authors — Makanin and Gorenstein — have been included in this issue, while Vladimir Sorokin, another shortlisted author, was published in the second issue of Glas. The closing interview with Alla Latynina, the first chairman of the Russian Booker Prize jury, gives a reflection into Russia's literary scene today. Despite Russia's present problems, the literary process continues.

Editors

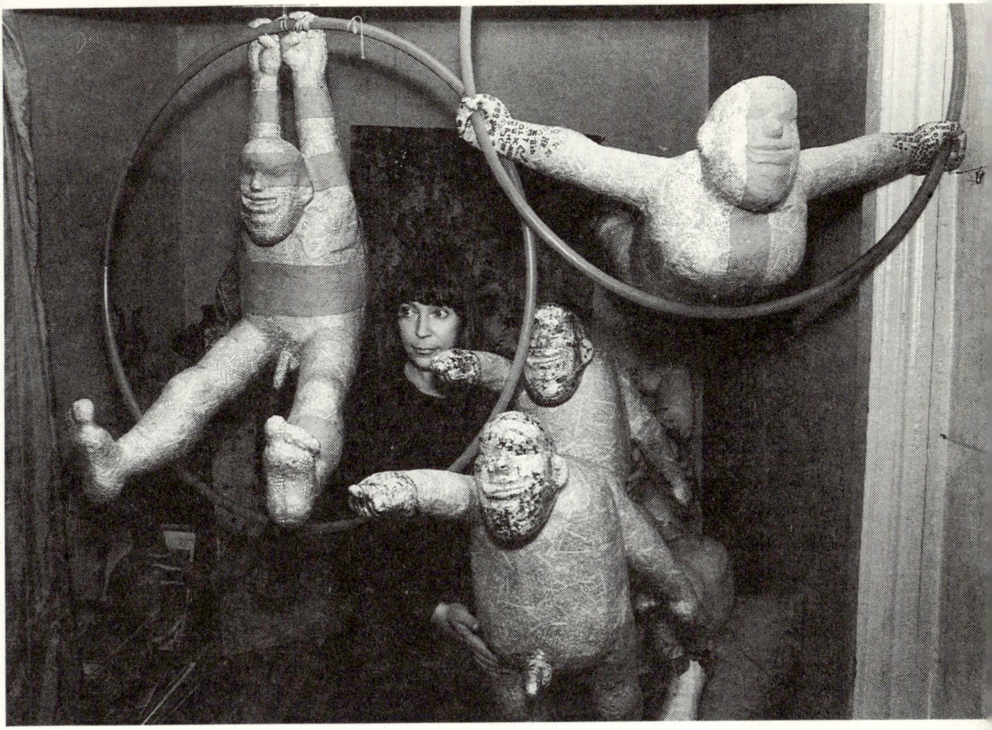

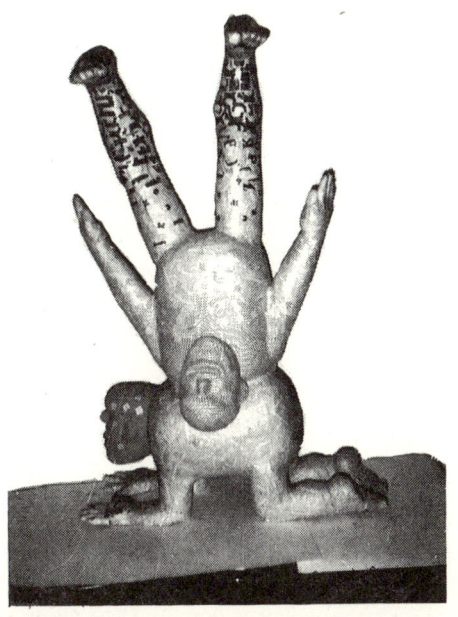

Victor
PELEVIN

THE BLUE LANTERN
MID-GAME
THE VIEW FROM THE WINDOW

The Blue Lantern

It was almost bright in the dormitory because of the lantern burning outside the window. Its light was blue and lifeless, and if it weren't for the moon, which I could see by leaning over from the bed a long way to the right, the effect would have been really sinister. The moonlight diluted the ghastly glow radiating in a cone from the top of the tall pole, making it gentler and more mysterious. But when I swung out to the right, two legs of the bed hung in the air for a second, and the next moment smacked down hard against the floor, and the dull sound seemed strangely in keeping with the blue strip of light between the two rows of beds.

"Stop that," said Crutch, waving a bluish fist at me, "we can't hear."

I began to listen.

"Have you heard about the dead town?" Tolstoy asked.

Nobody answered.

"Well, then. This guy went away for two months on a business trip. When he comes home he suddenly notices everyone's dead."

"What, just lying there on the streets?"

"No," said Tolstoy, "they were going to work, talking to each other, queuing up. Just the same as before. Only he can see that really they're all dead."

"How'd he work out they were dead?"

"How should I know," Tolstoy answered, "I didn't work it out, he did. Somehow or other. Anyway, he decided to pretend he didn't notice anything, and went off home. He had a wife, and as soon as he saw her he realised she was dead too. And he really loved her, so then he began asking her what happened while he was away. And she told him nothing happened. She didn't even understand what he was getting at. Then he decided to tell her everything and he says: 'Do you know you're dead?' And his wife answers him: 'Yes.' He asks her: 'Do you know everyone in this town is dead?' And she says: 'Yes, I know. But do you know why there's only

The Blue Lantern

dead people round here?' 'No,' he says. Then she asks him again: 'Do you know why I'm dead?' 'No,' he says again. Then she says: 'Shall I tell you?' The guy was scared, but he said: 'Okay, tell me.' And she says to him: 'Because you're a corpse yourself.'"

Tolstoy pronounced the final phrase in such a dry, formal voice that we felt something almost like real fear.

"Yes, a real nice business trip that guy went on..."

That was Kolya, still a young boy — younger than the others by a year or two. He didn't actually look younger, because he wore huge hornrimmed glasses that gave him an air of solid respectability.

"So now you're telling a story," Crutch said to him, "since you were the first to speak."

"That wasn't the deal today," said Kolya.

"That's always the deal," answered Crutch, "come on, get on with it."

"Let me tell one instead," said Vasya, "D'you know the one about the blue fingernail?"

"Of course," said a whisper from the corner. "Everyone knows the one about the blue fingernail."

"Ah, but do you know the one about the red patch?" Vasya asked.

"No, we don't know that one," Crutch answered for all of us, "let's have it."

"This family moves into an apartment," Vasya began slowly, "and there's this red patch on the wall. The children noticed it and called their mother to show her. But their mother says nothing. Just stands there and smiles. Then the children called their father. "Look, pa," they said. But their father was scared stiff of their mother. "Let's go," he says to them, "it's nothing to do with you." And their mother just smiles and says nothing. Then they all went to bed.

Vasya stopped speaking and breathed a heavy sigh.

"Then what happened?" asked Crutch after a few seconds' silence.

"Then it was morning. In the morning they wake up and they see one of the children is missing. Then the children go over to their mother and ask her: 'Ma, ma, where's our little brother?' And

Victor Pelevin

their mother answers: 'He's gone to grandma's. He's with grandma.' The children believed her. Their mother went off to work and in the evening she comes home and she's smiling. The children say to her: 'Ma, we're scared!' And she smiles again and says to their father: 'They won't do as I tell them. Give them a good beating!' So their father went and gave them a good beating. The children were even going to run away, but their mother put something in their supper, so they just went on sitting there and couldn't get up..."

The door opened, and we all instantly closed our eyes and pretended to be asleep. After a few seconds the door closed. Vasya waited a minute for the footsteps in the corridor to die away.

"Next morning they wake up and they see another one of the children is missing. There's only one little girl left. She goes and asks her father: 'Where's my middle brother?' And her father answers: 'He's in the summer camp.' And her mother says: 'You tell anyone and I'll kill you!' She didn't even let the girl go to school. In the evening the mother comes home, and she put something in the little girl's food again, so she couldn't stand up. And the father locked the doors and the windows."

Vasya stopped speaking again. This time no-one asked him to go on, and the only sound in the darkness was breathing.

"Then these other people come," he continued, "and they look in the apartment and see it's empty. A year went by and they moved new tenants in. When they saw the red patch, they went up and slit open the wallpaper — and the mother's sitting there, all blue, so bloated with blood she can't get out. She was eating the children, and the father was helping her."

For a long time no-one spoke, and then someone asked:
"Vasya, where's your mother work?"
"What's it matter?" said Vasya.
"You got a sister?"

Vasya didn't answer — he'd either taken offence or fallen asleep.

"Tolstoy," said Crutch, "give us something else about corpses."
"D'you know how people end up as corpses?" Tolstoy asked.
"Sure," answered Crutch, "they just up and die."
"And then what?"

"Nothing," said Crutch, "like sleep. Only you don't ever wake up."

"No," said Tolstoy, "that's not what I mean. D'you know what it all starts with?"

"What?"

"It all starts with people listening to stories about corpses. Then they lie there thinking: why are we listening to stories about corpses?"

Someone gave a nervous giggle, and Kolya suddenly sat up in bed and said very seriously:

"Stop it now, guys."

"The-ere," said Tolstoy, pleased with himself, "that's how it happens. The main thing is to realise you're already a corpse, and the rest is easy."

"You're a corpse yourself," Kolya snarled hesitantly.

"I'm not denying it," said Tolstoy. "But then you'd better think what you're doing talking to a corpse."

Kolya thought for a while.

"Crutch," he said, "you're not really a corpse, are you?"

"Me? How should I know?"

"And you, Lyesha?"

Lyesha was Kolya's friend from home.

"Kolya," he said, "you just think it out now. You lived in the town, right?"

"Right," agreed Kolya.

"Then suddenly they took you away to this other place, right?"

"Right."

"And suddenly you realise that you're lying there with all these corpses and you're a corpse yourself."

"Right."

"Right then," said Lyosha, "just think it over a bit."

"We kept on waiting," said Crutch, "thinking you'd work it out for yourself. In all my death I've never seen such a stupid corpse. Don't you understand why we're all here together?"

"No," said Kolya. He was sitting on the bed with his legs drawn up to his chest.

"We're here to accept you into the company of corpses," said Crutch.

Kolya gave out a sound between a mumble and a sob, leapt up off the bed and shot out into the corridor like a bullet; we could hear the swift retreating patter of his bare feet.

"Don't laugh," Crutch whispered, "he'll hear you."

"What's there to laugh at?" Tolstoy asked in a melancholy voice. For a few long seconds there was total silence, then Vasya asked from his corner:

"But guys what if..."

"Oh can it," said Crutch. "Tolstoy, let's have something else."

"Okay, well, the story goes like this," Tolstoy began after a pause. "Some people decided to give this friend of theirs a scare. So they got dressed up as corpses, came up to him and said: 'We're corpses. We've come for you.' He got scared alright and ran off. And they stood there and laughed, and then one of them says: 'Listen, guys, what are we all doing dressed up as corpses?' They all look at him, and they can't get what he's trying to say. So he tries again: 'Why are all the live people running away from us?'"

"Well, what of it?" asked Crutch.

"That's it. That's when they all realised."

"What'd they realise?"

"Everything, that's what."

They went quiet, then Crutch spoke:

"Listen, Tolstoy. Can you tell a story properly or not?"

Tolstoy didn't answer.

"Hey, Tolstoy," said Crutch. "Why're you so quiet? You died or something?"

Tolstoy said nothing, and every second his silence grew more and more ominous. I had to say something out loud.

"Do you know the one about the T.V. programme 'Time'?" I asked.

"Go on," Crutch said quickly.

"It's not all that frightening."

"Go on anyway."

I couldn't remember exactly how the story I was going to tell ended, but I reckoned I'd remember while I was telling it.

"Basically, there was this guy about thirty years old. He sat down this time to watch 'Time' on the T.V. Turned on the T.V., moved up his armchair to make himself more comfortable. First of all the clock came on, as usual. He checked his own clock to make sure it was right. Everything was the same as usual. Anyway, the chimes struck for nine o'clock. And then the word 'Time' appears on the screen, only not white, like it always was before, but black, for some reason. Well, he was a bit surprised, but then he decided they'd just done new titles, and he carried on watching. Everything was just the same as before again. First they showed some tractor or other, and then the Israeli army. Then they told everyone some academician or other had died, then they showed a bit of sport, and then the weather forecast for the next day. That was all. 'Time' was over and the guy tried to get up out of his armchair..."

"Remind me later on, and I'll tell you about the green armchair," Vasya put in.

"So he wants to get up out of the armchair, but he feels like he can't. All his strength's gone. Then he looked at his hand and saw the skin was all flabby and wrinkled. He got scared and made this mighty effort to get up out of the armchair and go into the bathroom to look in the mirror, but it was real hard to walk... Somehow he got there. He looks at himself in the mirror and sees that his hair's all grey, his face is a mass of wrinkles, and he's got no teeth. His whole life had gone by while he was watching 'Time'."

"I know that one," said Crutch. "It's just the same as the one where they play football with a hockey puck. This guy watches them playing."

Out in the corridor we heard footsteps and a woman's voice raised in annoyance. Instantly we were silent, and Vasya even began snoring unnaturally. A few seconds later the door swung open and the lights went on in the ward.

"Right, who's the chief corpse around here. You, is it, Tolstenko?"

Antonina Vasilievna was standing in the doorway in her white coat, and beside her was Kolya, with his eyes all red from bawling, looking fixedly somewhere behind the radiator.

"The chief corpse in Moscow," Tolstoy answered in a dignified voice, "is on Red Square. And what're you doing waking me up in the middle of the night?"

Such impudence put Antonina Vasilievna off her stroke.

"Go in, Kolya," she said at last, "and lie down. The camp director can sort out the corpses tomorrow. Let's hope they don't all get sent home."

"Antonina Vasilievna," Tolstoy said in a slow drawl, "why're you wearing a white coat?"

"Because that's the way things are done, alright?"

Kolya glanced quickly at Antonina Vasilievna.

"Go to bed, Kolya," she said, "and sleep. Are you a man or not? And as for you," she turned to Tolstoy, "if you say just one more word, you'll find yourself standing naked in the girl's dormitory. Got it?"

Tolstoy stared in silence at Antonina Vasilievna's white coat. She looked herself over, then raised her gaze to Tolstoy and screwed a finger into her forehead. Then suddenly she flew into such a fury that her face flushed bright red.

"You didn't answer me, Tolstenko," she said, "d'you realise what'll happen to you?"

"Antonina Vasilievna," said Crutch, "you said yourself that if he said one more word, you'd... How can he answer you?"

"As for you, Kostylev," Antonina Vasilievna said, "the director will have something special to say to you in his office. Remember that."

The light went out and the door slammed shut.

For a while — about three minutes, maybe — Antonina Vasilievna stood listening outside the door. Then we heard her quiet steps along the corridor. Then there was a loud whisper from Crutch:

"Listen, Kolya, I'll give it to you good tomorrow..."

"I know," Kolya answered sadly.

"Oh-ho, real good..."

"D'you want to hear about the green armchair?" Vasya asked.

No-one answered.

"In this big factory," he began, "there was this director's office with a carpet, a cupboard, and a big table with a green armchair standing in front of it. And in the corner of the office there was this red challenge banner that had been there for ages. And then they appointed this guy director of the firm. He went into the office, looked around, and he liked what he saw a lot. So he sat down in the armchair and started working. And then later his deputy director comes in and instead of his boss in the armchair he sees this skeleton sitting there. Well, they called the police, searched everywhere and couldn't find a thing. So then they appointed the deputy to be director. And he sat in the armchair and started working. They came in later and they saw a skeleton sitting in the armchair again. They called the police again and they couldn't find a thing this time either. Then they appointed a new director. He already knew what had happened to the other directors, and he ordered himself a huge doll the size of a man. He dressed it in his suit and sat it in the armchair, then he backed off and hid behind the drapes — remind me afterwards, I've just remembered the one about yellow drapes — and waited to see what would happen. An hour goes by, then another. And suddenly he sees these metal wires come sliding out of the armchair and wrap round the doll from all sides. One of the wires goes right round the throat. And then, when the wires have throttled the doll, the red challenge banner comes out of the corner, goes up to the armchair and covers the doll over with its flag. After a few minutes there was nothing left of the doll, and the challenge banner went back from the table into the corner. The new director slipped out of the room, went downstairs, took the fire axe off the wall, went back into the office and smashed at the challenge banner with all his might. And then he heard this great groan, and where he split the wooden base in half, blood came pouring out on to the floor."

"And then what happened?" asked Crutch.

"That's all," answered Vasya.

"And what happened to the guy?"

"They put him away. For the banner."

"And what happened to the banner?"

"They fixed it and put it back," Vasya said, after he paused to think about it.

"And when they appointed a new director, what happened to him?"

"The same thing."

I suddenly remembered that in the camp director's office there were several banners with the numbers of Young Pioneer Detachments painted on them; he'd already handed out the banners twice during ceremonial parades. He had an armchair in his office too, but not green, it was red, and it revolved.

"Yes, I forgot," said Vasya, "when the guy came out from behind the drapes he'd gone completely grey. D'you know the one about the yellow drapes?"

"I do," said Crutch.

"Tolstoy, d'you know the one about the yellow drapes?"

Tolstoy didn't answer.

"Hey, Tolstoy!"

Tolstoy said nothing.

I thought about the yellow drapes on my windows in Moscow, yellowish-green anyway. In the summer, when the door of the balcony over the boulevard is open all the time, letting in the noise of engines and the smell of exhaust fumes, mixed with the scent of some flowers, I often sit by the balcony in a green armchair and watch the yellow drapes swaying in the wind.

"Listen, Crutch," Tolstoy said suddenly. "The way people get accepted into the company of corpses is not like you think."

"How is it then?"

"It happens various ways. Only no-one ever tells anyone they're joining the corpses. So the corpses don't know afterwards that they're already dead, and they think they're still alive."

"So you've already been accepted, have you?"

"I don't know," said Tolstoy, "maybe I have. Or maybe they'll accept me afterwards, when I go back to town. Like I said, they don't tell you."

"Who's *they*?"

"Who? The dead."

"There you go again," said Crutch, "I wish you'd just shut it. I've had enough."

"That's right," Kolya piped up. "We've had enough."

"And you there, Kolya," said Crutch, "you're still gonna get it good tomorrow."

Tolstoy said nothing for a while, then he spoke again.

"The main thing," he said, "is that even the ones who accept the new ones don't know they're accepting them into the company of corpses."

"How can they accept them then?" asked Crutch.

"Anyway you like. Suppose you just asked someone about something or turned on the television, and they're really accepting you into the company of corpses."

"That's not what I mean. They must know they're accepting somebody when they accept him."

"Not at all. How can they know anything if they're dead?"

"Then there's no way to understand it," said Crutch. "Then how can you tell who's alive and who's dead?"

"Why, can't you tell?"

"No," said Crutch, "seems like there's no real difference."

"Well, just think for a moment which you are," said Tolstoy.

Crutch made a movement in the darkness and something struck hard against the wall just above Tolstoy's head.

"Idiot," said Tolstoy. "You almost hit my head."

"We're dead anyway," said Crutch, "who cares?"

"Hey guys," Vasya said, "shall I tell you about the yellow drapes?"

"Go screw yourself with your yellow drapes, Vasya. We've heard it a hundred times."

"I haven't," said Kolya from the corner.

"So what, do we all have to listen to it for your sake? Then you'll run off crying to Antonina again."

"I was crying because my leg hurt," said Kolya. "I banged my leg on the way out."

"And anyway, you were supposed to be telling a story. You spoke first that time. D'you think we'd forgotten?" said Crutch.

"Vasya told one instead of me."

"He didn't tell one instead of you, he just told one. And now it's your turn. Or else you'll definitely get it good tomorrow."

"D'you know the one about the black hare?" Kolya asked.

Somehow I knew straight off which hare he meant — one of the things hanging in the corridor opposite the dining-hall was a piece of plywood with an image burnt into it of a hare wearing a necktie. Since the drawing had been carefully executed in great detail, the hare really did look quite black.

"There. And you said you didn't know any. Let's have it."

"Once there was this children's summer camp. And in the main building there were all sorts of animals drawn on the wall, and one of them was a black hare with a drum. For some reason there were two nails hammered into its paws. And once this young girl was walking past on her way from lunch to the quiet hour, and she felt sorry for the hare. She went up and pulled out the nails. And suddenly she had the feeling that the black hare was looking at her as though he was alive. But then she decided she'd imagined it and went off to the dormitory. Quiet hour started. And then the black hare suddenly began to beat on his drum. And straightaway everyone in the camp fell asleep. And they began dreaming that quiet hour was over, that they woke up and went to their afternoon snack. Then they seemed to do everything as usual — play ping-pong, read and all that stuff. But they were dreaming it all. Then their stay in camp ended and they went home. Then they all grew up, graduated from school, got married and began to work and raise children. But in fact they were just sleeping. And all the time the black hare went on beating on his drum."

Kolya stopped speaking.

"One thing I don't get," said Crutch. "You say that they all went home. But at home they had parents and friends their own age. Were they dreaming too?"

"No," said Kolya. "They weren't dreaming. They were in the dream."

"Raving garbage," said Crutch. "Did you follow any of that, guys?"

No-one answered. It seemed like almost everyone had fallen asleep.

"Tolstoy, did you follow any of that?"

Tolstoy's bed squeaked as he leant down to the floor and flung something at Kolya.

"You bastard," said Kolya. "You'll get your face smacked for that."

"Give it back here," said Crutch.

It was his running-shoe, the one he'd thrown at Tolstoy earlier.

Kolya gave him back the shoe.

"Hey," Crutch said to me, "why d'you never say anything?"

"It's just that I feel sleepy," I said.

Crutch curled up in his bed. I thought he was going to say

something else, but he didn't. Nobody said anything. Vasya mumbled something in his sleep.

I looked at the ceiling. Outside, the lantern was swaying on its pole, and the shadows in our dormitory swayed in time with it. I turned to face the window. I couldn't see the moon any more. Everything was absolutely quiet, not a sound but the distant drumming of the wheels of a faraway night suburban train. I went on gazing at the blue lantern, and didn't even notice when I fell asleep.

© *Translation Andrew Bromfield, 1992*
From: Victor Pelevin, *The Blue Lantern* (in Russian),
Text Publishers, Moscow, 1992.

Mid-game

The place was virtually empty. Two naval officers in black uniforms sat at the table opposite. They were bald and had the complexion of corpses. A yellow cocktail stood untouched before each. They were drinking from a bottle of vodka on the floor under the table through a long plastic straw. They passed the straw from one to the other with the same cool precision as, no doubt, they brought to the buttons and switches on the control panels of their nuclear submarine.

"Might as well drink up and pack in," Lucy had just decided, turning to gaze out of the window at the green roof of the Manege with its innumerable machine gun turrets masquerading as dormer windows.

"May I have the, hic, per-leasure..."

Lucy looked up. One of the black-uniformed naval officers was standing peering expressionlessly into her face, his long arms swaying slightly at the sides of his body.

"What of?" Lucy asked in bewilderment.

"Of, hic, a dance. Dance is rhythm and rhythm begets freedom," the officer added somewhat incoherently.

Lucy was about to say something but surprised herself by nodding and getting to her feet instead.

A pair of black arms snapped shut behind her back like the lock on a suitcase and the officer manoeuvred backwards between the tables with little dance steps, drawing Lucy in his wake and doing his best to press his black tunic to her. It was not even a proper naval tunic, more a kind of oversized school blazer with epaulettes. The officer's movements were completely out of time with the music. Evidently he had his own small orchestra playing something slow and sentimental in his head. His breath smelled of vodka: not the hangover smell that emanates from a drunk, but the cold, pure smell of a chemical.

"Why are you so bald?" Lucy asked, distancing herself from the officer. "You're still quite young."

"Seven years in a coffin of ste-eel," the officer crooned softly, his voice rising on the last word almost to a falsetto.

"You're joking!" Lucy exclaimed.

"Coffin of ste-eel," the officer sang, and shamelessly pressed her to his person.

"You know what freedom is, do you?" Lucy asked, pushing him off. "Well, do you?"

The officer cooed.

The music ended and Lucy disengaged herself from him roughly, returned to her table and sat down. Her cocktail tasted disgusting. She pushed it away and for the sake of something to do opened the handbag on her knees and began counting the green five-dollar bills by touch, seeing in her mind's eye the patrician countenance of President Lincoln and the inscription "Legal Tender", which she misunderstood to mean "Lawful Tenderness". She had only eight of the banknotes left. She sighed and decided to try her luck on the second floor to give her conscience nothing to reproach her with later.

The stairs were cordoned off with a thick velvet rope before which a crowd of people stood hoping to be allowed into the restaurant. A narrow gap was blocked by a stool supporting the head waiter in a blue uniform with a yellow stripe of uncertain significance. Lucy nodded to him, stepped over the barrier, and went upstairs to the restaurant. She turned off into a tiled service room just before the buffet. By luck the waiter in there was Seryozha, carefully decanting left-over Champagne from a great number of glasses

Mid-game

through a plastic funnel back into a bottle already swathed in a napkin and standing in an ice bucket.

"Hello, Seryozha," Lucy greeted him. "What's tonight like?"

"The pits. Two scruffy Poles and a Kampuchean with a chopper. Come back on Friday. We'll have petro-Arabs for you. I'll sit you next to the sweatiest one."

"Those Asiatics give me the creeps," Lucy sighed. "I once worked with an Arab. You wouldn't believe it, Seryozha. He carted this damask sword around in his suitcase. He waved it around on this what's it..." Lucy demonstrated.

"Leather thong?" Seryozha suggested helpfully.

"Yes. He couldn't get it up without his sword. Didn't let it out of his hand all night. Even sliced the pillow in half. By morning I was covered in pillow feathers. Just as well he had an en suite bathroom...".

Seryozha laughed, caught up the tray with the Champagne and whisked it off to the restaurant. Lucy paused for a moment by the marble balustrade to look at the ceiling. It had an enormous fresco in the middle which, she vaguely felt, depicted the creation of a world she had been born into and grown up in, but which over the last few years had somehow disappeared. The centre was given over to a blurred salvo of fireworks like an enormous bouquet. In the corners stood titans, skiers, perhaps, in tracksuits, or perhaps they were students with notepads tucked under their arms. Lucy had never looked at them that closely because her attention was always monopolised by the streaks and stars of the fireworks, painted in the same, long-forgotten colours as those with which, for old times' sake, "morn sometimes still rosily kisses the walls of our ancient Kremlin: lilac, pink, and palest mauve." Calling to mind those toffee tins of yesteryear, and tooth powder, and dog-eared wall calendars bequeathed with a bundle of early Soviet bonds by a grandmother Lucy has already forgotten.

The sight of this painted ceiling always made Lucy feel sad. She felt sad now. She quickly left the restaurant and went downstairs to the cloakroom.

By the little hard currency bar on the ground floor Lucy bumped into a denizen of the Cosmos Hotel, dressed in a loose leather shift and an arresting green hat with a pompom. After a moment's mental exertion Lucy recalled that her name was Nellie. Why Nellie should have abandoned the concave and convex architectural planes of her pitch beside the Exhibition of Economic Achievements for these inhospitable parts she couldn't imagine, but Nellie replied to the question without her having to ask it.

"They've changed Security on the door at the Cosmos," she said with a smile. "They just refused to let an Englishmen back in who'd left his hotel card in his room. He was yelling at them to look him up in the register but they just stood there fish-eyed. How are things here?"

"Dire!" Lucy said. "I'm not here working. Just came in to sit around for a bit. There's some drunk sailors. Shall we try the Intourist bar on the tenth floor?"

"I've just come from there," Nellie answered. "Things were looking ugly. Anya's in trouble again. Her Counsellor from the Cuban Embassy had her snorting coke, and like the birdbrain she is she got so high she gave the waiter a twenty dollar tip. He turned out to be a true-blue Communist who'd been hit on the head in El Salvador. He told her, "If I'd got my hands on you in the jungle, you bitch, I'd have let the lads have their way with you and then sat you bare-arsed on a termites' nest. I shed my blood for this country," he said, "and you're dragging it through the dirt.""

"They'll just caution her and let her go. It's a good question who dragged our country through the dirt. What's making them so uppity? Vienna negotiations deadlocked again?"

"Nothing to do with it," Nellie said. "There's something new going on. Did you hear about Natasha?"

"Which Natasha? The one who got killed?"

"Too right. The one with a chess piece in her mouth who got dumped in a snowdrift."

"I heard. What about it?"

"I'll tell you what about it. The day before yesterday they found Tanya Polikarpova by the Cosmos With a chess rook in hers."

"Tanya's been killed?" Lucy went cold. "KGB up to its old tricks again?"

"I don't know, I just don't know," Nellie said thoughtfully.

Mid-game

"It's not their style. Whoever did it didn't take her currency, or her shopping bag full of foreign food. Just stuck this chess piece in her mouth. Beats me what chess has got to do with it. Bloody psychos!"

Lucy nervously rooted in her handbag for a cigarette.

"That's enough," she said. "Let's not talk about it any more. Not at night."

"Give us a cigarette," Nellie said.

Lucy gave her one, and while Nellie was lighting up from hers she took a close look at her. There was something familiar about her that Lucy couldn't quite pin down. It had struck her before that she had known that face very well, long ago, in some earlier life.

"Wait a minute," she said hesitantly, when the door had closed behind them and they were standing on the snow-covered steps outside the hotel. "That was never you in the first floor restaurant in the Nationale in that black dress with the brown?"

"Yup," Nellie smiled. "Yves Saint Laurent."

"You liar!"

Nellie shrugged. There was a Chekhovian pause, broken when a young man, who had been sheltering from the wind behind a pillar, took a step in their direction and with a fricative Ukrainian accent, but enunciating very succinctly, enquired,

"Hi, ghirlies. Not pushing ghreenbacks, huh?"

Lucy bestowed a withering look on his cony fur hat and tatty leather jacket, and only then at his rosy cheeks, ginger moustache and watery eyes.

"Hi, blockhead," she said. "They're really shipping you goons in by the cartload. Don't you even know what we call greenbacks nowadays?"

"What?" the young man asked, his rosiness suffused with a blush.

"Dollars. And we aren't girlies, we're ladies. And tell your commanding officer from me that your dictionaries are crap and ten years out of date."

"You shouldn't have torn into him like that," Nellie said when the young man had retired in confusion back to his pillar. "That's only Vasya, the duty policeman from the Bank for Foreign Trade. They send him round every week to find out the black market exchange rate."

"Right," said Lucy, "I'm off home. See you around."
"Let's go somewhere together for a drink," Nellie suggested, in a tone which took Lucy aback. She shook her head and smiled.
"See you," she said. "So long."

The taxis flew by without stopping, their green "For hire" lights twinkling mockingly. By the time she had walked with outstretched arm all the way to the Manege Lucy was really cold. Her face and hands were chilled and, as always when she was out in the frost, the dull ache in her breasts had started up again. She caught herself screwing her face up with the pain, remembered the wrinkle she had noticed appearing on her forehead, and tried hard to relax her facial muscles. A few minutes later the pain subsided.

Lucy could not shake off the echo of what Nellie had told her on the steps of the Hotel Moskva. "They really screwed Tanya up," she repeated pointlessly to herself, the actual sense of the words somehow not registering. The rook sticking out of Tanya's dead mouth she did, however, visualise very clearly. It became really cold, and her breasts started aching again. She could still make the last train on the underground, but that would mean a half-hour walk at the other end, trudging along on her own in her expensive fur coat down an ice-bound avenue named in honour of some political thug, and shivering in the wind's drunken guffaws as it whistled through the enormous concrete arches of the apartment blocks which flanked it. Lucy had just resigned herself to the fact that this was indeed how the evening was going to end when a small green bus drew up alongside her. Its military number plate proclaimed the arrival of the armed forces.

There was a naval officer at the wheel, the one who had danced with her at the restaurant, only now he was also wearing a black greatcoat. A field cap with a large tin badge was perched jauntily on his bald head. Lucy peered in to the semi-darkness of the interior and was surprised to see Nellie sitting in relaxed pose on a side seat next to the other sailor.

"Lucy," she cried merrily. "Hop in. They're jolly sailor boys and they're going right past my house. They're ... Where do you have to get to?"

"Krylatskoye," Lucy said.

"Krylatskoye as well? What do you know! We're neighbours, dear. Come on, pile in."

The bus leapt to a start, performed a dashing u-turn, and hurtled past the Bolshoy, the Children's World department store, and away down dark, howling backstreets dotted with half-ruined hoardings and black with gaping empty windows.

"Vadim!" said the second bald man. "And that," he nodded in the direction of the driver, "is Valera. Want some vodka?"

"Why not?" Lucy replied. "But only through a straw."

"What do you want to drink it through a straw for?" Nellie asked.

"That's how they drink it, through a straw," Lucy said, putting the thin, soft end to her lips.

She suddenly noticed music playing. There was a cassette recorder on the engine cowling by Valera. It was playing "Bad Boys Blues". Everything gradually became less complicated and, most importantly, began to feel good. The dark interior of the bus, the Navy's gleaming skulls, Nellie jogging her foot in time to the music, the houses flashing past the windows, the cars and people. The vodka was working. A yearning sadness, with an edge of fear brought with her from the Moskva, evaporated, and a straightforward girlish dream, so pure in its hopelessness, a simple longing for that suntanned, generous American boy possessed Lucy's heart so suddenly that she wanted to believe him when he sang that we would have no regrets, and would yet fly away in a time machine, even though we had been jolting along for so many years in a train going nowhere.

A train to nowhere, a train to nowhere ...

The bus drove out on to a main road bordered by ice-covered trees, and followed a lorry with a yellow signboard reading "People" on its tailboard. A heavy iron object was rolling around inside it, and the clanging metal seemed to bring Lucy to her senses.

"Hey, where are we going?" she suddenly asked, alarmed to find that the places flashing past were no longer familiar, and did not even look very much like Moscow.

"Oh, er, we need to fill up with petrol," Vadim said breezily. "We don't have enough petrol to get us to Krylatskoye. There's a filling station near here where you can get it for coupons."

There was something reassuring about the word "coupons", and Lucy again half closed her eyes.

"We are in the Navy, girls," Vadim said. "Serving on the Marines' nuclear submarine Tambov. It's just one great big underwater armoured train with a crew as close-knit as a family. Seven years already, girls..."

He took off his cap and passed his hand over his dully gleaming skull. The bus turned off down a narrow side road with what looked like concrete pillboxes spaced along the sides. They seemed to have left the town now and be out in open country. In the sky cold stars shone like the bulging, lascivious eyes of that Frenchman the day before yesterday, and the running of the engine seemed suddenly strangely muted, or perhaps it was just that the roar from lorries driving by had disappeared.

"The ocean," Vadim said, putting an arm round Nellie's shoulders, "is immense. Its boundless grey expanse stretches off in whichever direction you look. Above, far away, is the firmament of the stars with its floating clouds... The sheer weight of water... Enormous submarine skies, at first light green, then inky blue, and that's how it is for hundreds and thousands of kilometers. Gigantic whales, predatory sharks, mysterious creatures of the deep. And there, can you imagine, suspended in that pitiless universe, the thin, thin shell of our submarine, so very tiny... The porthole in the side shining like a yellow dot, while in there behind it a party meeting is taking place. Valera is making a report. And all around, think of it! The ocean... vast, and ancient..."

"We've arrived," Valera suddenly announced.

Lucy raised her head and looked from side to side. The bus was standing in a snow-covered plain some thirty metres off a deserted roadway. The engine fell silent and it became very still. Outside the window you could see a distant forest. Lucy was surprised to see that it was fairly light outside although there was no light source, and then she thought it must be the snow reflecting the diffused starlight. The vodka had left her feeling cosy and secure. The thought did cross her mind that something was not as it should be, but it immediately went away again.

"What do you mean, we've arrived? Are you kidding?" Nellie asked sharply.

Mid-game

Vadim took his arm from around her shoulder and sat hiding his face in his hands quietly giggling. Valera slammed the driver's door and a second later opened the door to the body of the bus. Clouds of steam billowed in from the frost. Valera slowly and ritualistically climbed the steps. In the semi-darkness his expression was not clearly visible, but in one hand he held a Makarov pistol, and under the other arm he was carrying a large, battered chess board. Without turning he slammed the door with a single thrust of his solid backside. The door's rubber piping squeaked in the frost. He held the board out to Vadim.

Lucy slipped off her bench, sobering up with terrifying speed, and retreated to the back of the bus, instinctively hiding behind Nellie's back. Nellie herself began backing away, stumbled over something on the floor and almost fell on Lucy, but saved herself just in time.

Valera stood at the front of the bus pointing his pistol at them. Vadim shook the chess pieces out on to the engine cowling and then stood stock still as if he had forgotten what came next. Valera was also motionless and the two of them seemed like silhouettes cut from black card. A green light was assiduously flashing on the dashboard, reporting back to the mind which created it that all was well in the complex mechanism of the bus.

"Boys," Nellie said in a quiet, frightened voice, "we'll do whatever you want, only put those chess men away..."

Her words seemed to galvanise the motionless sailors.

"Let us proceed," said Valera, and Vadim bent over a handful of chess men with his back to them. Lucy had no idea what he was up to.

Vadim kept striking matches, peering at a scrap of paper, and again bending over the brown leatherette on the cowling, where normal drivers keep bundles of petrol coupons, a tin for loose change, and their microphone. Valera was still standing there motionless, and it occurred to Lucy that his arm must be getting very tired.

Vadim finally completed his preparations and took a step to the side.

The engine cowling had been transformed into a bizarre-looking altar on which four thick candles were burning. The chess board lay open in the centre of the square so formed. The black and white armies had advanced far into each other. Their ranks had already been thinned out considerably and Lucy, whose perceptions had been immeasurably heightened by the horror of the situation, was suddenly struck by the great drama represented by the crude wooden figures on the chequered field, two irreconcilable forces bent on mutual destruction. The emotional charge of the situation got to her in spite of her life-long disinterest in chess, and she unexpectedly remembered a tale read in childhood about two kings playing chess on a mountain while their armies were locked in mortal combat nearby.

By the edge of Black's section of the board stood a small metal figure, a thin man in a jacket, with sunken cheeks and a mop of steel hair tumbling over his forehead. He was around twenty centimetres tall but, oddly enough, seemed enormous, and because of an effect of the flickering candlelight he seemed also to be alive and making pointless, darting movements.

"You," Valera said, pointing to Nellie.

Nellie jabbed a thumb into herself interrogatively, and the men in black nodded in unison. She walked forwards, pitifully swinging her French handbag, its strap clutched in her fist. Half way down the bus she paused and looked round at Lucy. Lucy smiled encouragingly, feeling the tears starting to her eyes. When she reached the two black figures Nellie stopped.

"You," Vadim said coldly. "A move for the White side, please."

"Which?" Nellie asked. She appeared completely calm and detached from the situation.

"As you choose."

Nellie moved one of the figures without a second glance.

"Please now get down on your knees," Vadim said in the same tone.

Lucy cringed.

"Hell," Valera said suddenly. "Knights can't move that way."

"It's really not that important," Vadim said reassuringly, taking Valera's arm. "It really doesn't matter..."

"Doesn't matter? You want him to lose again? What? Have they bought you too?" Valera shrieked.

"You," Vadim said tensely. "Get up and make a proper move."

Mid-game

Nellie rose from her knees, and glanced at Valera and the spike quivering in his left hand. It all happened very quickly as the penny dropped at last. She gave a heart-stopping, cat-like screech, seized the metal figurine by its head and shoulders, and brought down the cuboid pedestal on which it stood on Valera's black cap. As if on cue he collapsed into the space between the door of the bus and the steps.

Lucy covered her ears expecting Vadim to do something terrible, but instead he suddenly squatted down and shielded his head with his hands. Nellie swung the figurine once more, and Vadim howled with pain. She had struck his fingers, but he remained in the same position. Nellie struck again, and again Vadim failed to react, only protecting his hurt hand with the fingers of the other. Nellie spotted where Valera had dropped the pistol, flung the figurine to the floor and grabbed it. She aimed it into the space between the steps and the door: the metal partition cut off Lucy's line of vision.

"Get up out of there!" she said in a hoarse, mannish voice. "Fast!"

Hands in black sleeves appeared over the partition, and after them a bald skull and attentive eyes. Vadim was still squatting, pressing his black cap down on his head as if he were caught in a gale. Valera glanced at the girls, got down on all fours and began gathering up the chess pieces from the floor.

"Seven years in a coffin of ste-eel," he began to croon quietly.

Nellie fired a shot into the roof. Valera jumped to his feet and threw his hands up. Vadim only drew his head even deeper into his greatcoat.

"Listen carefully," Nellie hissed at the two black officers. "You stay where you are; and you," she trained the pistol on Valera, "get in the driving seat. And if you so much as think of braking in the wrong place I'll blast a hole right through the middle of your bald-spot. You see if I don't."

"This one here," Nellie said, indicating a green fifteen-storey tower block. "Drive right up to the entrance, baldie. Now open the door."

The door hissed and opened.

"Sit in the bus for five minutes without moving, you vermin. Understand?"

For some reason Lucy picked the figurine off the floor as she was getting out and shoved it under her arm. Valera clenched his fists, grimaced, and groaned quietly. Vadim stayed as he was, shielding his head with his hands.

They walked backwards to the entrance, and only when the lift doors closed behind them did Lucy begin to relax.

"Were you very frightened?" Nellie asked.

"Just a bit," Lucy answered. "They're psychos, both of them. They'd have bumped us off and dumped us in a snowdrift to wait for spring. With chess men in our mouths. Hey, it must have been them did in Natasha and Tanya..."

"You've only just realised that?" Nellie asked. "I knew the score as soon as I saw the chess board."

"What move was that you made?"

"Haven't a clue," said Nellie. "I forgot how to play chess a long time ago."

Nellie's flat was in a state of exquisite disorder. The door to the one living room was open and the light had been left on, evidently since Nellie had gone out. There were clothes strewn all over the place. Flacons of expensive perfume littered the floor like bottles in the den of an alcoholic. A portable Japanese television stood on the floor by the window, and beside it an enormous cassette recorder. There was a sour smell which Lucy immediately recognised as spilt Champagne, after it has evaporated for several days and been transmuted into glue.

Pride of place was taken by a double bed so vast you didn't at first even notice it. It sported a blue duvet with contrasting sheets.

"She brings clients home too," Lucy thought, as she scrutinised the metal man she was still clutching. "There's nothing so terrible about that, then. Other people do it as well."

"Karpov," she read out the writing on the grey paper stuck on to the stand.

"Well he's certainly Soviet," Nellie said, taking off her leather shift.

Lucy looked up at her in bafflement.

"Karpov," Nellie explained, taking the item off her, "versus

Mid-game

Korchnoy. Get it? That's what that nutter was on about. Take your coat off. I'll just be a minute."

Lucy took off her fur coat and hat and hung them on a set of antlers which served as a coatstand, donned two odd slippers, and went through.

"I could do with a drink," she said.

"I've got a half-bottle of Jogging Vanya," Nellie responded from the bathroom.

Lucy didn't understand immediately, but then remembered that in circles close to the Beryozka hard currency food store on Dorogomilovskaya Street that was what they called Johnny Walker, rumoured to have been the tipple of the late Comrade Andropov. "Heavens," the thought suddenly struck her. "It all seems so recent. The snowstorm on Kalinin Avenue, the campaign for discipline, the young face of that American Girl Scout on the television, the slanting blue "Androp..." signed under the typewritten text of his reply." What must his stern spirit be whispering now to the soul of Samantha Smith, who survived him by so short a time. How fleeting life is, and how fragile we are.

Nellie quickly cleared away the most obvious traces of debauchery: the over-full ashtrays, the inside-out tights dangling from the back of an armchair, a grapefruit skin, the biscuits trampled underfoot, until all that was left on the carpet was a pile of magazines and the iron Grandmaster wrested from the enemy. Nellie reached out with the black remote control unit and opposing teams of brightly coloured ice-hockey players flashed silently over its screen. Then the hockey rink was replaced by a short, pudgy man in spectacles standing beside a wall-mounted chess board.

"Events took an unexpected turn as the present match in the world chess championships continued," he said more and more loudly (as Nellie pressed the volume button). "Black had a clear overnight advantage, but the game took an unexpected and interesting turn after a paradoxical move by the White knight..."

"Listen to them," Lucy said. "They're always going on about chess. I can't stand it. Please switch it off."

"Hang on a second. Let's just hear the weather."

Chess pieces clattered over the board.

"One of the two officers, I'm sorry, bishops, central to the

37

black position found himself in danger, and the coup de grace, if I may put it that way, came when the challenger himself, analysing the game overnight, failed to take full account of the consequences of what appeared at first to be an ill-considered move by the White knight."

A close-up of the commentator's fingers and the silhouette of a White knight appeared briefly on the screen.

"Black's white-square bishop is obliged to retire."

The chess men clattered once more.

"... while the situation of the black-square bishop becomes, to all intents and purposes, hopeless."

The commentator prodded first the White, then the Black figures on the board, circled his hand in the air, and smiled sadly.

"How the match ended we shall, I hope, hear in time for the evening news bulletin."

A snow-covered field appeared on the screen, enclosed on two sides by long fences and ending in a forest. The edge of a roadway was to be seen at the bottom of the screen and the white figures of tomorrow's temperatures glided along it, most of them preceded by a minus sign resembling a silicon brick.

"I wouldn't mind taking a brick like that," Lucy thought, "and bringing it down on bloody Valera's bald head..."

"Do you know what music that is?" Nellie asked, moving slightly closer to Lucy.

"No," Lucy answered, moving slightly further away and feeling her breasts starting to ache again.

"They always used to play it after the news programme Time, but you don't hear it very often now. It's a French song called *Manchester-Liverpool*."

"But those are English towns," Lucy said.

"So? It's still a French song. Do you know, for as long as I can remember we have been travelling on and on in that train. I don't remember what it used to be like in Manchester, and now I don't suppose I shall ever get to see Liverpool."

Lucy felt Nellie again moving closer, so close, indeed, that she could feel the warmth of her body through the thin fabric of her dress. Nellie put a hand on her shoulder in what could have been simply an affectionate gesture, but Lucy knew exactly what was coming next.

"Nellie, what are you..."

Time ended, but what then appeared next on the screen was not eternity but an announcer, and then some ramshackle factory with a lot of glum-looking workers in flat hats standing around in the middle of it. Next there was a reporter holding a microphone, and then a lot of broad-cheeked men in suits sitting at a table. One looked Lucy straight in the eye, hid his indecently hairy hands under the table, and started talking.

"We've no business getting up to this sort of thing," Lucy whispered, mechanically repeating the words of the snout on the screen. "The workers aren't going to like it..."

"The workers aren't going to get it," Nellie murmured breathily in reply, her movements becoming increasingly shameless. The bewitching heat of Anais Anais radiated from her, with just an astringent hint of Fiji.

"Oh, what the hell," Lucy thought, laying her hand on Nellie's shoulder with an unexpected sense of relief. "Let it be my final test..."

Lucy was lying on her back looking at the ceiling. Nellie was pensively examining her profile with its delicate down of face powder.

"Listen, girl," she whispered. "Promise me one thing. Promise me you won't just get up and walk out, no matter what I tell you. All right?"

"I promise, Nellie. Of course I do."

"You haven't noticed anything odd about me?"

"Of course not."

"Well, all right... No, I can't go on. Kiss me... That's good. Do you know who I used to be?"

"Heavens, Nellie, what difference does it make?"

"No, I don't mean like that. Have you heard about transsexuals? The sex-change operation?"

Lucy felt a sudden wave of fear breaking over her. It was even stronger than the fear she had felt in the bus, and her breasts again began to ache painfully. She drew away from Nellie slightly.

"Yes, Nellie. What about it?"

"Well, then," Nellie gulped. "Only hear me out. I used to be a man. My name was Vasily, Vasily Tsyruk. I was the Secretary of a Regional Committee of the Young Communist League. I used to walk around in, well, a suit, and a collar and tie, wearing a waistcoat and chairing endless meetings... carrying dossiers on people around in my briefcase... agendas, minutes... Well, anyway, I would be going home in the evening, and on the way I had to pass this hard currency restaurant, limos, women like you, everybody laughing, and me walking past in this prissy waistcoat, with my YCL lapel badge and my prissy moustache, carrying my prissy briefcase to cap it all, and they would all hoot with laughter and pile into all these cars! "Well," I thought, "so what. I'll soon be a Party member, and before you know it I'll be an instructor in the City Committee." I had it all going for me. "I'll live it up in restaurants that'll put this one in the shade. Never mind the town, I'll paint the whole world red..." But then, one evening I went to a Solidarity with the Palestinians party and this drunk Arab called Avada Ali went and threw a glass of tea in my face, and people in the Regional Committee of the Party started asking questions and wondering why Comrade Tsyruk got tea thrown in his face when it never happened to other comrades. Anyway, I got an official reprimand and it went down in my file. And me already a candidate for Party membership! I practically went out of my mind! And then I read in the Literary Gazette about this Professor Vishnevsky who did this operation for, well, queers, only don't think I was gay... I was just reading about how they inject these hormones and change your whole personality and way of thinking, and my old personality and way of thinking had really let me down. Anyway, to cut a long story short, I sold my old Moskvich and went for six operations one after the other. They injected me with endless hormones, and a year ago I came out of the clinic with my hair long and feeling a different, er, woman. Everything seemed different. I walked down the street and even the snowdrifts didn't seem real. They were like the cotton wool round a Christmas Tree. Then I suppose I got used to everything, only recently I have had this feeling everybody is looking at me and that they know all about me. And then I met you and I thought, right, I'll test whether I really am a woman or... Lucy, what's wrong?"

Lucy had moved away and was sitting by the wall pressing her knees to her breasts with both arms. There was a silence.

Mid-game

"Do I disgust you?" Nellie whispered. "Am I disgusting?"

"So you did have a moustache," Lucy said, and tossed back a lock of hair from her face. "And perhaps you remember you had a deputy called Andrey Pavlov? Only you called him Creep."

"I do remember," Nellie said in amazement.

"You even sent him out for beer. And then you saddled him with a personal dossier over that poster propaganda cock-up, when someone drew Lenin on the propaganda board wearing gloves, and Felix Dzerzhinsky without a shadow!"

"How do you know all...? Creep? Is it really you?"

"You even gave me that nickname. What did I do to deserve that? Was it because I hung on your every word? Because I sat typing up the minutes of all those meetings till eleven o'clock every night? It was nearly my turn to join the Party then as well, you know. Heavens, everything could have been so different... Do you know what I have been dreaming of for the past two years? I wanted to go sailing past your Regional Committee in a Mercedes 500, and I wanted Tsyruk, you, that is, to be standing there with his Tatar moustache and his briefcase full of minutes of meetings and just to look him straight in the eyes from the rear seat, and then look through him as if he wasn't there. Do you understand?"

"Andy, baby, that wasn't me... It was Sherstenevich in the Party Bureau said the admin deputy should carried the can. After all, what a scandal! The oldest Party member in the region was just nipping down the shops for his yoghurt and what does he see?! He nearly went berserk, the silly old fart. Andy, sweetheart, is it really you?"

Lucy wiped her lips on the sheet.

"Have you got any vodka?"

"I've got surgical spirit," Nellie said, getting up. "Just a mo."

Modestly covering herself with the crumpled sheet she ran to the kitchen. Crockery clattered and glass fell to the floor and shattered. Lucy cleared her throat and spat at length on the carpet, once more fastidiously wiping her lips on the sheet. A minute later Nellie returned with two half-filled crystal tumblers.

"Here... I don't even know what to call you..."

"Call me Creep, the way you always did," said Lucy, and tears shone in her eyes.

"Let bygones be bygones, dear. Come on. Let's drink to our meeting up again. Ooof! Reminds me of Astrakhan. Do you remember, when they volunteered us for that building work? But tell me, who did your operation?"

"A cooperative," Lucy said, casting a glance at the packaging for French tampons scattered over the bedside table. "I reckon they botched it. Instead of American silicon implants they shoved in some good old Soviet rubber. When I was working on a platform with a lot of Finns near Leningrad I kept squeaking something rotten in frosty weather. They often hurt."

"That isn't the rubber. Mine often ache too. They say it goes away with time."

Nellie sighed and fell silent.

"A penny for them," Lucy said a minute later.

"Oh, it's just... Sometimes, you know, I feel as if I still am following the Party line. Do you know what I mean? Only times have changed."

"Aren't you afraid everything will go back to how it was?" Lucy asked. "Cross your heart?"

"Not really," Nellie said. "If it all comes back, we'll see. We're qualified personnel after all, you and I. And you can always sew it all back on in a week or two if need be."

Out in open country a watery winter twilight was falling and a small green bus was driving along a deserted road. Sometimes the red lettering of a collective farm sign would leap towards it, to be followed by a succession of ugly buildings, and then a sign bearing the same name crossed through with a thick red line.

Inside the minibus were two officers in black. One, the driver, had a bandage on his head on which a naval cap perched precariously. He was crooning to himself. The second officer was also bald and black, but it was his hands that were bandaged, and he had chocolate all over his tear-stained face. He was sitting in the body of the bus on the seat nearest the driver. A box of chocolate meringues lay open on his knees.

"But I do as you tell me," he said, his body racked with stifled sobbing. "I have done ever since I was little. I imitate everything you do. You went mad ages ago, Barbara, you really did. I can see

Mid-game

that now. Just think what we look like, with our bald heads, wearing sailors' vests, sailing around in this tin can drinking all the time... And that chess..."

"We are at war," the second said. "We are engaged in a struggle without quarter. It's just as hard for me, Tamara."

The first officer covered his face, unable to talk for a moment. Gradually he regained his self-possession, took a meringue from the box, and crammed it into his mouth.

"How proud I used to be of you!" he began again. "I even felt sorry for my best friend for not having an elder sister. I followed your lead in everything I did, did everything just like you... You always pretend you know the meaning of life and how we should live in the future, but now I've had enough. I'm worried sick every time I have a medical, and going out at night with this spike... No more! I'm leaving you. I've had enough."

"But what about our cause?" the second asked.

"What about it? If you really want to know, I don't give a toss about the chess."

At that the minibus veered sharply and almost ran into a snowdrift by the road side. The first officer grabbed the rail with his bandaged hands and howled with pain.

"No! I've had enough!" he yelled. "From now on I'm going to think for myself. You can sail with the Tambov if you like. Do you hear? Stop the bus!"

The officer was again convulsed by sobbing. He groped around in his jacket pocket and tugged out several coloured booklets. He threw them down on the leatherette cowling. Then the cartridge clip for the pistol was consigned to the same place, followed a moment later by a worn plastic dildo attached to a tangle of straps and bits of elastic.

"Stop the bus, you bastard!" he shouted. "Stop, or I'll jump out anyway!"

The bus braked and the front door opened. The officer leapt down into the road with a wail and ran without a backward glance diagonally across an immense square of virgin snow bordered by the road, the forest, and some distant fences. He ran towards the snow-bound forest and the moon, which was now unambiguously white. He floundered off with the gait of a clumsy churchman, but for all that crossed the square quite rapidly.

Victor Pelevin

The second officer gazed silently after the black figure which was gradually diminishing on the flat white field. Sometimes it stumbled and fell, but each time it rose again to its feet and ran on until finally it disappeared from view. A small glistening tear crept down the cheek of the man in the driver's seat.

The bus moved off and the officer's face gradually became expressionless. The teardrop suspended from his chin fell off on to his uniform, and the trace it had left on his cheek dried up.

"Seven years in a coffin of ste-eel," he crooned quietly as he drove to meet another day, and the road rushed towards him, as broad and empty as life.

Translated by Arch Tait
From: Victor Pelevin, *The Blue Lantern* (in Russian),
Text Publishers, Moscow, 1992.

The View from the Window

This winter, no matter where I might be, or whatever I might happen to be doing, I often have the feeling I'm really standing at a window, looking out on the world.

Sometimes there's newspaper stuck over the window, and I see the black maggot of human thought, set free at last by the authorities, crawling along one line after another.

Sometimes the window is convex and bluish, like a television screen, and a short distance beyond it a young man appears, suspended in the cold winter air. He controls himself remarkably well, and you can hardly tell that his teeth are really chattering from the cold, even when he smiles as he recounts the events of the day. When he's finished, some invisible hand covers him with the Russian tricolor flag and I assume that behind its shelter they are restoring him with vodka or hot tea.

The window is constantly changing, but no matter how it might appear at any particular moment, what lies out there beyond it is really always the same — a roadway, a few shops, a children's playground, blocks of flats with flickering lights in the windows,

The View from the Window

and people wandering about over snow-covered pathways. Up overhead there is the croaking of emaciated Russian crows, exhausted and disillusioned by perestroika, and up beyond them, majestic winter clouds go drifting by: the usual view of the usual Russia from the usual Moscow mentality. But you only have to shift your gaze just a little to see something new, and sometimes you can even hear voices coming up from the street.

The sight that seems most often to lie beyond the pane of glass is an immense dark plain, almost empty, on which smoke is rising from scattered bonfires, with a few people seated around each of them. A large effigy of Yevtushenko is ablaze on the nearest bonfire, and a crowd of writers in tattered literary overcoats are warming their hands at the flames. The buttons on their coats bear Gogol's profile in bronze. They are staring morosely into the darkness, trying to give the impression that they are gazing into the far distance. An effigy of Gorbachev is blazing on the next fire, with a few people trying to warm themselves beside it. A bit further on there's an effigy of Yeltsin, and further on again there's Yegor Gaidar, and even Peter the Great. A lot of effigies have already burnt away, and the thin smoke rising from the heaps of ash swirls in the slipstream of the cars that occasionally drive past — "Mercedes", hastily cobbled together out of the tin cans that arrived as humanitarian aid. But neither the effigy of Yevtushenko, nor the flames of the bonfire can dispel the darkness, they merely emphasise how thick and dense it really is, and it seems as though daylight will never come.

The wind carries crumpled newspapers through the air above the plain, and now and again the people sitting round the bonfires catch them. The newspapers have different names and advocate different political movements, but it's hard to understand how these sheets of grey paper borne in the wind can really move in different directions. One of them flutters past my window — I catch it, crumple it up and toss it into a small bonfire on which my own tiny effigy is burning.

...I am actually astonished at the patience with which I used to wait for the collapse of "all this", as we used to call it. But who could have thought that we too were a part of "all this"? Ever since we were born we have drifted along on a huge iceberg of frozen blood, and when the sun appeared in the sky, naturally we were happy to see it. But after a while each of us in turn suddenly found himself floundering in the water with no apparent chance of ever getting ashore.

We were in such a hurry to sink our floating concentration camp, and each of us diligently and honestly bored his own few holes in its bottom. Then when it finally began to keel over and sink, we suddenly realised that we were its passengers, and the guard dogs who had barked and snarled at us for so many years from behind the barbed wire had long since left and gone to read lectures on perestroika in small American universities. But we have no time to think about all this, because the waters are closing over our heads, and the struggle to swim ashore and get back to the window requires an immense effort of will.

When the window is back in front of me again, through the glass I see an immense crowd seething around a huge motionless figure wearing a huge metal cap. The figure is illuminated by searchlights, and it casts squat, stumpy shadows across the crowd in various directions — they seem even more massive than the figure itself, and the shadow of the clownish cap looks very much like horns. Hundreds of ropes have already been thrown around Lenin's neck, and he clearly cannot remain standing for much longer. Somehow one of the ropes finds its way into my hands, and I pull on it with all my might. It doesn't shift at all, because we are not merely toppling a metal Golem, we are trying to rip something out of our own selves, something that has been part of us since the day we were born. Then suddenly there are voices crying out in joy and hope, someone shouts out that the statue has begun to sway, and I feel the rope in my hand going slack.

"It's falling! It's falling!" The shout goes up all around, and we are all swept up in a wave of euphoria as we see the immense statue, which always seemed the most unshakeable monument in the world, lean over centimetre by centimetre until it finally begins to topple. We wait with bated breath until suddenly we notice that the immense man of metal with his arm extended into emptiness is falling right on top of us. We start moving back, cries of terror go up on all sides, but it's too late to run — first we are engulfed by the shadow, and then we are crushed against the earth by a blow of monstrous power.

The View from the Window

When the power of vision returns, the window is more than ever like a television screen, and floating in the air beyond it is a figure in a black cassock — after what has just happened, this seems quite appropriate. The figure in the cassock opens a black book with a cross on the cover and begins to intone:

"And death shall enter in at thy window..."

This just isn't frightening any more — very few evenings now pass without a discussion of the end of the world, because you just can't help thinking about it, even in the morning — especially since the evenings and the mornings are equally dark.

In general, anyway, the end of the world arrives with the end of every human life, and so the apocalypse is a purely statistical concept; it is the time when the majority of the population is going through the end of the world. But is it only our country or actually the world? There's never been a case when cancer starting, say, in the lung, killed the lung and left it at that. The whole body dies. We are not quite dying yet, rather, as Gorbachev used to say, "the process is gradually becoming more and more irreversible". The government — which occasionally runs past the window, is doing everything it can to turn the current of events in a different direction, and sometimes very intelligent heads do emerge from the raging waves for a few seconds. But what can our escape from Gorbachev's torture-cell of price on non-existent goods, or the renaming of metro stations built in the thirties after the old historical names of the streets they stand on, or even the regular setting of the clocks one hour forward or one hour backward actually change? It probably won't even do any good if they carry out their plan to rename some of the planets in the sky above the restored Russia and the independent Ukraine. It won't even do any good to hand over power to the Soviets of Paratroopers' Deputies — there is only the faint hope that all of these black and white apocalyptic steeds with their terrifying riders have already been eaten up by the class-conscious workers of some distant coal-mine.

...There's the sound of shooting outside the window, and just to be safe I duck down. Now I can't see anything. I can close my eyes and try to calm myself by thinking about something less disturbing the cinema, for instance. Of course, the most expensive and opulent horror film of the last fifty years is now being shot in Russia: but the horror is of a rather specific kind. You can't get a taste of it simply by walking around the streets and looking at the faces or the price-lists in the empty shops. There is nothing particularly horrifying in all that — this country has seen worse. What's important is something else: we are all bound to each other by thousands of invisible threads, which transmit our feelings like the current in the general power-supply. There's no need to read the newspapers or watch the television to understand that a psychic storm of immeasurable violence is raging in the skies over Russia. You only have to close your eyes to be struck in the face by an invisible wave of other people's terror and despair, and while the shots are still rattling away outside, there's time to wonder what brings this exaggerated and irrational terror into our lives. It's obviously not just the uncertainty about tomorrow and yesterday. Animals don't know what they're going to eat tomorrow, but still for millions of years they've carried on walking and flying and swimming about. Even miles down under the sea, in the eternal darkness, there are half-blind fish resisting the pressure of thousands of tons of water on every side. They're not squashed flat as a pancake for the simple reason that their internal pressure is equal to the external pressure. But if one of these fish is pulled from the depths up to the surface, it will explode like a bomb.

We are the same kind of fish. For seventy years we have lived under the pressure of tons of terror, which has permeated everything around us so thoroughly that we have ceased to notice it. It has become an integral part of ourselves, and now that they have tried to drag us up to the surface in a few short years, up to freedom and the sun, we feel terror advancing on us out of the future. But there is no terror in the future — what we are feeling now comes from inside us. We are being torn apart by the terror that used to be balanced by the inhuman pressure applied to our souls. They keep on pulling us up higher and higher, and we've already swollen perceptibly, but if only we don't burst in the next few metres, at long last we shall finally glimpse the sun.

The shooting finally dies down, and I can risk a glance out of the window again. Now, thank God, all I see is what is really out there — an empty courtyard covered in snow, lighted street-lamps

The View from the Window

and a slope of ice up which two young children are dragging a sledge. They are arguing about something and laughing so loudly that I can hear them through the glass, I suddenly come to, throw open the window and see that the world beyond it is the same as always, the sky is calm and clear, and I can even see a few stars. There is a cold wind swirling snowflakes in the air, and it's quite obvious that nothing terrible will ever happen outside the window unless we really want it to happen.

Because the world is not what we see through the window. It is each of us, looking through our own windows.

© *Translation Andrew Bromfield, 1992*

Authors of books about Russia, interested in the opinion of their Russian colleagues about their work, are welcome to send us books for review. They will be read by Russian specialists in the field with a knowledge of English and offered to publishers for possible publication in Russian translation.

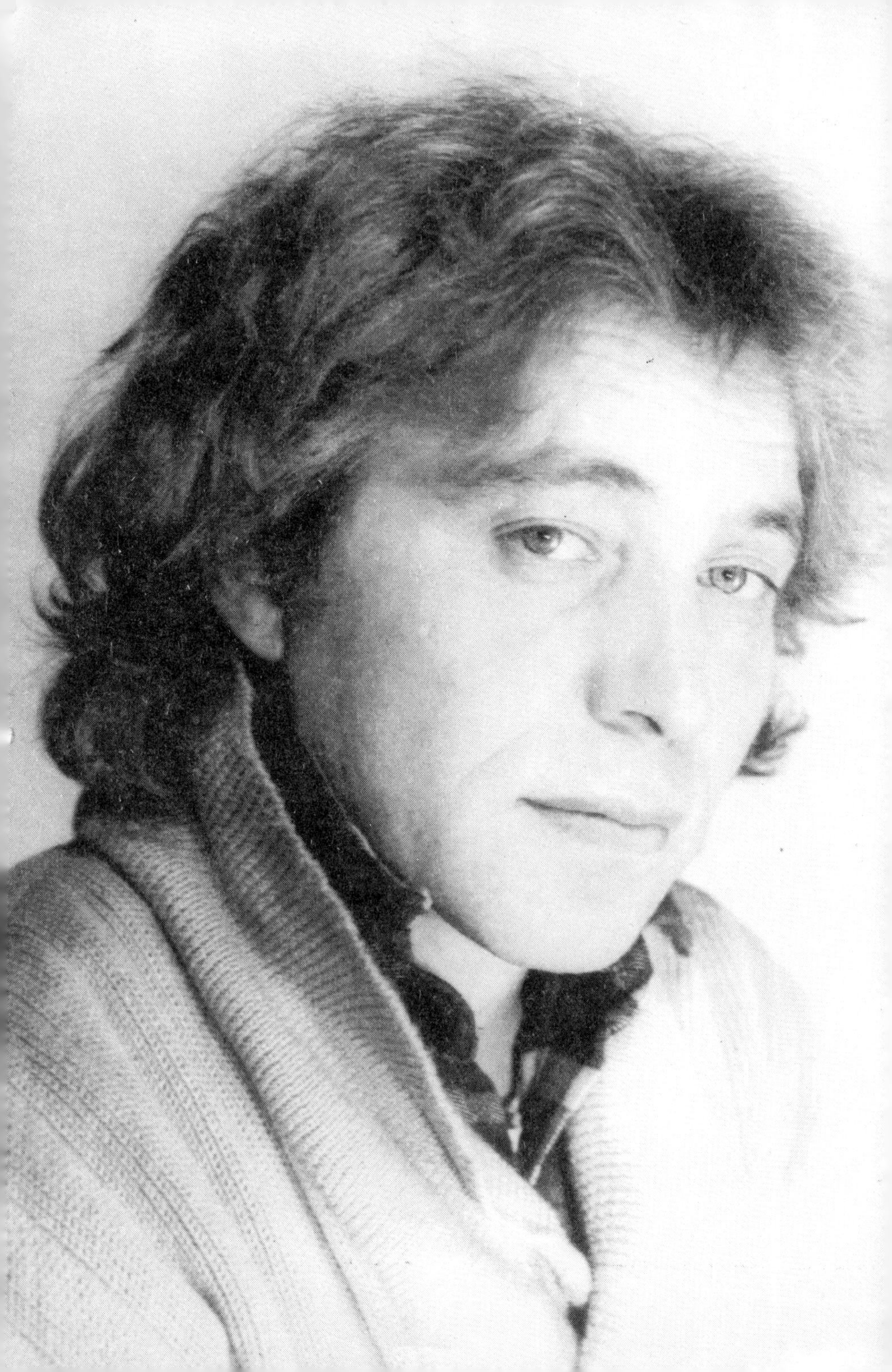

Zufar GAREYEV

FACSIMILE SUMMER

I noticed him immediately they got in the train in Moscow. He was a clean-cut, gangly, American-looking hunk with an in haircut, spiked but short. He was wearing shell-suit bottoms with webbing on the pockets and showing off three quarters of his lanky ankles. In white socks.

You could run a similar description on me. You might say, "She was a girl of about eighteen with a sultry look, a punk haircut, and wearing an Xtra Large jacket." I'm very in too, apart from my eyes. I know just how they look: heavy, weird, like I'm not getting enough. Take them away and I'd have a perfectly pretty face and no one would ever suspect. A girl ready for plucking. A girl like a thousand others. Who cares whether she's got a name. Even if taking the eyes away is going too far, they can always be concealed. Just keep the eyelids half-closed so people don't notice and snarl, "Oh, so that's the kind you are," before they kick you out. Ouch! "We don't want you here! We're out to have a good time, we're cool. We buy ice creams and in the evenings flit about the metro stations" (and glide past the blue aquaria of the cafes).

So anyway, there am I sitting and wondering who he's with. He can't just be on his own. Everybody has to be with somebody.

Too right. There's mumsy sitting right beside him, then some girl, probably an older sister, and another woman. Auntie? More kids nearby, with their parents. Off on a two-day family outing to the Preventive Therapy Sanatorium, aka the trade union guest house in our village, I expect.

Mum's in a tizz:

"Dima, at least have a sandwich."

She ferrets around in some carrier bags. Sounds of rustling polythene. Auntie isn't going to blow away in the wind from the look of her. Maybe be a high-up bureaucrat. She declaims from the newspaper:

"In the Moscow region the temperature will be twenty-two degrees. Wind easterly, becoming northerly later. Temperatures gradually becoming cooler. 197 Hear that, Anya?"

Mother's persistence has vexed Dima.

"Leave it out!"

She is a small, bustling woman, like a monkey. An ingratiating smile hovers permanently about her lips.

"Well, how about a nice apple. Or some of granny's pies. She put them out specially."

He reads my look. He blushes.

"Leave it out, I said."

She has a mouth full of white teeth, false, an unspeakable wig, flame-coloured, small veiny hands, and gold dripping from her fingers and ears.

I go out to the vestibule. He's going to come out after me in a minute. He does, only not alone. A fat friend in glasses comes with him. They stand across from me, Tubs playing with his cigarette, Dima lethargically propelling a sweet round his mouth with his tongue. I smell oranges.

"Mamselle is travelling far?" he asks, the incarnation of cool. It is not so much a question as an ironical asseveration.

His fat friend is put out and retreats. Just before pulling the door to behind him he turns round. Can this be jealousy?

"To Fryanovo, monsieur?" I enquire. "For the Preventive Therapy?"

A wry smile.

"*En famille*, worst luck!"

I shrug.

"Children love their parents and parents love their children. *Que faire?*..."

A mutual silence.

"*Vous etes des amis?*"

"With Valera?" A shrug.

I was right. Valera is an embarrassment. I double-check my results by saying cattily,

"Perhaps he hasn't had breakfast yet. He seems very hungry..."

Dima blushes. I've caught him off balance. He rapidly adapts to the new circumstances:

"What joys would life hold for him were it not for the odd burger."

He has betrayed his friend. *Pour moi!*

"Does he have a complex about his awfulness, I wonder?"

"Hardly!"

He smiles, unable to conceal his pleasure.

"He dogs my every move and gives me little prezzies with goofy notes like, "No, I am not sentimental...""

"Perhaps he'd like to join us for a moment?"

"What for?" My whim strikes him as odd, but he looks into the carrriage and beckons Valera.

Valera shambles clumsily through the door. I have turned to look the other way, as if Dima and I hadn't been talking at all. Or perhaps Dima has been trying to chat this girl up, muffed it, and now she's clammed up on him.

Valera is a heavy breather. He's still playing with his cigarette, unable to decide whether to light it. Outside the window an industrial landscape of building excavations, chimneys, and rust-brown rivulets is crawling by. Dima's pretty little face bobs cattily over his friend's shoulder.

"Off you go now, Valera," he says, giving him a thump on the shoulder.

Valera crawls off back to the carriage, his tail between his legs.

"He can go eat a bun."

We gas on, and then it is Fryanovo. I rush to find a telephone, intending to tell grandma in Moscow that I've arrived safely, will meet her as planned on Monday, won't phone again before then, and send my love to mother. I figure I should be able to fit that in and still catch up with the boys: my grandmother's house and the famous Preventive Therapy Sanatorium lie in the same direction. But of course there has to be a queue for the phone, then our telephone is engaged for ages. So there isn't time to fit it in and they've gone before I'm finished.
I think. The first thing they'll do in this heat is go for a swim in the river. They all do. I'll catch them on their way back.

I go out of the house, down the street to the river, and spot them straight away. They are swimming. No need for girls just now as they embrace the water, the blue sky, the summer, their white trainers and colourful rugby shirts strewn over the grass...

O summer mine! It is not for me to plunge into your tousled greenery. My hair and my jagged thoughts will snag on you and jerk me back, my neck will snap and my eye glaze over in mid-flight. To jump I must not dare, but grit my teeth as best I can. Endure, but jump? Never!

I take up my position by the fence. A Zhiguli drives past,

covering me in red dust. The river is not so improperly proximate that someone could say,

"Look at that girl over there. Eyeing us over, she is. Bet she knows where it goes."

I wait a while for them to come back, and then I think,

"Why don't I saunter down to the kvas stall for a glass of fruit juice? I can see them just as well from there, ducking into their thin shirts, and still be back in time."

I walk there without looking back. Another Zhiguli comes towards me, bouncing and jiggling in the soft potholes, and bouncing and jiggling the red-haired ladies inside it. I feel quite ill, imagining they are all wearing wigs in this incredible heat, hot enough to melt your brain. There is no juice. It's sold out. The kiosk assistant is plump. His signet rings, damp with kvas, gleam dully in his puffy fingers. He looks at me with curiosity. I can see him out of the corner of my eye. He is probably thinking,

"She's a bit of all right. Looks like she's got a bit of a chip on the old shoulder, though. Funny that. Girls don't usually have chips on the old shoulder. Simple creatures they are. Either laugh or else they cry."

I look away and see the boys are already out of the water and pulling on their clothes. One is hopping, trying to shake the water out of his ears; another is already stooping over his trainers. I return to my station by the fence. The road curves round towards me here. They are strolling lazily along, a disorderly gaggle making no real effort at conversation, just exchanging the odd remark. Dima is not exactly in the centre of things; rather peripheral, in fact. I am heartened. No rivals. I'm bound to get somewhere with him. Okay, so his tubby pal is tagging along beside him and has already glanced anxiously in my direction several times. I can't decide how best to position myself. Turning away to face the fence would be affected and silly, and anyway I would not get to see Dima properly. Staring straight at him would be too brazen. I'm not a prostitute, after all, or a half-wit. I turn sideways on to them, my eyes on a diagonal. None of them look my way as they go past, except Valera of course. I feel sorry for him, poor clumsy clot. He is, after all, protecting the air I drink.

Dima is sucking a sweet. I seem to smell a faint, cool, citrus fragrance.

They pass me and then laugh raggedly. He glances round quickly, furtively, and immediately turns away again.

How I love this. You will be walking along the street, a group of boys and girls coming towards you. The eyes of one or other of the boys, the least predictable, less often a girl, linger over you. A little enigmatic splinter of me has lodged in his heart. I understand myself only too well. I want to pick them up off the street, at random, unpredictably. I want them to be from the street. The street is so vivid, and so mysterious. It stops in its tracks, it moves on towards the metro, flows towards bus stops. It has a thousand eyes, and hands, and hidden, timid, evanescent desires, with no one to extrapolate them but me.

In the evening I am back at the fence. I can see the broad, well-lit entrance of the Preventive and Therapeutic nicely. The veranda is also brightly lit and has tables dotted around, and there is a dance floor with sparkling fairy-lights of red, yellow and violet. Who knows, when he's had a drink or two he may fancy taking a stroll along the road where that girl was standing earlier. I wait. No dice. I head for the dance floor myself. The new arrivals are standing on the sidelines, sceptical observers of the provincial scene. He has spotted me. I vanish into the shadows. That should have been enough. He will find a reason and ditch the others. I move off and deploy myself at the exact spot where our eyes met during the day, where the road curves lovingly towards the fence. I stand there for a long time and begin to wonder whether life may be outsmarting me. A good twenty minutes pass before he appears in the distance. He approaches.

"Hi," he says.

"Hi," I reply. "Let's go."

We go in the direction of my house. He asks,

"Where are we going?" and I hear in his voice the unasked question, "Her place?"

I say, "My place."

He is slightly unnerved, I can tell, although he is hardly going to let on. He just very straightforwardly consents:

"Let's go."

I have to bring him out of his shell. It's no good trying to love him tenderly like a small child, from the great height of my long experience of life.

He asks, "What's your name?"
"Oxana. Oxana Sorochenko."
"Right. Mine's Dima."
"I know."
We talk about this and that.
We come to the house. I say, "You are a student somewhere. College?"
"Sherlock Holmes in a skirt! But which one?"
"A good one. I know a lot of other things about you too."
He is very quiet for a moment, before giving me a wary look. I realise he's just decided I'm a psychopath. The conversation immediately ceases to gel. He has closed up on me. He probably just wants to make his escape. My eyes have probably got their heavy, weird look and he has noticed. I bet he is thinking I am not really eighteen years old, which I am, but a good thirty, which I am not, and if I try getting in to the dance floor torches will suddenly shine and I'll be asked,
"Your ticket please, madam. Gate-crashing! We saw you."
Everybody will turn round and start shouting, "There she is! That's her!"
He sits in grandma's rocking chair, his eyes half closed. He wants to make it clear that in a minute he is going to land me such a punch in the face. His contempt for me, filthy slut that I am, has been building up all this time and now...
"That rocking chair is sixty years old."
Some conversation I've started, but there's nothing to be done about it now.
"Great," he replies. "That's really good." He rocks purposefully, keeping his eyes half closed.
"You want to go, then?" I ask.
"Are you trying to get rid of me already?"
"You don't mind being here?"
"No. I don't mind."
I don't believe him for an instant.
"You do mind. You just don't want to admit it."
"No," he assures me, "I really, absolutely do not mind. What makes you think I do?"
I begin to calm down, but something is nagging at me, telling

me he does mind really. I'm not going to get to kiss him. He'll push me away. Somebody else's spit: Yuck! He would just want to push me off, run to the bathroom, have a good bath, rub himself dry, put on a pair of clean shorts, stretch out in bed and fall sound asleep. Hands outside the blankets, as recommended in books for parents on the family and marriage. Up in the morning, slip out of the sheets, rustling and tangling round your legs, pulled along after your body. Falling off abandoned...

Then down to the river. Stroll along the shingle, your own man, belonging only to the sun and the sky and the water, and the clean, washed grass by the shoreline. Come back here, give me a dirty look, try to work out how to get away from me.

I peel an orange and offer him half. He eats it, cupping his hand underneath.

"Want a sweet?" I ask.

He doesn't see the connection.

"A sweet?"

Suddenly I fling myself on the divan and start wailing.

I cry and cry. Without turning round or getting up I say,

"Go away. Forget all about me. I'll stay here on my own."

I lie on my stomach, pressing my hands under myself, listening. He is fussing, something jingling in his pockets, change or keys fixed to his belt with a key-ring, small bright, nickel-plated objects. I look up. He is bending over his trainers, making the tongues stick out a bit more. That's it. *Fin.*

"Got anything to drink?" he asks hoarsely. "My throat's dry."

"In the kitchen."

I trail after him. He turns the light on, stands there blinking in the brightness.

He has something to drink and says,

"I'll phone. What's your number?"

I write it down on a piece of paper which he shoves in his pocket. I must seem very pathetic at this moment, because he gives me a smile, although it turns out pretty twisted and unconvincing.

"You won't be lonely without me, eh, Holmes? I want you to be a good girl now."

"I'll be good. Don't I get your phone number?"

He writes it on a scrap of newspaper. Who knows, perhaps he really will ring:

"Hello, Holmes, no sweat over the other night. Let's meet up."

Then I tenderly run my fingers over his punkoid haircut and whisper,

"You will ring, Dima. You will ring me, won't you?"

"Got to be off now," is his reply.

"I'll come part of the way with you. Don't want you getting lost."

I have no sooner said it than I am convulsed with inane laughter, evidently a nervous reaction. I roar with laughter, flailing my arms and sending a glass crashing from the table. I notice in passing the astonishment on his face. I am walking in front, staggering all over the place, unable to control my guffawing.

We come out to the road and he says,

"Don't come any further."

"Why not?" I ask.

"Just because." He crumples. "Just don't."

I shrug.

"Goodbye, then."

I wait until he has disappeared and then head again for the dance floor. The fairy-lights are still there, and someone is singing somesing from one of Leontiev's songs,

"The mists of memory swirl above us.
You seem a dream..."

I sit a while on a bench. There's a boy who can't take his eyes off me, a funny boy with round, mad eyes. First he asks me if I have any matches, then he wants to know the time, then he says hasn't he seen me somewhere before.

Suddenly I spot Dima and Valera heading off for the station. I follow them. I can't help myself. I just want to see him off, without being seen. They just make it to the train in time. They jump in and the doors immediately slam shut behind them. I go back home.

I am thinking. "Now I can ring him tomorrow, and see him perhaps. Tomorrow I'll go back to Moscow."

What a beautiful morning, everything dredged in silvery dew. I come in to the station in Moscow, firmly close the door of the telephone kiosk behind me, and dial Dima's number. Engaged. "If at first you don't succeed..." I can wait. I wonder who's at home with him: his father? His grandmother?

"Can I speak to Dima, please?"

"Who shall I say is calling?"

"We are students at the very good college together. Please don't be alarmed."

I re-dial. Engaged, and again engaged.

His pal Seryozha or his mate Andrey has rung him up to chet.

"Hiya, Dimbo."

"Oh, hi yourself."

And so on. Very laid-back, nothing heavy. The in way of conducting a telephone conversation this summer, a half-conversation, fag in mouth, interspersed with yawning, the collar of your light summer jacket turned up against the wind which has, as the newspaper predicted, changed direction. There will be a nip in the air for the next few days. The wind tugs and tugs at the collar of that insubstantial jacket, and tugs and tugs at your words. A conversation blows away on the wind, away from the town to bio-degrade in the country without harm to the environment. Not a conversation to stir you up or weigh you down. The words have just a hint of something coming from the heart, just a hint of ideas and human breath, a quarter part, an eighth, slipping out the corner of a mouth.

At last I get through.

"Can I speak to Dima, please?"

"Sorry. You must have the wrong number. There's no one called Dima here."

I have the wrong number. There is no one called Dima there. There never has been and there never will be. At least now I know the score.

I come out of the kiosk. I stand for a moment and then go over to the flower-sellers near the platform without even knowing why. I suppose I just want some lilac. There's always a good choice of flowers, but when I spot the lilac I know that is what I am looking for. I go up to the woman selling it. Her lilac has a smoky, almost ashen hue. I shoulder my way through to it, sorry that I am not wearing a white dress today. I so wanted it. I should just send them all to hell and pull it on, even though I can't stand white, or dresses. At the school-leavers' ball last year some of us girls wore lilac, but only for a hoot. I stand there like an idiot in the midst of the station bustle wishing I was wearing a white dress. I look at the lilac for an age, and then say,

"Be a dear, let me have just a tiny little spray for fifteen kopeks."

"A right one we've got here," the woman retorts. "Think I'm going to mangle my lilac for you for fifteen kopeks?"

What a cow! I shove fifteen kopeks her way, quickly snap off a tiny bit, and head smartly for the platform. I can hear her shrieking behind me, "You got no conscience, you hooligan, you!"

I run to the train and stand in the vestibule. When the creaking carriage moves off I fasten the sprig of lilac in my hair. It is only a little piece, but I can feel a coolness from it. It has an orangey tang to it. That is why it had to be lilac.

"Mamselle is travelling far?" Oh Dima, you narrow, faithless little boy.

I look out the window and raise my hand to my hair. This girl was travelling very, very far. The day before she had been going round saying,

"Listen everybody, I'm going far, far away."

"Well, well." Everybody was amazed.

"Yes," the girl said, "I am leaving and going far away." She measured up the white dress.

"Really!" people protested to her. "How can anyone go far, far away in this day and age?"

"You can," the girl replied, cutting out the pattern.

"How can you travel in a white dress, especially if you are going far, far away," people asked in perplexity, and some of them got quite cross.

"Of course I must wear a white dress," the girl explained to them. "It absolutely must be white. How can you not understand that?"

Then many of them pursed their lips disapprovingly.

But the girl sat working all night at her dress, hunched over it and glancing out the window. Suddenly she gave a start. Rosy-fingered dawn was colouring the window pane. With cold fingers she started doing up the buttons of her dress.

Zufar Gareyev

For breakfast she drank only a glass of cold, clear air, with an ice cube, by the window, throwing her head back so that her long hair cascaded downwards. Her teeth chattered against the tumbler because she was so excited.

She set the glass down on the window sill, walked to the railway station, and boarded the train.

The doubting people came to see her off. She waved her hand to them, and they shouted to her and ran along the platform as the train moved off. Where was this town far, far away that she was going to?

"It's far away," the girl cried, "beyond the Urals, beyond the Celestial Mountains of Tien Shan, beyond the Carpathians and the Alps. It's a tiny town with quaint, crooked streets and little houses with roofs of red and green."

"And is there lots of lilac there?" the people shouted, running along the platform.

"Yes, there is lots and lots of lilac!"

She would put a tiny sprig of lilac in her hair as she walked through the streets. She would roam them for a long, long time wanting neither to eat or drink or sleep or worry about anything at all. She would have no suitcase and no flat and nobody would look at her crossly and ask her where she worked and what she thought she was doing with her life.

"Really?" people shouted. "Will it really be like that?"

Would people really not ask questions or give orders? Some were horrified at the thought, and everybody ran along the platform shaking their grey heads. "It's not possible! No. It's impossible. Oh, heavens, no, never, never..."

They ran and became more and more breathless until finally they began to gasp and suffocate and tear at their clothes and fall down. They clutched at each other with weakening hands, and they shrieked and trampled each other underfoot. They cried out in horror, and there was nothing, absolutely nothing left that any of them could achieve in their own lives. And all that remained for each of them was to whisper,

"Good luck, dear girl. *Bon voyage!*"

Translated by Arch Tait

May We Recommend

to our Russian-speaking readers

SOLO

EXPERIMENTAL AND AVANT-GARDE WRITING

A bimonthly magazine, 100 pages
Editor: Alexander Mikhailov
Editorial Board: Andrei Bitov, Evgeni Popov,
Zufar Gareyev, Vladimir Zuyev

"SOLO is a direct descendant of METROPOL. It is the only literary journal in Russia solely devoted to new talents whose chances of success in today's market economy are just as slim as they were under total ideologisation.
In the general atmosphere of confusion in Russia today, SOLO carries confident young voices, it spotlights contemporary nonconformists in the provinces and the capital alike. If you want to know not just the present but also the future of Russian literature,
SOLO is your best reading."   Andrei Bitov

With the material selected by such prominent figures in contemporary Russian letters as Andrei Bitov, Evgeny Popov, Alexander Mikhailov, Zufar Gareyev, and Vladimir Zuyev, SOLO is a hallmark of impeccable taste.

SOLO won the Russian Booker Special Prize for magazines

GLAS is preparing an issue on Young Voices mainly based on SOLO publications.

For subscription contact: Kubon and Zagner
Buchexport-Import, Hebstrasse 39/41, Postfach
340108, W-8000 Munchen 34, Germany
Tel: 089-522 027   Fax: 089-523 2547

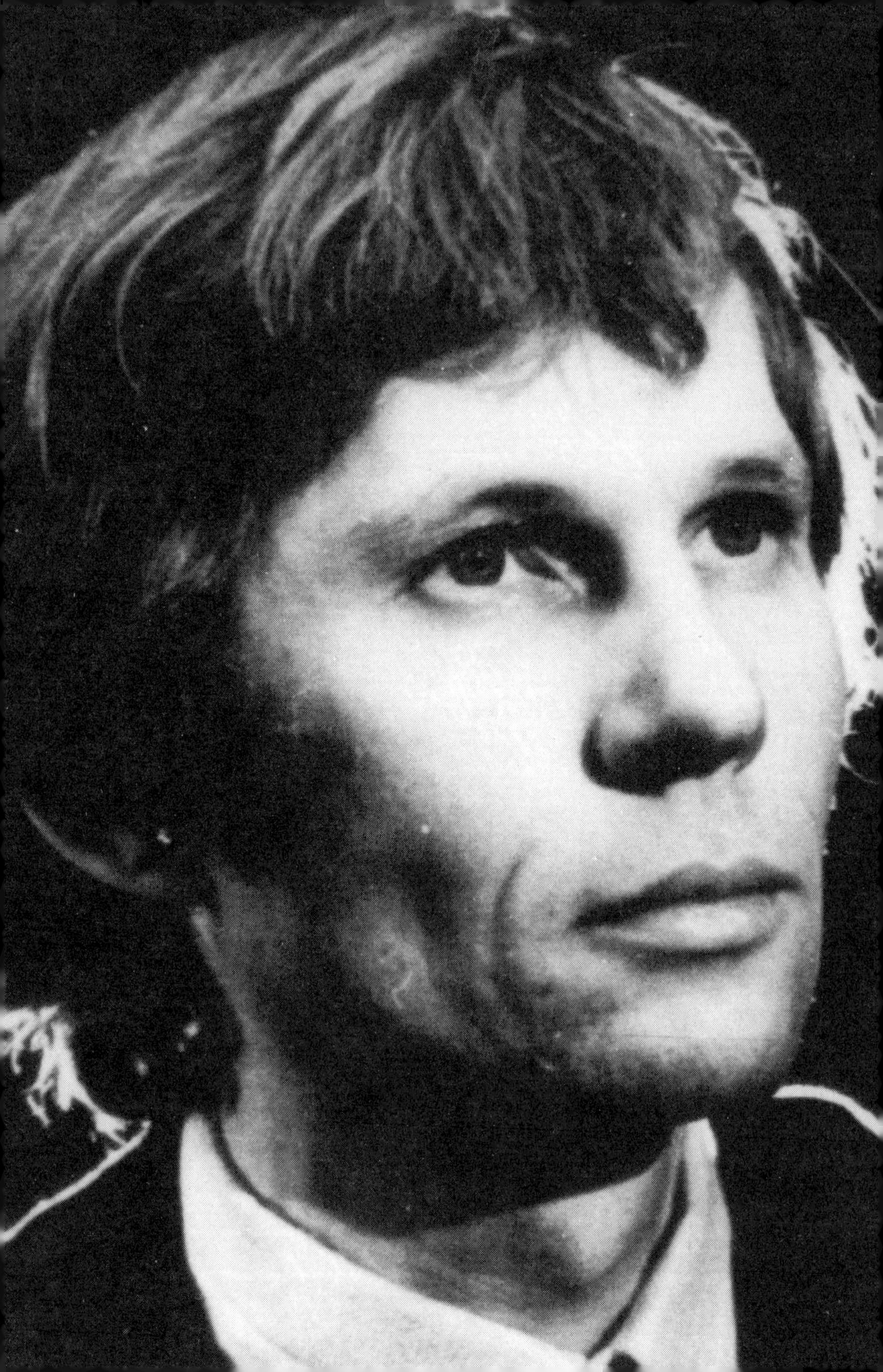

Yevgeny
KHARITONOV

TEARDROPS ON THE FLOWERS

Only yesterday, and where is it now? Old crowds have mutated into new crowds, a mood has passed, and lovers are ex-lovers.

Life assumes new forms I can't adapt to: Vocational Training Institutes, pop groups, Swedish love communes. Encircled by a world which has no place for me. I hear the young say. "You are no longer of interest to us, but you are admirably qualified to understand us, so we shall show you our genius. Understand it." I know, though, that when it is at last my cue they will run off, except for some who will stay out of politeness. And those who run off will be the ones I fancied, and those who stay will be the ones I don't.

I am an old man now and new things bother me, the ever-changing fads designed to make us obsolete.

I planted the flowers facing me, but they have turned away to face the sun, and now I am in the row behind.

Once upon a time I went out to my grave to sit a while, and eat an egg to my health. I sat and I sat, and what did I see? I saw nothing. I couldn't see, only hear. And smell. So there I sat, smelling, and a little flower came flying up to me, flapping its little arms and legs. "Hello, little flower," said I. "What do you want of me?" "Give all of your life to me," said the little flower. "Here you are, little flower," I said. "Take all of my life, and give me in return all of my death." Then I died, and he grew where I had been.

I had not the strength for living, and couldn't find the pulse anyway. I wanted fixity, motionlessness. All I ever asked for was a corner where I could rest, bide a while, have a smoke, be still, stretch out my legs, or maybe just turn up my toes. I always pretended, of course, that I only had to fall in love truly to find hope. I would catch fire, burst into life, my real, exotic temperament would blaze forth. How could it be expected to blaze forth until it had something to feed on? Of course, nothing much did come its way. For that I would have had to fight, and know how to provoke interest, and I was no good at that. I spent all my time concentrating things in writing. I got into writing because I wouldn't have been any good at standing up straight: and I was no good at sports.

Mostly I made friends with girls, away from the roughness and fighting. Playtime scared me. Hordes of crude, truculent, heartless, unfeeling, spiritually stunted adolescents rushing out to punch each other up. I would press up against a wall with my eyes shut, or stay in the classroom.

(Shall we start now on a disentangling of causes and effects, or shall we recognise that the cause was not what caused it?) Your author, at all events, became ever more isolated, and scurried ever deeper into his dead end. Goodbye. May you too find your dead end in life.

Is everything in my life by now really so settled and obvious, with no nook left out of which something unexpected might turn up? Perhaps that's a prerogative of fresh young things, and it's time now for me to join the grumblers.

"Do you enjoy grumbling?"

"Very much so. A most accomplished grumbler, I am. Hey! Where do you think you're going? Can't you see I haven't finished grumbling to you yet?"

Today I was hit by my hundredth birthday. Everything there is to say I have already said and thought in my life.

A poet hasn't, after all, got that much he can say. He just repeats himself again and again. It's a trial to read his collected works and see how a person can go over the same ground again and again.

For all that, the aim remains constant: to break through to truthful utterance, which is bliss. To give voice to truth uncontestable.

Despite which, the germ of untruthfulness is lodged within each of us, and all because prudence bids us stay on good terms with each other.

I brushed against her. Heaven forbid she should think to sway back against me. Nevertheless, brush against her I did out of a humane sense of obligation, because from the way she was looking at me I could tell how much she wanted that. She probably thought I just didn't approve of all that common cuddling. Actually, it was not a sense of obligation that made me do it, but more that I did not want her to stop liking me. I did not want to see active dislike in her eyes, and a coldness because I hadn't touched her.

It does get to you rather when some girl who has been pursuing and doting on you, and thinking it an honour that you deign to be escorted by her or let her invite herself round, suddenly drops you. Even if she has been beginning to get on your nerves, it makes you want to continue the cruel game you have been playing with her; cruel because you were deliberately being polite and solicitous when that was the last thing she wanted. Your friendliness was a ruse to keep her from being forward and coming on too strong when, wittingly or unwittingly, she had been wanting it for ages. Why weren't you getting on with it? Poor girl. Until now she had known where she was in her dealings with men, or lads, and the male of the species in general. You had pout and flounce. Certain things they mustn't be allowed to get away with. You must be haughty, raise their hopes sometimes but then, once you had them horny, become unapproachable again. Suddenly all these tactics she had been assimilating since childhood, from her mother perhaps and her girl friends, these feminine wiles which were supposed to enable her to outsmart any man, were something he was better at than she was.

It was she who had to keep phoning, to try to engineer an invitation to come round, to work out ways of sitting next to him; and it was she who was reduced to a frazzle. She was on the receiving end of smiles of amity when that was not at all what was wanted, and which were quite the wrong sort of smile anyway. She had been invited to stay the night, although as yet she had no inkling of this, because she would not be coming alone, but bringing a girl friend who would be bringing a boy from the club, and because afterwards the boys and girls would be sleeping in separate rooms. She may still have hoped that this was all just her well brought-up host being respectable. Everything was wholly inexplicable, until somebody at last explained what was going on, and she was left with a wound in her heart which would never heal. To allow at least a scab to form she has resolved to stop going to the club. If by mischance she should meet you in the Underground she will be civil, asking how things are, but terminate the exchange just a little curtly. You

Teardrops on the Flowers

aren't exactly stung, but you want the game to continue. You suddenly rather wickedly wish her in love with you again. Not that you are upset, altogether, but you do feel just slightly miffed by the idea that somebody can fall out of love with you. You even sometimes think it might be a good idea to ring her up on some suitably practical pretext, just to set her little heart a-flutter and make her want to devise a reason to ring you up, when needless to say you would again talk to her in the old way, within the bounds of your humane sense of obligation, even though there is cruelty in your humaneness. You like her being unable to catch you out as to where the cruelty lies, even though she knows it is there, but at the same time can't imagine what you can be guilty of, when all there is on the surface is civility.

At least this game still amuses me, so I can't completely have lost interest in people, or in life for that matter.

In the ordinary course of events, the woman at your side ought really to be in love with you. She should be someone who has heard all about you from your own lips, and with whom meaningful glances can be exchanged over some silly, good-looking young post office clerk; or tender golden-tongued songster with a voice bigger than his throat (but a chicken for all that); or a boy going by in the street, or one who's come to repair the fridge. You can't exchange that sort of glance with your straight peers, who only share such looks with their friends a propos of mare-like women trotting by. It is nonetheless important (as well as being agreeable) that this confidante who understands you and your every mood so well should be (platonically) in love with you. Try, even so, not to be left alone with her. When you and she are together in public she can read your glances at other people and interpret all your moods. You are talking to a young man who has come to the club to see you. It is clear from certain amusing inconsequentialities in the conversation how much you fancy him, and how little he understands where you are at. Who will provide an audience for your darkling smile, who can pick up the nuance in an apposite remark, a solitary word deftly slipped in but rich with all your very special experience? He understands nothing; she sees it all. Who could you find better able to savour your sad maxims?

What kind of woman should she be? Not intellectual, that's for sure: not the sort of woman friend who's as up on everything as you are yourself. How are you to make something of a person every bit as intelligent as yourself? No intellect, if you are to have any prospect of success. Then you can goad her, order her around, swear at her, even, possibly, knock her about a bit. And love her for it. She doesn't want to be physically large or, heaven forbid, liberated, and of course she should be young: and stupid, so you have no qualms about telling her she is a silly cow. She should keep asking you how things should be done, and sing while she is doing them, or rather, hum quietly so as not to disturb you.

Any respect for her as a person and you're dead. How can you imagine someone naked and looking up at you from below if you are on terms of understanding courtesy with you? You would be making a mockery of her dignity as a human being.

S. noticed I was enervated as long ago as 1961, so what can you expect nowadays. It showed in Physical Education lessons at school, and in my coordination. I am hopeless at jiving. Good jivers bounce; the music pulsates through them and they devise a succession of rhythmic figures as they respond and react to it. God grant arhythmic me just to remain on an even keel.

In my compositions I try to collect as much as I can, droplet by droplet, in order to produce a tight, saturated, compressed lump, a vision of life, concentrated and condensed. I do it for my soul, and I do it to pretend to others that in my own life I am no less dazzlingly intense and resilient.

Art can be a thing composed from fragments, lots of itty little bits and pieces glued together to form a whole. The pieces are assembled and something extra inserted. Or art can be a gasp! A song! A bullseye scored! A javelin hurled and soaring home! If there be talent. The first kind of art can have sophistication, and entirely merit your putting on your spectacles to scrutinise it, or listening intently to what is in there for the hearing. But talent takes your breath away, catches you up and carries you off into the empyrean.

Teardrops on the Flowers

The first kind of art can sweep you off your feet and call you to join forces with it to do battle or to love. It is a song which teases you to sing along. But with the second there's no question of your joining in. Your part is to listen with delicacy and succumb to enchantment, to catch a soft, far distant music. The first blares at you until you practically have to block your ears or give up and say, "Aargh, take me!" The second demands that you pick up the libretto and read it carefully, while the words of the first you have no trouble remembering as you pound the rhythm out on yourself. "Hey, that really says it all!" and all pile in together.

There is something strange about the second kind of art, something as weird and hypnotic as the life of fish in an aquarium, another mode of being you look at or listen to as something apart from yourself: while the first infectiously draws you into the dance, brings the tears to your eyes, and makes you want to sing and dance at the same time. The first calls to people, while the second is apart from people, absorbed in its sacral, secret patterns, capable of enchanting even through glass. The first sweeps people off their feet and makes their hearts beat faster. The second you have to penetrate, and there is pleasure in the very reading of it and the penetrating. While the first itself does the penetrating, and seizes, pierces, and drags you along; and may afterwards seem to have been vacuous.

I really should get into pop culture. How many times I've longed to. What sophistication can rival its vulgarity? Alla Pugacheva finishes belting out her latest hit in my flat, only to start up again ten windows along.

Where is love, sweet, swooning, ineffable love, for hard-to-please old me. I've got the flat, the evening, some remnant of youth, and it's summertime, but I haven't got the friend I need. So I'll go on remembering those four months, less and less veraciously, gradually forgetting that even that time things were not really right. No! I take it back. Everything was great. At least let me keep my ability only to have to think something was great for it to have been so. Only it got in the way of my writing, and was no help at all in integrating the different parts of my life (because nothing which prevents you from living alone is compatible with my kind of writing). The only solution is to get a cat and magic it into a seventeen-year-old schoolboy who looks like me, only prettier.

    I would put a saucer out in the kitchen for him, and take him for a walk every morning. He would scratch at the door if he wanted in, and be at home to greet me. He would be lying curled up at my feet as I wrote these words. And I would perform experiments on his body and register the readings with my heart.

    I need a younger brother who needs an older brother.

    The door was heard to open. I came in and over to me. We embraced with dry, careful bodies, not wishing to seem too ardent or to crowd each other, very close, knowing all there was to know about ourselves, real lovers. We have a shared childhood behind us. Only we couldn't have children.

    I once fell out of one world and into another, and now I live in the gap between two worlds. A world of family and loyalty where I was looked after, and a world without families, of infidelity, where you look after yourself.

    Here comes old age, where old men look much like old women, and little old ladies look much like little old gentlemen. How awful!

    Something (and I Know What) holds me back from doing something they would say was really good and successful. You should have nothing in your life: no successes, no familiar faces, and then! And then!

    Only then would your soul have its desire, and your face the necessary palor (the red blotch on your nose notwithstanding).

    If only everything were like that life would take a different course: but "if onlies" don't come to pass, because I am at home in yearning.

    I shall never find happiness: of course not. I am incapable of feeling it. For some reason I can always see its down side, an insight I could do without. It irritates me that I know that I could do without it. I know you can know too much; but still I know it.

Teardrops on the Flowers

Yesterday I seemed to be within an ace of what I long for, and I blew it by being too clever by half.

Oh, my demon. Will I ever be free of this knowing?

It's all just shapes, and correlations between objects. Which objects exactly is immaterial to this knowingness. Everything is functions and circuits. Perhaps spirit is in there somewhere, but not soul: or heart. A heart needs something to grow up against. More specifically, it needs to cling to who you are; what you like; what makes you cry; what makes you close your eyes with joy; what you were taught as a child; how you were spoiled when you were little.

A person needs an anchor and a faith to share. Not just any anchor and not just any faith, but his own particular Anchor and his particular Faith. If you share our Faith, be one with us; but if all you are looking for is a faith, then you might as well go to hell. God is on our side. And no, it's not that you might as well go to hell, but you really will Go to Hell. God is on our side. Not just any god, the Real One. Don't take me for a mathematician!

Preserve the nation. Preserve our people. What for? Why not encourage an influx of new blood? Isn't the alternative degeneration and stultification? Why is every species and every individual so desperate to preserve itself from outside interference? Because there's a law of self-preservation? At all events, if there is a higher law which requires that a body should be open for the successful functioning of its metabolism, we have no plans to rise to that level. Our instinct is identical with the law of self-preservation and it is, not to allow our present selves to be destroyed. That is what our intellect, and indeed our heart dictates! (How wise of God to endow us with anti-Semitism.)

I should have been a soldier: new soldiers drafted in every year; you're doing your bit for the Motherland; and you're bound by regulations which haven't been dubiously devised by you for yourself.

Nothing is such a turn-on as the agile movements of the young as they run, jump, charge about, soar on the horizontal bar, somersaulting, their vests working up and their trousers working down to the coccyx, records of all that hot, youthful energy. Where there is health and youth, there too there is war!

MY IDEA OF HAPPINESS

Going into a bathhouse and simply, effortlessly scoring. Unfortunately I can't do it. I'm hopeless at chatting up. You need low cunning. It's no good just going over, as I once did on a railway station at the age of nineteen, and naively propositioning an agreeable deity sitting on a suitcase. He reacted as if I were diseased. You need cunning and you need the knack, all of which grates on the Soul of the Poet. Well, all right then, so what do you have to do? Don't pose, for a start. Keep your cool. Don't get too involved with him, and when he starts wondering why you're talking to him anyway, don't start being afraid he's going to bawl you out or laugh at you. Don't be afraid of getting your fingers burnt. Do remember nobility of spirit has no place in courtship rituals and the making of conquests, which demand both agility and a readiness to crawl, and possibly a familiarity with and willingness to resort to the language of the gutter. You need an up-to-date grasp of contemporary values, and the ability to sustain a conversation if you are not to get precisely nowhere. B. is amazing the way he can touch them up on an overcrowded bus. He puts his hand straight on their flies, the targetted fifteen-year-old quite often gets a hard on, and presses right back at him. If he pulls away and swears at him, it just runs off Boris. He even turns nasty himself, demanding to know what is going on. Or so he says.

Anyway, to return to bathhouses. You really do need to know what you are doing. It's no good being embarrassed. Slide up the bench to him and get chatting. If he says something rude, just move on without feeling you've been humiliated or lost your dignity. In this life happiness is turning your own trick, won with your own fair hands, not one somebody else has found, and you managed to grab a bit because they did you a favour. Get out there and do your own cruising. Don't be a Chekhov character in a shitty closet. You need strong nerves. Don't lapse into mute, hopeless melancholy. Go for it. Stalk them, feel your way, spy out the land like a Jack London hero. Lie, if you need to, make promises, get them interested, and then go for it! Don't settle for exquisite sorrow. Right now there's no one around to admire it anyway. Heaven knows. I used to rely on fellow feeling. I thought you could score by being understanding. You end up getting so understanding you decide to back off because he doesn't really seem to want it, out of fairness. Who's doing who a favour?

Let us turn now to the hunt and the mug's morality of waiting to be asked. We kid ourselves there is something attractive about that tragic pose in *Death in Venice*, when all there is behind it is cowardice and a lack of initiative. Remember, you don't even have an audience to admire your tragic indecision and hopeless gazing at the object of your love. Phaedra paralysed in her hopeless passion is all very well in the theatre, although she would still look good if she were getting somewhere. Even so audiences in Moscow went away or dozed off over that Italian film *Portrait of a Family in an Interior*. Who wants to look at some admirable old gentleman who may be wanting who knows what? If there's something he wants, why doesn't he come out with it? The truth of the matter is he's scared of getting his old bones broken or being called a rude name, although of course he tells himself it's just that he doesn't want to upset a young man needlessly, and that he's very tactful and aware that his quarry has quite different interests. Well he may, but the fact is that old men doing nothing and getting nowhere is a dismal spectacle which just makes everybody feel miserable and worried they'll end up like that themselves. Another point to remember: if you spend an age working out how to make a move and wondering what to say, you're in for a long wait. You hang around hoping he'll notice you and start chatting you up himself. No chance. He needs nothing. You've just got to get in there and get on with it. The longer you put if off the more inexorable the paralysis. Oh dear, you're going to start thinking, it really would seem strange if I were to start trying to talk to him now. He's seen me looking at him: he might think I've got designs on him!

And then of course you need to know where to look for it. For instance, there was that girl who came round to say hello from Alex. She got a temporary residence permit for Moscow working for a domestic services firm called "Zarya". It's just the same as in the old days when country girls came to the city to find work as maids, only now the maids come through "Zarya" and do home visits, and tend to be embarrassed about writing home about their new job. So there all these young single girls are, living in their hostel, or rather in an ordinary flat the firm gives them, with a kitchen, bathroom and three rooms with two girls crammed into each. "And do you," I enquired, "by any chance also have young men coming to work for you in "Zarya" in return for a temporary residence permit?" No. They didn't have boys; it was purely girls' work. There were, however, boys who polish floors and clean windows, but they were Muscovites, not boys from the country.

There you have it! All you need to know about scoring in Moscow. You phone for a floor polisher. He arrives, takes his shirt off and gets down to his floor polishing. You put on some music (better get Sasha to copy some of the latest groups), offer him a vodka or three. The pictures on the walls speak for themselves, and start him asking questions. So much easier to be interesting in your own home. There are always attractive young men working for the post office, of course, but they mend the telephone in no time at all. Floor polishing takes time: time for me to spread my net. Pity they aren't country boys, though. Now where would you find country boys? Of course! In Rural Vocational Training Institutes. How to establish contact, though? Tricky, until you remember that in the vicinity of student hostels are canteens where students eat. In the canteens are toilets. Leave your phone number there, appending a false name just in case. I was once telephoned by a youthful voice of a kind to raise your hopes which asked for Victor. "Victor? There's nobody of that name here. You must have the wrong number," I said despondently. He rang again. "Is Victor there?" "What number are you dialling?" "Such and such." "Well that's the right number, but there's nobody called Victor here." A week later somebody else phoned, also for Victor. (Have you noticed you can fit six telephone dits into the interval between two of the *dahs*? And three just about fit into a *dah*.) Oh my goodness, what had I done! Victor was the name I had subscribed beneath my telephone number in the summer. I'd forgotten all about it. In the summer the students had gone home to their mummies, and now here they all were back for the beginning of the academic year.

Perhaps I ought to seek out a military unit and spy on their routine to see what time they get out on leave. There might be a suitable nearby spot there too where I could leave an open invitation and my telephone number. Or in the Suvorov Military Academy. I remember once on the train from Kaluga cruising a whole succession of empty carriages until suddenly, a carriage with lovely military cadets! I sat down on a vacant bench. Along came another man up to the same game, saw the cadets, and decided to sit beside them. "Is this seat free?" he asked. Naturally he immediately aroused their suspicions, they gave him a dirty look, and told him to push off. Nice try, all the same. Quick reaction, not a moment's hesitation before initiating the conversation. The longer you think about it, the harder it is to get started, and don't be afraid of getting the brush off. "Oh, well," you could see him think. He did push off, and went on his way, but then started to cry.

THEM

Beneath that hard shell of masculinity, then, every man is hiding a soft heart of melted butter. You know you are going to have to do a lot of flattering, indulging, and coaxing before he opens up for you like a flower. The probability is that all men would all love to open up, and don't for fear of being taken advantage of. That solid shell of invulnerability is defensive.

You know, there is an age of man when he wants to cuddle but somehow there are no girls around yet, so he and his friend sit with their arms wrapped round each other, or one stretches out on the other's lap. It's not what you think, though. Not naughty homosexuality. It's just that he had nowhere to put the warmth inside him, so he leans on his friend for the time being. The crux of the matter is that I never wanted to move on from that temporary state. In fact, I had a passionate desire to stay in that delicious state forever.

But what about THEM: the red Indians and seafarers who love to explore? How am I to do justice to their inner world, when they (our worlds) are so different. Their love of adventures and sailing ships is alien to us and makes us turn up our noses. We do not read the same books, about caves, and Indians, and pirates, and kindred nonsense.

For all their youthfulness and rosy cheeks, you sense they have within them the soul of a red-neck. I, on the other hand, even having lived among them and assumed the aspect of a hard man, have the soul of a soft, frightened, shivering little boy, though I keep it well hidden behind a facade of stern eyes firmly in their eye sockets. While they, for all their youthful, vulnerable, lightweight appearance, bear within them the germ of a red-neck. If we were the same age, they would hoot with laughter at me. We could never get on together if I were young. I would never be able to abide their crassness and spiritual immaturity, their tales of how they got drunk and talk of cars. I would have no place among them. They have no conception of meekness, dissimulation, or guile, of what it feels like to be afraid of being the odd one out, or to wonder what another boy may think about you, or be afraid he might not like you. All right, all those things are present in them too, and yet they are not same things, and they are not present to the same degree. As for the things they find amusing: getting drunk in the countryside and chasing a duck out of a pond on to the bank and wringing its neck. (Heartless butchers, one of their girls lovingly called them.) They had no feeling for the duck, or for the peasant woman who owned it.

Undoubtedly there was something that needed to be overcome at a particular age; a need to leap for the parallel bars, without being afraid you would fall off. Lord love us, though, what's a boy to do later on when he finds those who have overcome and conquered nothing so utterly delightful, those who have had the courage to tarry in that earlier state! What heroic resolve to stay weak!

Reading made me a dreamer. Or perhaps it was the other way round, and my disinclination for energetic games set me among the readers and dreamers. At all events, it was soon a closed circle. I began to live in daydreams, and as if that weren't enough, as I grew older my aspirations grew less, before finally vanishing completely.

Goodness, how I am drawn to that pillow, to lie down and rest on it.
"Good day to you, Divan Divanovich!"
"Good day to you, Slobodan Sleepitov."

Teardrops on the Flowers

I hit on the idea of connecting the front door bell to a bellpush by my pillow, so that when I was lying there in the dark going to sleep, hoping someone might be just about to come to see me, I could surreptitiously press the button and the harsh ringing of the bell would fill the entire flat. It was a game for playing with your heart and, sure enough, my heart stood still.

You ought always to be ready for the worst, and then it will be easier to bear. Just to be on the safe side when I was little, I always thought as I was pushing my feet into my gym shoes that a mouse might have crept into them. If there had been one, at least I wouldn't have a sudden fright; and if there was not, and of course there never was, you could think, "Wow, thank goodness for that." It's a pity though that nowadays you are always ready in your heart for the mouse, and can't just take things as they come. Even now when I pick up the telephone receiver, I am ready for it to be the investigating magistrate, and when it isn't, I still think. "Thank goodness for that." Having an investigating magistrate in your heart doesn't make for easy living. That's just what Christian morality wants too: everyone feeling they are in the dock the whole of their life, and not having a good time.

Two books are being written: the one that we are writing, and the one that is being written about us. We are the kitchen writers who write in the living room, and read in the kitchen to our visitors. But a more dread tome is being written about the kitchen writers by Them, and it is locked behind seven seals, and read to no one.

In those two books there are two main questions: "Who is answerable?" and "What are we going to do about it?" To this the answers are: "Nobody is answerable," and, most importantly. "We do not need to do anything about it."

A writer must have a pretty fair idea of the disposition of forces in a city for the KGB to want to recruit him.

You've already done them a favour by their having got to hear about you. Everybody the KGB take an interest in is already complicit with them, since if they call you in they have at least managed to find out about you.

But we can't suppose that anything they can do we can do. Let's face it (face what?) Let's face it anyway, what are we (they) to them (us)? What we? What us? Shit!

That character (Tyurmov) is bound to phone again tomorrow.

They may not bother putting me inside, just as long as they can keep me shit scared.

I gave Gulya a guitar to take my manuscripts to the West, and have been thrice, nay, a tenfold punished for the fault of giving away a guitar someone had given me as a present, and for not making an open-hearted gift of it but for giving it in return for a favour. My nemesis is that none now shall learn the burden of my lay. Having given the guitar away I was unable to learn to play it, and now I never will, because you can't buy them any more for love or money. For the rest of time all that remains for me is to write delicately wrought prose of no interest to the simple-hearted young, while my songs everybody would have loved. How justly God has punished me.

> *Now none shall learn*
> *the burden of*
> *my lay.*
> *(Caw! Caw!)*

No, talent is not some young man amazing us by the ease with which he can compose a song or put together a stack of poems in next to no time. Talent is doggedness. When nothing is coming out right, but still you are damned if you will do anything else, even if nothing ever comes out right for the whole of your life.

Please, all I want is to fill up just this one little sheet. You have made up your mind, and what preoccupies you now is not what you are going to fill it up with, but just the task of filling it up with something. Three-fifths of a page left. I'll never get it filled, unless by writing that I'll never get it filled. That's true weakness (fit for heroes). Nobody will ever know how heroic I was. Will anyone ever

Teardrops on the Flowers

critically analyse my work? No chance. What's at stake is more important than will they won't they. There's a curious occupation (they thought, seeing me intermittently jotting things down on a scrap of paper. Oy, you, up in the Circle, behind the pansies,...). Perhaps I should try thinking something about them. Whew! Thank heavens. Not, not thank heavens just yet, two more lines to go before it will be thank heavens. Only one more now. Now only half of one. Now I don't know how much more. Right! That's it.

For the first five years or so I would write one poem every couple of months or so. One time I took six months over a poem, working flat out: no going out, no breaks, just half a year spent composing it until I got it more or less right. I would never have admitted to anyone how hard I found producing it. I'm deeply impressed now when I look back at the extraordinary potential for diligence I once demonstrated.

So what was going on, and what is it that continues to be going on? I spend my time constantly mulling over one and the same thing, just one thing, constantly. Only when I stop thinking about that one thing all the time do I copy it down and put it in my collection. That's the long and the short of it. Only things which are new and fresh really work.

I am a little mouse. Hither and thither I scurry, looking for a crust of bread.

How many extraneous strata have been laid down in the course of my life, burdening me, when what I need is a light structure, unencumbered (if somewhat convoluted).
And I need children too.
Right then:
He married a woman. He was happy with her. They had children. The children did well. They had useful, interesting jobs, and more than once achieved official recognition for their work. They helped each other; they loved each other; and God loved them. They had friends, and they got together with them on official holidays. But their flat was falling down. It had seemed all right when they moved in.

Dear, oh dear. Isn't everything unstable. Isn't it sad how nothing seems to last forever.

Without a good job and contacts how can you fix up a proper future for your son? We wouldn't want him ending up in the Vocational Training Institute. He's not too keen on booklearning. Kicks over the traces a bit. Bit of a loser, really. We and the wife did our best to make sure he would grow up along the right lines, get a good schooling, grow up a respectable man with a higher education, in a good profession, but he got in with the wrong crowd. What can you do? Perhaps the army will knock some sense into him. After he's demobbed he can go to college and get some professional qualifications. Just so long as he doesn't turn into a self-employed artist, or a poet. That's all we need. Or a genius. Lead a normal life, that's the best thing to do. Get a hobby he quite enjoys, within reason. And give us some grandchildren, too. Then we'll be happy.

Of course, I haven't produced any children to make my parents happy (yet), so perhaps he'd better not take me as a role model.

I started daydreaming that I was not a genius, but just a chap who was good at his job. A utilitarian age calls for specialists. Right: I would be a children's writer, proud of having my work officially recognised. In any case, what a splendid vocation: using language to inculcate the attitudes I delight in those who will grow into young men. After all, your childhood impressions determine the kind of adult you become. How important Yevgeny Shvarts's children's plays were to me. Damn him for being a Jew (God bless him). How gentle and humorous and warmhearted they were. (Only we weren't allowed any Emperors with No Clothes, or Dragons Doing Battle with Authority.) And other children's writers like Arkady Gaidar, and Samuil Marshak. There's really no reason to be ashamed of doing something useful: the children would be in my hands, and would speak using my words.

Weak boys (and girls), please pass it round that I am a tyrant. And I will love you.

Right, then:

Teardrops on the Flowers

His mother is a lonely woman who smokes and rates love above everything else. You do meet ageing women like this, and some even have an only son, and want to show how liberal their views are, and think they are not the same as everybody else, and that this is something to be proud of. Oh, I am not like all those other mothers. I am very understanding. I don't mind if he isn't like the other boys, either. The main thing is to be free and to love, isn't it. What does it matter whom. Who cares if it is another man: after all, I am a woman who smokes, and is very understanding, and never goes to bed before three o'clock in the morning. (How completely ridiculous! Mothers are there to keep you on the straight and narrow.) So, where were we: she has a young, effeminate son, and let's say I come home with him and stay the night. The mother and I have a tacit understanding. She is glad her son has such an agreeable gentleman friend. We put our heads together to decide what to do with him to make sure he doesn't go off the rails, and everything turns out for the best for him. I am direct with her, like a son-in-law, and she and her son have their own girlish discussions, which they don't let me in on, on how to handle a man. She gives him positively gynecological advice, and gets him the best quality Vaseline. No. Hammelis cream, anti-septic and sphincter-relaxant. They are more like girl friends than mother and son. Oh, one other thing. Mother-in-law and I decided at one of our family meetings that it was time for the boy to take The Decision. I spared no pains, and took him to see a proper surgeon, in Hungary. His mother and I were worried to death, but everything went well. Now I wear the dried amputated member in a rather large locket as a memento of our sacrifice.

1. "He beat me and taught me everything there is to know, and then passed me on to a Georgian who did with me whatever he wanted. With men it's important to know how to behave, of course, I had no rivals. After they'd been with me they lost the notion of going with girls, I was that devastating. I knew every nerve in a man's body, and how to play on it until he was groaning in ecstasy and oblivious of everything. I could get anything I wanted off them: the star from the Kremlin tower, if I wanted.

"He fucked me until I bled, until I passed out, and he taught me everything there is to know. I am grateful to him for that now, because afterwards there was no one to rival me at my art. How he taught me? He would beat me if I did not come at the same time as he did. Even if I did, he would beat me all the same, but once and for all I learned to come at the same time as a man is coming in me. How he would beat me up just using my stretched dick. He'd stretch it (when I had a hard-on) and strike it, or slap it, or punch it on the nose. I just screwed up my eyes like a kitten. He taught me only to answer to a woman's name, and to be that woman in body and soul. He never asked me whether I wanted it or not. He would just masterfully seize my head and thrust me down to his dick. And afterwards he would beat me again. The men I serviced later might go wild, and kiss and bite my little hole they so loved to get their lousy sausages up; but he was a real man, only beating and teaching me. He would even make me bring the belt, and obediently take down my trousers, and lie down in front of him bum uppermost. That was my training in the university of life, and after that I did the work my degree qualified me for. But you know all about that."

(*Pants Off*: a Novel)

2. A man fell head over heels in love with a certain young man, but he (the young man) decided he had had enough after one time with him. The man kept phoning and wanting to come round, but the young man did not really need it any more. All the same it was quite fun simply to let the man have his way, without love, like a slut. The young man enjoyed being screwed, admittedly, but when it was over, that was it. There was nothing more he wanted from the man, except to be rid of him. But he kept ringing every day, desperate to come round. So then the young man decided to tell him he had made up his mind to live with a certain woman who had supposedly been his girlfriend yonks ago, and who he had started seeing again. Sorry about that. When the man rang up he would keep saying. "Sorry, I can't. She's at home; I can't talk now. Sorry." Then one time he gave in, and when the man rang again, he told him to come round, because she was out today. So there he was waiting and waiting for the man to arrive, and in the meantime psyching himself up with fantasies (about the Georgian), until he

Teardrops on the Flowers

couldn't stand it any longer and decided to jerk off while the other was on his way. As soon as he'd come he thought, "What use is he to me now? I'll only have him lying beside me all night trying to kiss me and stopping me sleeping. Fuck him!" (The other man was on his way on the bus by this time; now he could hear him coming up the stairs to the flat.) The young man quickly put out all the lights and pinned a note to the front door saying he was sorry, he couldn't see him, he'd had to go away on urgent business. The man rang the doorbell. The young man was standing inside the flat on the other side of the door, not breathing. He bent down to the floor, and started miaowing to kid on that he and the imaginary woman he'd been going on to the other about had got themselves a family cat, and had gone out and left the cat mewing on its own.

Thus that night did he keep himself pure and free from abomination; perhaps the cross helped too, which he slipped on as the doorbell rang, admittedly with the intention of looking prettier.

Well now, is all this ME or NOT ME? (as I said one day when I had been looking through these patterns I make). It certainly seems to be me; but then again, it also seems not to. If I were in a literary magazine surrounded by other writers, then it would be me; but being here alone on a desert island, just me on my own, it can't be, but anyway...

Why, oh why can't I just fly right away into the lovely world of wonder-conjuring words, unshadowed of distress, gay columbine, cloud-mapleen, saved-soul-stirring, blond-brow hazel-eyed, kiss-curled, seventeen-autumnal, navy-red starring

For heaven's sake, stop worrying. Everything you write will be fine. And even more so everything you don't.

Translated by Arch Tait

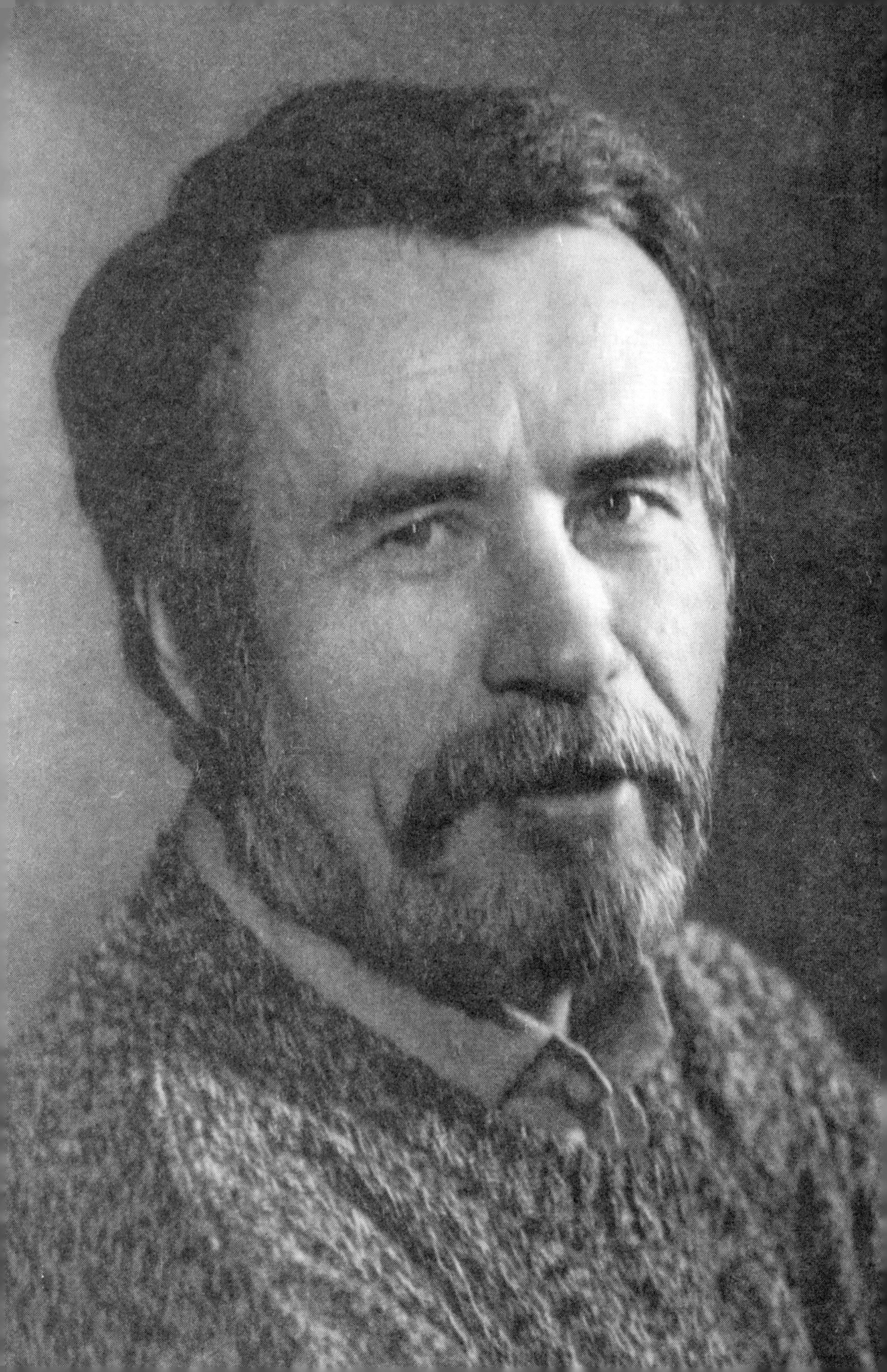

Vladimir MAKANIN

KLYUCHARYOV AND ALIMUSHKIN

1

Suddenly one man noticed that the more luck he had in life the less a certain other man had. He noticed this quite by chance and quite unexpectedly. He didn't like it. He was not so hard that he could be having the time of his life while through the wall from him someone else was sobbing his heart out, and that was the situation in a nutshell. Very nearly. There was nothing whatever he could do to change it or to help. It's not everything that can be changed or helped, after all. Then he started to get used to it.

One day he couldn't take it any more. He went to see him — the other man — that is, and said, "I am having a lot of good luck, and you are having bad luck... I feel really bad about it. It's getting to me."

The man who was having bad luck didn't understand. In fact he couldn't believe it.

"Rubbish," he replied. "The two things are quite unrelated. I am having bad luck, that's for sure, but it's got nothing to do with you."

"All the same, I'm really upset about it."

"Rubbish... Forget it. Don't let it worry you."

He went away and got on with his life, but he carried on being a bit upset, though, because things went from bad to worse for the other man; while he was really in luck. The sun shone on him, women smiled at him, his superiors at work were easy to get on with, and his home life was idyllic. At this point he had a mental conversation with God.

"It isn't right," he said. "The way it's working out, one man's happiness comes at the expense of another man's unhappiness."

God said, "What's wrong with that?"

"It's mean."

God thought and thought, and then he gave a sigh and said, "There isn't enough happiness to go round."

"Come again?"

"That's right. Just you try keeping eight people warm with one blanket. How much is each one going to get?" Then God flew off. God just disappeared without giving an answer, or at least not a proper answer. He just shrugged the problem off with a joke, really.

After that the man stopped thinking about it. Ultimately there's a limit to how long you can go on thinking about the same thing. Ultimately it just starts getting you down. That's pretty much all there is to the story. What really matters, though, is the details... Klyucharyov worked in a research institute. He was a mathematician, I think. Yes, a mathematician is right. He had an ordinary sort of family, lived in an ordinary sort of flat, and lived on the whole a perfectly ordinary sort of life. Bright patches and dark alternated and averaged out, and came to a total which people designate as "an ordinary life."

Klyucharyov stood out among all this ordinariness mainly, perhaps, for his somewhat affected sense of humour. On the way home from work one day he found a purse with maybe ten roubles in it, lying on a path in the snow. Quick as a flash he said to himself, "Well done. This is the sort of thing that makes life worth living."

Still smiling, Klyucharyov immediately wrote out an ordinary sort of notice. "Blah, blah, found a purse, anyone claiming it call at," and put his address at the bottom. He fixed the paper to a nail on the noticeboard of the nearest block of flats. It was winter. In order to write the note and stick it to the nail he had to put his briefcase down in the snow. The impaled slip of paper flapped in the wind, but stayed firmly fixed. There was nothing all that surprising in the fact that nobody responded to the notice that day or the following day. What really was surprising was that the day after that his head of department, a cantankerous old sod who crushed anything that showed signs of life and who quite obviously wished him no good, suddenly suggested that Klyucharyov should write an article for a major scientific journal. He didn't even try to push himself as "co-author." It was this detail which made Klyucharyov tell his wife when he came home, even before he'd got through the door, "I've got a winning streak starting."

Now Klyucharyov's wife was a quiet, unassuming woman, and good luck of any kind worried and even frightened her. She took it very badly, for example, when nobody came to claim the purse.

A little later that evening Klyucharyov's wife said she had something to tell him. She had forgotten to tell him earlier, but now she had remembered it.

"Don't tell me," Klyucharyov laughed. "Your friend phoned?"
"Yes."
"That was really difficult." It was a humorous little dig at a woman his wife had once worked with. She and his wife had been friends at the time and by inertia she still counted as a friend. They worked now in different places and had not seen each other for ages, but from time to time they still phoned. They would talk about their children, or what they had managed to buy. The phone calls were becoming less and less frequent. As time went by this relic of feminine friendship seemed destined to wither away and die, but in the meantime it was alive and well and coiled within a telephone flex.

His wife was silent. It annoyed her that her friendship was withering away and that their socialising over the telephone was already a butt for her husband's humour. In order to soften the impression, Klyucharyov prompted her, "What was the thing you had to tell me?" Then his wife told him that Alimushkin was having trouble at work. Actually, people said he was going downhill...

"Alimushkin?" Klyucharyov really could not remember who he was, so he just shrugged. By now he was used to the fact that his over-anxious wife could work herself into a state over just about anybody; but then he remembered the man. He had seen him twice. "Is Alimushkin that chap who was really sharp and witty?"

"That's him," said his wife.

She added straight away that perhaps Klyucharyov would like to go round to see him some time. She had written his address down specially. His wife's tone of voice was perfectly serious, and even rather touching. Klyucharyov mechanically took the slip of paper with the address, before snorting to himself in exasperation. Aren't women marvellous! Only a woman could suggest you should go round to some character you hardly knew and say, "Hi there, old man, I hear you're going downhill."

"Why on earth should I go round to see him? I've only met the man a couple of times in my life."

"Well I've only seen him once."

A most telling piece of logic, admittedly.

"I'm sure you agree," his wife kept up the attack. "It's much better and less embarrassing if a man goes round to see him."

"Better or worse, I'm not going. I'm too busy."

They did not quarrel about it. The Klyucharyovs were a quiet, stable couple. His wife even admitted that it was maybe asking a bit much to expect Klyucharyov to go off like that on some wild goose chase. They changed the subject and talked instead about their 16-year-old son who was making quite a mark as a sportsman. More precisely in competitive gymnastics.

2

Klyucharyov would have forgotten his wife's strange request, but for another telephone conversation that same evening. This time it was Klyucharyov who rang his friend Pavel. An expression from one conversation can often wander off and find its way into another. Expressions only have a short life and probably they too want to live as long as possible. Be that as it may, instead of saying hello, Klyucharyov humorously asked his friend, "How are you doing, Captain? Not going downhill, I trust?"

Pavel replied, "No, I'm not going downhill. What are you on about?"

Klyucharyov laughed, and had to explain the joke. It didn't mean anything. It was just a catch phrase, They knew this chap Alimushkin, for instance. He was going downhill.

"Alimushkin?" Pavel repeated. "He works at the same place as I do."

"Get away." (It's a small world.)

"We slave in adjacent offices." Pavel added that Alimushkin was all right, but he'd got himself in some sort of a pickle. Something wasn't working out. He just couldn't get on with his work.

"Why not?"

"Christ knows. He's a loner. To tell the truth, I steer clear of loners."

There they were in full agreement. Klyucharyov didn't like loners either.

"I'd sooner be stuck with an alky," Klyucharyov said. Then all at once he remembered something else about Alimushkin. "Hang on a minute. How can he be a loner? He used to be a real wit, sharp as a razor."

Pavel only sighed before replying with a great and eternal truth: "He's gone soft."

That same evening Klyucharyov went out for a bed-time stroll around his apartment block, what he called "letting some fresh air in." He walked the well-trodden paths in the snow, and couldn't get the phrase, "He's gone soft," out of his mind. Suddenly an odd thought occurred to him. What if he was having his luck at this Alimushkin's expense? He remembered his boss suggesting he should write the article, and the purse, and smiled at himself. What a daft notion. Just one of those ideas that pop into your mind, something to kick around. There was a frost. The stars were out overhead. He walked on looking up and thinking what a lot of stars there were, and how vast the sky was. Those stars must have seen no end of human successes and failure and long since grown vacant, and frozen into indifference towards everything. The stars did not give a toss. Small chance they would start involving themselves, sending one person success, and another failure.

Klyucharyov did not, however, manage to get the notion out of his head the next day either, and for this reason. He had been invited round to Kolya Krymov's. Even before he had got his overcoat off in the hall he could hear the phrases flying: "What? You haven't heard about Kolya Krymov's new passion?" Or again, "Kolya Krymov's new passion will be here any minute," or even, with a hint of fairground haranguing, "Put those glasses down. Get your hands off that bottle. Hold your horses. Any moment now Kolya Krymov's new passion will be among us." Such were the jokes which filled the air. The men and women were all around thirty-five, and all of them were sure that the best way of having fun together was to take it out on their host. Kolya Krymov wasn't complaining: if anything it was good for the ego. Finally she arrived. Her name was Mrs. Alimushkin. She was a very beautiful woman.

Klyucharyov asked Kolya through the general shouting match at table whether he was going to marry her. He and Kolya were close friends. Kolya Krymov (while everybody was falling over themselves looking after Mrs. Alimushkin, and some poet was inscribing a book of his poems to her) was in expansive mood, and so he answered, yes, he was. He blushed slightly. Kolya Krymov liked to formulate things precisely, and so he said that one affair too many might look like debauchery, while getting married one more time only looked as though you were still searching... Just then it became apparent that one of his guests had overdone the vodka, and Kolya Krymov went off to see him out and get him into a taxi. Thus ensued a brief conversation between Klyucharyov and Mrs. Alimushkin.

They were sitting near each other with Kolya Krymov's empty chair between them. Klyucharyov began talking to her for want of anything better to do, and certainly without anything of that sort in mind. He asked her, "What's your old man been getting up to?"

"Sod him," the lovely replied. "He just keeps on and on about how he's going downhill..."

"Bit of a moaner, is he?"

"Not really. More of a loner. Doesn't say anything for hours on end."

She had a kind of brazen beauty. There was something provocative about her. Klyucharyov had never known a beautiful woman of that kind before. Of course he had seen them in the street. They always had somebody escorting them. Sometimes there were two escorts.

The conversation came to a halt, and Mrs. Alimushkin started it up again. It didn't cost her a thought. She could talk the hind legs off a donkey, and her eyes were bold.

"To tell you the truth, I'm through with him. I'm staying at a girlfriend's flat. I do as I please, go out to parties, and enjoy myself."

For a moment her eyes were very close to Klyucharyov's. He said, "I don't suppose it was after you moved out to stay with your girlfriend and enjoy yourself that he started going downhill?"

"Come off it!" she said. "It was the other way round."

He could see she was telling the truth. That was the end of the conversation, and Mrs. Alimushkin turned to talk to the neighbour on her left. That notion of his came back to Klyucharyov again though. He thought, if I were really having my luck at Alimushkin's expense, his wife would have given me the eye today. It's the perfect moment. Instead it's Kolya Krymov she's giving the eye. Shame, that."

He left the party slightly the worse for wear and slightly distraught. He wasn't too sure what he was feeling. He wondered what to tell his wife. (He hadn't warned her he would be late.) He pulled out the slip of paper with Alimushkin's address. It was quite close and so... he went to see him, to have at least some excuse. Alimushkin was asleep. It was past midnight and an odd time for a visit. Klyucharyov didn't know how to begin.

"Were you asleep? People say you are going downhill," he said, trying to make it sound almost like a reproach.

Alimushkin said nothing. He just stood there looking half-doped. He yawned. Klyucharyov felt a bit awkward, and opted for a more formal approach.

"I do hope you remember me. We have met before. In the library a few times, and once at friends."

Alimushkin nodded. "I remember now." He was still half-asleep. Remembering his manners, he asked, "Cup of tea?"

"No thanks. Just thought I'd look in," Klyucharyov replied with a smile. He made the smile as friendly as he could. "Tea's the last thing I need. I've had more than enough to drink as it is."

Then Klyucharyov left.

When he got home and his wife started going on about the smell of drink on his breath, Klyucharyov became indignant. "Do us a favour, will you! I only went because you insisted. 'Find out what's going on, how he's doing...' You and your Alimushkin. I was stuck at Kolya Krymov's for two hours because of him (Klyucharyov allowed himself a degree of elasticity with the facts), and then I had to go round to see Alimushkin. The man's alive and well. He looks as fit as a fiddle — and he sleeps like a log."

Klyucharyov was walking down the corridor. He was taking a break from work for a minute or two, or maybe ten. He believed that this refreshed the brain, and so he walked with a light and confident step. He was walking past the door of a large, well furnished office, when who should be standing in the door but his nibs and his nibs's deputy. The Director of the research institute had his hat in his hand. Something was bugging his Deputy and he was trying to make some point. The Director was smiling a twinkly smile.

The Deputy Director's gaze happened to fall on the passing

Klyucharyov, and he said, "Well, take Klyucharyov. He's capable, hard working, he's got a higher degree, and you're still holding him down at research associate grade."

"Perhaps you're the one who's holding him down," the Director parried, twinkling.

"Me?"

"Yes, you," twinkled the Director.

Klyucharyov was no more than a yard away from them. He made no attempt to capitalise on the situation. He was simply walking by minding his own business, although you can't very well just go away or walk on past when people are talking out loud about you and looking straight at you.

"There's no need to argue about it," he said to them in a quiet, reserved voice. "I'm the one who's holding me down."

They smiled. They were pleased that he hadn't tried to capitalise on the situation. The Director said, "I must be off. Good Lord, I really must be off," and headed for the way out.

The Deputy Director hurried after him saying, "It's high time Klyucharyov was made a head of department."

"Do it, then," replied the Director.

An hour later, and quite unconnected with the conversation between the Director and his Deputy, since it came through quite a different channel, Klyucharyov heard that his article had been accepted by the journal and would shortly be published. When he got home, however, his wife again told him, "My friend phoned. There's been a development." The development was that poor old Alimushkin's wife had walked out on him. She had left him for good, swapping their flat for two smaller ones. Taking advantage of the fact that Alimushkin was going downhill ("He has no initiative! He seems half-doped all the time!"), his lovely wife had fixed herself a bijou little one-room flat, and dumped the somnolent Alimushkin in some damp squalid little bed-sit. That was where he now lived. That was where he was now going downhill, Klyucharyov's wife said. Klyucharyov could not but note that Alimushkin's failures seemed still to be running neck and neck with his own successes.

The following evening a further development was reported over the telephone. Troubles never come singly. Alimushkin had been fired. He had got something wrong or otherwise made a hash of it, and to cap it all he had thrown some important papers into the wastepaper basket. They would have been within their rights in sending him to court but had taken pity, merely sacking him instead. The real problem was not, apparently, the important papers or the wastepaper basket. His lethargy and indolence had really got up everybody's nose, and this had been the last straw.

"How does he keep going?" Klyucharyov asked. He didn't have Alimushkin's spiritual dimension in mind; he just wondered where the money was coming from.

"I don't know," his wife replied, and just because she did not know she asked Klyucharyov to drop in on Alimushkin and check once more how he was getting on. "Drop in on him," she said. "It'll only take a minute." She reminded him that ages ago they had seen Alimushkin at some friends', and he had been the liveliest person there, really witty and sharp.

Klyucharyov asked his wife, "Supposing he hadn't been witty and sharp, would you feel sorry for him now he's in trouble?"

"I don't know."

Klyucharyov latched on to that "don't know" answer, and said, not without a certain amount of glee, "You should be ashamed of yourself, dear heart, only feeling sorry for the chosen few." Feminine intuition got her out of that one too. She said, "I don't know. If he wasn't witty and sharp he'd be something else. Quiet and sentimental, perhaps. You'd feel sorry for someone like that too."

Next morning the Deputy Director invited him to become head of department. It was a straightforward offer with no strings attached, and Klyucharyov turned it down. He said he had no wish to topple his boss, having worked with him for good or ill for many years. This was the truth, but what was even more true was that at present Klyucharyov did not want the bother. He didn't need telling that he was on a winning streak and that the good things were not going to go away. He had a clear if inexplicable feeling that someone up above had firmly and confidently pulled on the reins and was in the driving seat instead of him, Klyucharyov; that needless to say whoever it was up there knew what he was doing and wasn't going to get it wrong.

Klyucharyov and Alimushkin

"Come again?" the Deputy Director asked in puzzlement, "You mean you don't want to be head of department? Are you afraid of the responsibility?"

"Yes. I can do without the hassle. I work a lot as it is."

"We know that."

"I work a lot, and I don't want any more for the moment."

Klyucharyov allowed himself to answer bluntly. It was as if he were probing and testing his luck for durability. He could, after all, always come back tomorrow and say, "All right, now I want it. Now I'm ready for it. I'll take it."

He went round to see Alimushkin. The first thing he asked was, "How on earth have you managed to end up in a tip like this, fellow? Why did you agreed to split the flat?" Alimushkin did not reply. He looked awful. He was lethargic and indolent and clearly not well. He stared Klyucharyov in the face and mumbled, "I... don't remember you." Then he turned and looked in another direction. Fixedly.

"Whether you remember me or not is beside the point. What possessed you to agree to live in a tip like this?"

Alimushkin did not reply. His brain was working a bit behindhand. He had only just managed to recollect his guest's face.

"Aren't you... Klyucharyov?"

"Yes."

Klyucharyov meantime looked around. He had realised, of course, that the lethargic Alimushkin had not done well out of the flat swap, but it had never occurred to him that a live human being could be shoved in a hole like this. The room was tiny, peeling, with leaks everywhere and no furniture. Just a rusty bedstead and a table. And one chair. Next door a solitary old man was living in an equally appalling room. The old man was ill, unsociable, and deaf as a post.

"He doesn't even say hello to you in the kitchen," Alimushkin informed him lethargically. "Doesn't say a thing."

"You don't say a lot yourself."

"No..."

There followed a long, awkward silence.

"So, here you are."

He nodded: yes.

"Do you go out at all?"

"No."

"Forgive my asking, but where do you get the money from to keep body and soul together?"

"I've got a few roubles left. I'm eating my way through them."

"And after that?"

There followed an even longer silence. Finally, instead of replying, Alimushkin said quietly, "I...," he looked at Klyucharyov as though wondering whether he would laugh at him. "I play chess."

Klyucharyov did not laugh. He said, "Good for you."

"There," Alimushkin indicated a small chess set with his eyes. The board was scuffed. The chessmen were set out. "I used to play... When I was a boy."

"Who do you play with?"

"Nobody. Just on my own. Analyse my game."

Klyucharyov suggested they might play. There was nothing for them to talk about. Alimushkin played really badly. Klyucharyov played several games with him and left. He was in a wretched mood. He would have felt better if Alimushkin had at least played passably.

3

There was an odd moment while he was there; one which somehow stood out. In one of the awkward silences Klyucharyov wondered, "How can a person's life have gone off the rails just like that?" Klyucharyov was no fool and realised that what happens to one man today can happen to another tomorrow. That's how people are born. That's how people die. He asked Alimushkin, "Tell me, how did it happen that things stopped working out for you?"

Alimushkin was silent. He wasn't quite sure what Klyucharyov meant. Then he tried hard to understand (The effort was written all over his face) and he told Klyucharyov, "No. It wasn't as if anything in particular happened. There was no reason. I just felt I was going downhill. That was all."

"Did it start when your wife left you?"

"No. Before that."

"U-huh," Klyucharyov seemed to take heart. "It began when you ran into difficulties at work?"

"No."
"Well what did it begin with then?"
"I can't remember."

Klyucharyov registered impatience. A mite irritably he started again, "But everything can't just go wrong for no reason. Think hard. Try to remember. It's important for me to know this too. It's important people should know how it started."

Alimushkin scratched his head, furrowed his brow. "No... I can't remember."

It was time to go because now one silence was running into the next. Klyucharyov looked around. There was a kettle, but so little tea in the jar beside it that he kept quiet. That was when he suggested Alimushkin should play him at chess. Klyucharyov beat him easily the first time, and the second, and a third. He got up to leave.

"See you again."

Alimushkin gazed vacantly in front of himself. Then he reached out lethargically for a pen. He was going to write out the last game to see where he had gone wrong.

"It's supposed to be useful," he mumbled.

Those were the exact words he mumbled: "It's supposed to be useful." The words brought out exactly his own utter uselessness and emptiness. Klyucharyov couldn't get them out of his mind. They haunted him. That was why when he got home he decided not to tell his wife the truth. It was a simple matter. His wife was busy with their son and daughter, laying down the law for some act of mischief they had committed. Klyucharyov said casually, "I went to see Alimushkin. He's really not in such a bad way, you know. He was very talkative, and perfectly calm."

"Good."

"He's taking chess up seriously. He's almost planning to make it the centre of his life."

"Oh good, I am pleased."

"Before you know it, it'll be Grandmaster Alimushkin."

When someone is listening to you uncritically talk is easy. So Klyucharyov put in for luck, with just a suggestion of solemnity in his voice, "I respect a man who can start a new life."

His winning streak continued, and began to resemble a thief in reverse, an anti-thief. You keep your left pocket covered, but he shoves things in your right one. "Here you are, pal, and welcome. Go on, take it. This moment is yours." At work everybody was eager to talk to him and eager to smile. A man with a future, they were saying. Even the Deputy Director smiled. He rambled on for a bit, and then said, "... and by the way, Klyucharyov, we've decided to give you an extra eighty roubles a month."

"Thank you."

"I pushed it through myself, with the Director's blessing. That's a rise of eighty roubles for a start."

"Thank you."

"We appreciate good workers, especially when they're unassuming."

The Deputy added (confidentially: he didn't say this sort of thing to everyone), "Some people try to elbow others aside through office politics and to clamber over their colleagues' heads on their way to a cushy position. I can't stand that."

Half an hour later Mrs. Alimushkin rang. Somehow she had managed to find out his office telephone number and had got straight through to him. Later she admitted she had secretly copied the number down at Kolya Krymov's. For some reason she felt it was something that had to be done secretly. She said hello and invited Klyucharyov round. She didn't spend much time beating about the bush, because she was a beautiful woman and knew it. She got straight to the point, without embarrassment. "That evening," she said, and paused: it was the characteristic pause of today's woman: "I really got the hots for you."

"Is that right?"

"I really did. Come round and see me, please. Today."

He went. He wasn't in the least bowled over by her voice, or her eyes. He didn't like beautiful women. He had never known any. He found life easier and more comfortable that way. He sat in her armchair and looked round her flat. A very bijou little flat it was too, the furniture out of this world. Klyucharyov said, "I thought you were getting married to Kolya Krymov." What this meant was, "You have asked me round. Are you teasing, or is this a little secret behind Kolya Krymov's back? Just what exactly are the rules of the

game?" But Mrs. Alimushkin simply replied, "No, I'm not going to get married."
"Why not?"
"I don't like him. He's nothing special. There's nothing to him."
"Make him into the man you want."
"I don't feel like it. Why should I bother?"

Klyucharyov did not embark on a coy, humorous conversation leading in a certain direction, even though it was a direction he quite fancied. Instead of being predictable, Klyucharyov behaved unpredictably. He behaved against his programming. Suddenly he became angry with Mrs. Alimushkin. He told her fairly rudely that there was actually quite a lot to Kolya Krymov, and quite a lot to the husband she had abandoned, and that she should get herself married and not make a fool, first and foremost, of herself. He realised as he said it that he was talking a lot of silly nonsense. She was, after all, a woman, and had a perfect right to choose.

In his briefcase, which he didn't open, were two bottles of wine. He had brought them for a purpose, and he knew perfectly well what that purpose was. Something had come over him and addled his brains, and here he was talking nonsense. He went on and on to her about getting married, and she was perfectly right when she said — He was about to leave, and already standing at the door: "What a bore you are. You'll be the death of me."

After all this excess of good luck, Klyucharyov's wife also wasn't quite feeling herself. She was frightened. In her case this expressed itself in a secret premonition of some nameless imminent disaster or misfortune. Without actually putting a name to the real reason, she had decided to ask her mother, Klyucharyov's mother-in-law, that is, to come and stay. "It would be a good idea for her to come and stay with us for a while. You never know, someone might fall ill, or something else might happen," she said, giving the game away.

"But why should anything happen?" Klyucharyov laughed.

Klyucharyov laughed. He was his old, jolly, humorous self again. He wanted to laugh out loud when he thought back to how he had behaved and what he had said to a beautiful woman who had invited him home. "What an oaf!" he chided himself. He pictured her cheeks and her lips, and his spine tingled delectably.

His wife phoned him at the office (from her office). "Is that you? My friend just rang me again. About Alimushkin."

"Not going downhill, is he?"

"Be serious."

"He's taking a hell of a long time to go downhill. I'm beginning to think he isn't going to make it."

"Don't..." His wife began whispering down the telephone. She was vaguely frightened of something and this was why she was whispering to her husband, "Do be careful, dearest." Then she whispered, "Don't talk so carelessly about other people, dearest. I do wish you would just be a little more thoughtful about them, dearest. I know how kind you are, but if you would just be a bit more thoughtful about other people as well." On she whispered. It was leading up to a request, to go and visit poor old Alimushkin once more. That was what was agitating her again.

Something quite different was agitating Klyucharyov. What was the best way of getting his wife's friend to put a sock in it. Why did she keep blathering on and on? Why couldn't she just mind her own business?

"Hello there!" Klyucharyov called out. He had gone round after work (bowing to the inevitable) to see Alimushkin, but there was no response to his greeting. Klyucharyov went into the room, and his face grew long. His face took on an expression appropriate to misfortune, because Alimushkin was lying in bed, and a figure in white was standing beside him. A doctor.

"Don't try talking to him," the doctor said. "He can't speak. He's had a stroke."

The doctor explained that the stroke could have been worse, but that it was a stroke nevertheless. He said he needed peace and quiet and someone to look after him.

"No, no," the doctor commanded. "You keep quiet, Alimushkin! Don't even try to talk. You won't be able to in any case."

Klyucharyov asked, "Has he lost the power of speech?"

"Temporarily."

"Can't he move around?"

"He can get to the loo by holding on to the wall, but certainly no further."

Klyucharyov went over nearer to Alimushkin, taking care

where he put his feet, because there were cockroaches scuttling over the floor. The room was gloomy. Alimushkin smiled a half-smile, one-sided because the facial muscles on the other side were paralysed. Klyucharyov gave him a wink, as if to say, "Hello there, what's this you've been up to?" Alimushkin held out a hand. Klyucharyov shook it.

The doctor must have been from the emergency service. He dug around in the papers on the table, before saying, "Give me a hand, would you? I take it you're a friend of his."

"Yes."

"Somewhere among these papers should be the address of his mother."

"His mother?" Klyucharyov asked in surprise.

"Well, he's going to need somebody to look after him."

"What about hospital? Surely he'll go into hospital?"

"There's nothing in particular a hospital can do for him, and moving him in his present condition would be inadvisable."

Klyucharyov nodded. Right. Like everybody else, Klyucharyov believed you couldn't argue with a doctor. He asked, "Are you going to get his mother to come, then?"

"I'm not. You are." The doctor, as if he too considered Klyucharyov to have something to answer for to the patient on account of his successes, gave him a stern look. That at least was how Klyucharyov took it, although in fact it was the usual look of a doctor hounded and harassed twenty-four hours a day. "You are. I must be off. I've already tried twice to send a nurse round, but at the moment she's tied up looking after a more acute case."

Klyucharyov nodded. He found the address and sent a wordy telegram off to Ryazan province. Luckily the post office was no distance away, and with no suggestion of a queue at the window, as Klyucharyov wryly noted. Alimushkin was really in luck.

When Klyucharyov got back from the post office the doctor had gone. Alimushkin apologised for all the trouble he was causing, gesturing the apology with his arm as if to say, "Sorry you're having to do all this". With another gesture he invited Klyucharyov to play chess with him, if he wasn't in too much of a hurry. Alimushkin could reach the chess set by himself. It was by the bedhead. Klyucharyov hardly looked at the board. He moved

103

the chessmen and looked at the floor. It was teeming with lacquered cockroaches.

Klyucharyov went straight from Alimushkin to see his wife's friend. He had finally tracked her down. He had the address on a scrap of paper. Flat 27, 9 Pirogovskaya Street. He had found it in his wife's diary, which he had surreptitiously fished out of her handbag... Now he was at her door. He introduced himself. "Hello, my name is Klyucharyov, I believe you've been on friendly terms with my wife for many years, haven't you? Oddly enough, we haven't met before."

Such was Klyucharyov's tone of voice, friendly almost. In point of fact, however, he was extremely annoyed, and at any moment this would surface. He was only beginning what he had to say.

"I'm glad to meet you," his wife's friend said. She was fairly solid, plump even, and slow moving, Klyucharyov could just imagine her sitting talking on the telephone for days at a time, with a bosom and a backside like that. He could feel the anger rising in him. "You'll have to forgive me, I'm going to be very blunt. I've had more than enough of your carrying on on the telephone..."

"What?" She didn't understand. She was a slow mover.

Trying to control himself, Klyucharyov made his meaning clearer. "Stop telephoning my wife about that unfortunate man Alimushkin. Stop working her up and upsetting her. Just behave yourself, will you? Have a bit of consideration for an ordinary, moderately happy family which does not need you weighing it down with all the troubles and woes there are around in the world."

"But I didn't think just phoning..."

"Well try thinking now. It's really not that difficult to understand. You don't give the woman a moment's peace."

His wife's friend was silent. She was at a loss. Klyucharyov apologised once more for his bluntness. Then he asked her, "Do you go round to see him yourself? Alimushkin, I mean?"

"Very rarely."

"Well you carry on going round to see him now and again. All right? And leave us in peace."

His wife's friend was plainly hurt. Slow moving and fat, she liked nothing better than talking on the phone, and here she was being deprived of a splendid reason for phoning. She didn't care in the least about Alimushkin, but for heaven's sake people, and girlfriends especially, have to have something to talk about, and for heaven's sake they do have to keep in touch.

Klyucharyov spelled it out one last time. "I want you to understand that your phone calls are upsetting my wife. They are driving her to distraction. People want to live and enjoy life. But you are being a pain in the neck. We have any number of friends and relatives who are ill without having to resort to Alimushkin..."

He had said what he had come to say, and wanted now to hear her reply. Finally, pouting her lips, she brought herself to say,

"I won't phone her up any more."

"Oh, no. That's not what's needed."

"What do you want, then?"

"Ring her one more time and put her mind at rest. Think up something pleasant for her. Tell her Alimushkin has got better, he's fit and well. Everything's fine. And he's going away... to Madagascar, if you like, on a business trip."

"Why Madagascar?"

"Or anywhere. Just to put an end to the whole saga. To stop my wife from asking you about him any more. Do you understand?"

"Yes."

"I'm going now, and I want you to ring her. Are you sure you understand?"

"Yes."

"Nice meeting you."

He left. Snow was falling outside. Snow fell now morning and evening.

When Klyucharyov came to see him the next day after work Alimushkin was flat on his back, motionless and speechless. When he saw Klyucharyov he began to gulp for air. He wanted to say something in greeting, and he couldn't smile. He couldn't manage even a half-smile now. "He's had another stroke. A bad one, the doctor said," murmured the quiet little old woman from Ryazan fussing by Alimushkin's bedside. This was his mother, summoned by telegram. Klyucharyov comforted her, and he gave her a sum of money to take care of all the things she would need money for. The old woman's head bobbed like a Chinese doll, and she started to cry. "God bless you, my dear." Klyucharyov left her sitting at her son's bedside. The old woman sat motionless. She couldn't believe this misfortune, this sorrow which had left her son, who was so strong and full of life, and who had already "got his papers to be an engineer," lying now flat on his back and unable to utter a single word.

It was not at all that Klyucharyov wished to save himself from having to remember and think about Alimushkin. He wanted to save his wife from that. She was just too highly strung and sensitive. Klyucharyov decided that the illness would be protracted, and that he would visit Alimushkin from time to time, and that he would tell his wife nothing.

He told her nothing, and nobody asked, because the house was in turmoil and full of shouting and excitement, and people had other things to talk about. Mother-in-law had arrived. Her arrival was a fairly stately affair. There was a present for Klyucharyov's wife, and a present for Klyucharyov's son. Naturally there was a present for Klyucharyov's daughter too. The presents were not very expensive, but chosen with love.

By the following day he had no further need to trick his wife, because she said to him herself, "Sorry I was such a bore and kept asking you to go to see him..."

"Who?" Klyucharyov asked mildly.

"Alimushkin."

His wife happily informed him that her friend had phoned and that at last it was good news. Everything had worked out all right for Alimushkin. He was fit again. He was witty again... His wife began to relate the details. The details were curious and even fanciful, because her telephone-hogging friend really had done her best. She had put her heart, her energy, even a certain talent into this last fitful flicker of a topic she was having to end. Now Klyucharyov's wife told these details to him. She was so happy. She smiled, and talked and talked, and Klyucharyov listened. He listened with unfeigned interest, and even questioned her on some points.

"Where did you say he is going to on business?"

"Madagascar."

Then the Klyucharyovs had something else to talk about, something moreover which concerned them deeply and which was much nearer home. Their son had won first place in the competitions for nearly every class of apparatus. He had been awarded nine point seven on the horizontal bar, an astonishing result for a young boy. Well-known coaches were taking an interest in him, and there were plans to enter young Denis Klyucharyov in competitions at national level.

"Well done, son!" was Klyucharyov's reaction.

His wife, needless to say, showed no signs of enthusiasm.

Indeed, Klyucharyov glimpsed in her eyes the familiar fear that something might happen. The horizontal bar is a dangerous piece of apparatus. Her son promptly interrupted the conversation to reassure her. "Don't worry, mum, I'm not going to fall off the horizontal bar. I'd lose two points if I did." He laughed. He was proud and full of life. It was tempting to say, like father, like son.

4

On Friday Klyucharyov accepted the Deputy Director's offer. His acceptance was couched only in general terms, but to all intents and purposes, he had said "Yes." The Deputy Director immediately started taking him from one office to another, as if to say, "What do you think of your future colleagues? Will they do?"

"They'll do fine!" was Klyucharyov's response. A new department was being set up in the institute. It was being formed by merging two laboratories and adding various research associates from here and there. It was a new department, so Klyucharyov would be getting his promotion to the higher echelons without having to topple or clamber over anyone else.

Right now that was what was in his mind, while the Deputy Director was going on about what a splendid department it would be. Powerful, up to the minute, and, he was sure, with everyone pulling together. "Do you hear, Klyucharyov?"

Klyucharyov said, "Of course I do. You've said it twice already."

"And I'll say it a hundred times," said the Deputy Director laughing. "I'm seducing you."

"I'm seduced already."

"I'm going to carry right on seducing you so that you don't change your mind."

"Am I up to it?"

"Oh, come on. Don't give me that!"

In mid-sentence the Deputy Director shook hands with one of the researchers as he walked past, winking genially as if to say, "Carry on, carry on. Don't let me distract you." He nodded to two more, and shook hands with yet another. He and Klyucharyov were walking past the desks, talking in low voices.

"Choose yourself a good secretary. Do you see those three girls over there?"

"Yes."

"Take a good look at that red-haired one."

"The glum-looking one?"

"Yes. She's smart, and meticulous. She'll keep all your files and papers in perfect order."

"Thank you."

They were talking in low voices. Then they went out into the corridor.

"Let's take a look at Lab Six now," said the Deputy Director. On the way to Lab Six Klyucharyov stopped to light a cigarette. There was something he had to say, and he thought it would be as well to get it off his chest straight away.

"There's just one thing," was how he began. "When somebody promotes a person, that somebody leans on his protege later on. I won't take that."

The Deputy Director laughed. "That's fine by me. Be your own man."

"I mean it."

"And so do I."

The Deputy Director patted Klyucharyov's shoulder.

"Don't go anticipating trouble where there is none. Nobody's planning to lean on you. Not me, at any rate."

The Deputy Director was a cheerful man with a sense of humour. Klyucharyov too was a cheerful man with a sense of humour. People like that always find a common language. It was just that Klyucharyov had a feeling that it would be as well for him to be on his guard at this particular moment.

Klyucharyov and Alimushkin

When Klyucharyov got home everybody already knew all about everything. In the hall and the rooms the atmosphere of a small family celebration was almost tangible. Kolya Krymov had already rung to congratulate him. Pavel rang, also with congratulations. It transpired that Kolya, and Pavel, and other friends would be gracing them with their presence that evening. Mother-in-law was beaming. She was pleased to see the Klyucharyovs going up in the world.

"Tonight I'll feed you like gods!" she announced. True to her word, she shot off to "The Gifts of Nature" and brought back a very impressive-looking loin of venison. Roasted and dripping with juices the crimson red joint on an immense white platter was going to look completely irresistible. The loin was roasted in the oven some forty minutes. Before that it was well larded with butter so that, driven out by the heat, the deer's blood would form a golden brown crust to sear the diner's soul. The joint was ready. Klyucharyov went off for the wine. He had just got back when Mrs. Alimushkin phoned.

Mother-in-law was displeased. Klyucharyov went to the phone, when she thought he should be polishing the floor, or at the very least opening the bottles. That really was a job for the man of the house.

Mrs. Alimushkin said, "I want to thank you." She went on to explain what it was precisely that she wanted to thank Klyucharyov for: for advising her not to spread herself around, and to get married. She really had seen sense now, and found an agreeable man who was a professor and not too old. And very kind, he was, and very much in love with her... She spoke with the merest trace of irony in her voice, and Klyucharyov could tell which way the wind was blowing. It was not difficult.

He said, "I'm very pleased for you."

Mother-in-law was just saying, "What's he thinking of, blathering away like that on the telephone."

His wife explained, "It's to do with his work, mother."

"He's on the job, more like."

"Mother!"

Klyucharyov went on, "I'm very pleased for you," and laughed. "You won't be needing me any more, then."

"Whatever makes you think that?" a sing-song note of suggestiveness came into the voice of the lovely Mrs. Alimushkin. "You put me in my place, and quite right too. I understand that. I'm going to be a good girl now. But after all, in future... I might need some more advice."

"From me?"

Mother-in-law said, "As if I don't know what they are talking about."

"Mother, don't be so suspicious."

"And you don't go making excuses for him. Why doesn't he stop blathering on the telephone. He'd be better employed polishing the floors."

"Mother!"

Mrs. Alimushkin said, "I really would like to have a wise friend. No more than that. Just a wise, true friend. All right?"

"Yes," Klyucharyov smiled. "I know. A wise, true friend, like in the films."

"Is that himself he's calling wise?"

"Mother!"

"I'm not going to ask you to come round in the next few days, but all the same, you will come to see me sometimes, won't you. It doesn't need to be an evening. I don't mind if it's a working day, or only once a month. All right?... And sometimes, not often, I shall phone you. And ask you for some good advice. Do you mind?"

"Go ahead and phone," said Klyucharyov.

"Let her phone. Just let her try. One of these days that sweet little voice will find me on the other end of the line, and then she'll get what's coming to her."

"Mother! You ought to be ashamed of yourself. What makes you so sure he's even talking to a woman?"

"What would make me think he's talking to a man?"

The guests arrived. Some came on their own, some with a partner, bringing wine in their briefcases and kind words in their hearts. Klyucharyov's wife welcomed them and sat them down at the table. She had a smile for everyone. She was no longer afraid of their spate of good fortune, or thinking that the gods would be angered and something happen. She had got used to it.

It was just this change that Klyucharyov detected in her expression. That was why (everybody around him was noisily congratulating him on his success), when they gave him a chance to speak, he began by teasing his wife.

"Success is a great thing," he said, raising his glass high. "But, oddly enough, the person who gets used to it fastest is the person who is afraid of it."

He looked over towards his wife, and everybody laughed.

"Good for her for getting used to it," somebody shouted out.

"Quite. Good for her... But she's got used to it already, and now she's going to want more. Now she's going to want more success. That's human nature..."

"I shan't," said his wife, laughing. "I shan't want anything of the sort. It makes me frightened."

Everybody laughed, and shouted, "You will! You will! You will want more success!"

They all clinked glasses when Klyucharyov proposed a toast, and the toast he proposed was, "Here's to success for everybody!" Then they ate and drank, and when the party was nearly over Klyucharyov's wife started showing photographs of Denis performing complicated exercises. The photographs were passed from hand to hand. They really were very impressive. One immortalised Denis for all time just as he was soaring to his highest on the horizontal bar. Their son was frozen on outstretched arms, his slender gymnast's legs pointing vertically towards the sky. The exercise was called "Sun." This was the first time Klyucharyov's wife had shown these photographs. Before she had been afraid that showing them might be tempting providence.

The guests departed, pleased with their hosts, and their hosts were pleased with their guests. Klyucharyov's wife and his mother-in-law cleared the table. Mother-in-law had had a little too much to drink and was humming something to herself.

Klyucharyov and his wife lay in bed and talked quietly about all sorts of unimportant things before going to sleep. First he yawned, and then she did. The children were asleep. It was after midnight.

"She'll be going away, then?" Klyucharyov asked, meaning mother-in-law. He yawned again.

Vladimir Makanin

"She's already bought the ticket."

"Flying?"

"Why do you always want mother to go by plane?"

"M-m... It's more comfortable, faster."

They said nothing for a while. Then Klyucharyov said he would go to the library tomorrow to get some books he'd ordered, and probably look in while he was at it to see how Alimushkin was getting on.

"I'll go round tomorrow. Just to see how he's doing."

His wife said, "You won't need to go round to Alimushkin any more. My friend rang to say he's flown off to Madagascar."

"He's gone already?"

"Yes."

"When?"

"She said at ten o'clock this morning. She said to tell you that Alimushkin had flown off, and his mother had been there to see him go."

Klyucharyov said nothing for a moment. Then suddenly he needed a cigarette and went out to the kitchen. His wife was already asleep.

Translated by Arch Tait

From: Vladimir Makanin, *Stories*,
Khudozhestennaya Literatura Publishers, Moscow, 1988.

May We Recommend

to our Russian-speaking readers

VOLGA

Published since 1966, *VOLGA* is a literary monthly journal based in Saratov on the Volga. It has established its reputation over the past few years through publishing new works which border on the avant-garde but remain accessible to the general reader.

The journal has become a major cultural centre attracting the best talents in the country. Many of Russia's foremost writers prefer to publish their work in this provincial magazine rather than in the capital.

VOLGA was among the first in Russia to publish Sasha Sokolov, Evgeny Popov, Vladimir Sorokin, Zufar Gareyev, Vyacheslav Pyetsukh, Sigizmund Krzhizhanovski, to name a few. In the pre-glasnost era these and other *VOLGA* contributions were known only to readers of samizdat; they have since become nationally famous.

Address: 3 Cosmonaut Embankment, Saratov, 410002, Russia

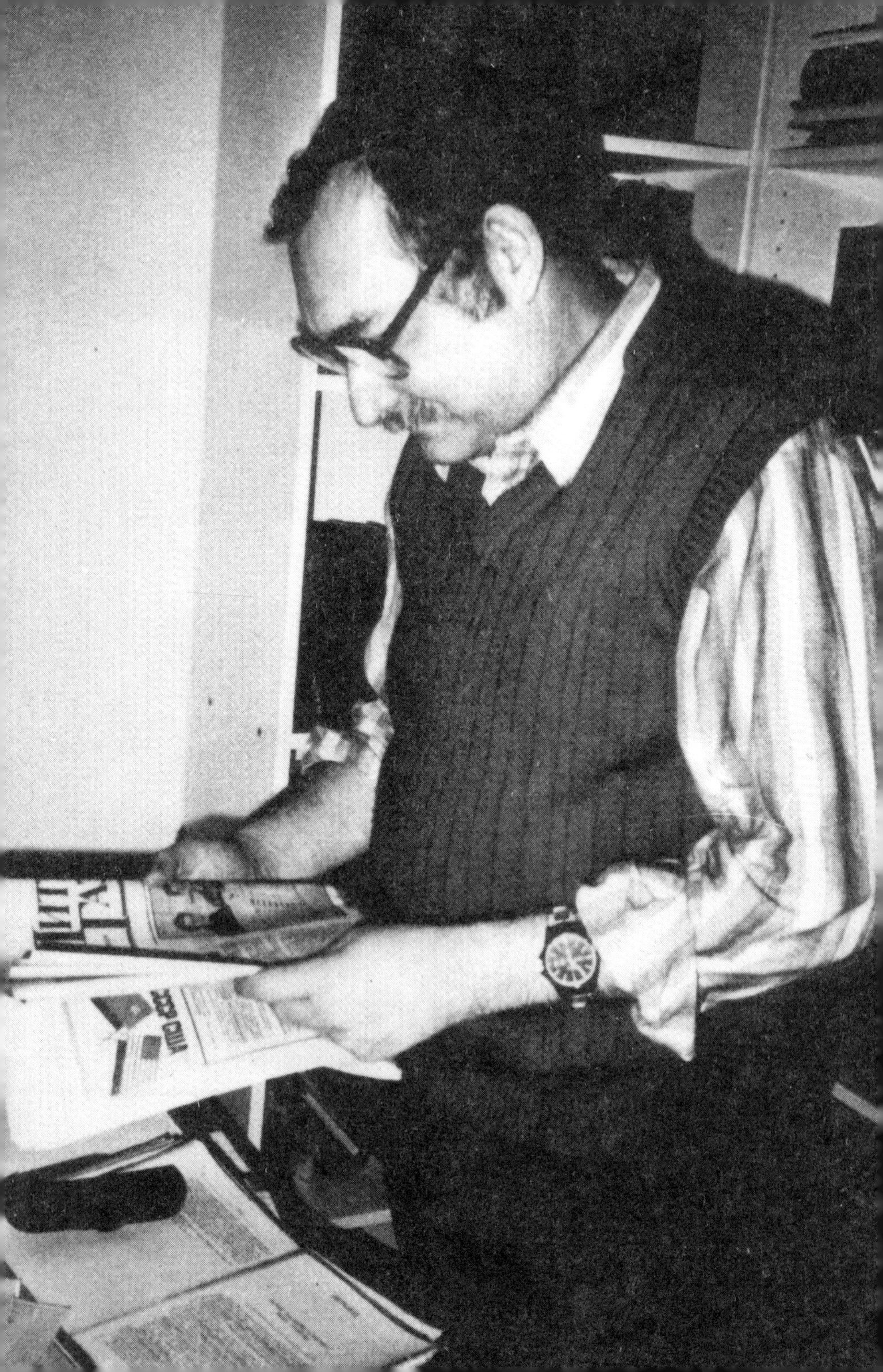

Friedrich GORENSTEIN

BAG IN HAND

Avdotya woke up in the early hours and immediately remembered about her little bag.

"Oh, my, my..." Avdotya began keening, "Oh, oh... Carrying that can of milk yesterday, the handle broke, it's all worn out... I have to stitch it up before the shops open."

She glanced at her little old alarm clock. Once upon a time that alarm clock used to get Avdotya up out of bed together with the others... Who? What's it matter... What personal history has Avdotya got nowadays?

Soviet citizens remember all the detailed ramifications of their personal history, thanks to the innumerable forms they have to fill in so very often. But it was a long time since Avdotya had filled in any forms, and of all the various state institutions her interest was reserved for the grocery stores. For Avdotya was a typical grocery-store granny, a social type unrecognised by socialist statistical science, but actively involved in the consumption of the product of socialist society.

Before the weary working population comes pouring out of its workshops, factories and institutions in the evening; before, worn to a frazzle by rush-hour travel on public transport, it squeezes itself into the hot, cramped gas-chambers of the shops, Avdotya has time to dart around them all, like a little mouse... She'll pick up a few Bulgarian eggs in one place, a little bit of Polish ham in another, a Dutch chicken in yet another, a bit of Finnish butter somewhere else. The topography of the food-hunt, as it were. She never even thinks any more about the taste of a good Russian apple from Vladimir or a sweet dark-red cherry, and she gathers berries outside Moscow to eke out her pension, not for eating.

Off she'll go, bag in hand, into the woods that are still left alive — as if she's just going to another grocery store to buy a few raspberries and strawberries from old Mother Nature — getting there before the alcoholics who follow Michurin in expecting no favours from nature and are collecting raspberries to make drink. They'll strip the woods so bare there'll be nothing left for a bird to peck at or a squirrel to gnaw on. They'll plunder their younger brethren and then squat heavily on the shoulders of their brothers and sisters among the working people.

Our Avdotya will sell a little bagful of raspberries from the

Bag in Hand

Moscow woods — a rouble for a fifty gramme glass — then she'll buy a kilo of bananas from Peru at a rouble ten kopecks a kilo. She'll sell a few bilberries at a rouble fifty a glass, and buy some Moroccan oranges at a rouble forty a kilo. It's a fine life under socialism. The western peace fighters are quite right. It's just a pity their visual propaganda doesn't make use of our Avdotya's weighing scales and Avdotya's added value.

* * *

Avdotya the grocery store granny was an old hand at shop-plundering, she was experienced, and her weapon was her little bag. Old Avdotya loved her little bag, and as she made ready for the working day she would croon to it:

"Ah, my little provider, my own little Daisy-Cow!"

Her plan was all drawn up in advance. First to "our shop" — that's the one next door to her house. After that to the bread shop. After that to the big department store. After that to the milk shop. After that to the "deli." After that to the shop run by the Tatars. After that to the vegetable stall. After that to the bread shop opposite the stall. After that to the shop beside the post office...

* * *

It was never calm in the big shop. When you plunged in there, the waves grabbed you and bore you away... From the grocery section to the delicatessen, from the delicatessen to the meat section... And always elbows on every side, elbows and shoulders, more elbows... The good thing was they couldn't nudge you here — there was nowhere to fall. But an elbow to the face, the "mug" — nothing could be simpler.

Now they've wheeled out a trolley piled high with flat tins of herring. This kind of situation is mannah from heaven to Avdotya... No queue or order of any kind, straightforward pillage. Free-for-all grabbing. It's not the cunning of the fox Avdotya requires here, but the cunning of the mouse. Just like a circus act: hup, one, two — and the trolley's empty. People look around to see who's holding what. The men have grabbed one or two... Some folk have grabbed nothing but empty air, they're furious. The leaders of the pack are the strong, skilled housewives, with three or four tins. A few little old women are up there with them. Avdotya has three tins in her little bag.

If the grocery store grannies ever combine forces, then they're formidable. Once seven old women, including our Avdotya, stormed a counter in chain formation. The leader, Matveevna, who's in hospital with a fracture just at present, was holding herself up with a crutch. They pushed everyone aside and they got their Polish ham. Of course, you always have to assess the situation in advance. For instance, it's pointless getting involved in that kind of situation over there in the meat section... Something's just been wheeled out, but just what isn't clear. Something between a scrum and a scrimmage. A few people smiling stiffly — the ones who try to make a joke of their brutality. But most of the faces are seriously vicious. This is work...

Ooh, you get away from there, Avdotya. You've grabbed your herring, now get out. Herring's not like nice smooth broth, it tickles as it slips through your guts, and it hurts when it makes you belch... But you still want it anyway. You can't always be doing what the doctors tell you, you have to please yourself. Some potato will fix the salt, and a sip of sweet tea will settle everything down. Now you've got your fatty herrings, you get out of there, Avdotya, while you're still in one piece. Get out, Avdotya...

But it was a bad day, nothing going right... Avdotya realised the situation too late. There was no space left to turn around, not even room to draw breath... And there was a new smell — homegrown coarse tobacco and tar, tar from new roads in the satellite towns...

They've arrived... There are the tourist buses outside the supermarket. Every bus a requisitioning detachment's mobile headquarters to which the plundered purchases are carried back. The entire bus weighed down with bundles, sacks and string bags. The troops move off in various directions — men and women with fine strong arms: and the scouts are nimble boys and girls. A freckle-faced girl comes running up.

"Uncle Parshin, aunty Vasilchuk said to tell you they're selling vegetable fat."

"What kind of fat's that, lop-ears?"

"Yellow," says freckle-face, nodding gleefully. "I got inside and saw them giving it out... And someone gave aunty Vasilchuk a shove with his shoulder..."

But uncle Parshin's not listening anymore:

"Vaniukhin, Sakhnenko! Get the milk-churn!"

Off runs the combat crew with a forty-litre churn... Oh, so many of them... Oh, it's just too much... And now they've shoved in another churn.

"Ooh, he... help. Help!"

The satellite towns work smartly. Transporting sausage, cheese and grains through the air. It's harvest-time. If you don't reap, you don't eat. And if you don't eat, when you pick up the Party newspaper, you get annoyed. And ideological wavering is not a good thing. And who are the satellite towns anyway? They're the best fighters in Russia... "Just as long as we're fed, we'll give anyone a thrashing... Just whistle for us, Central Committee, just give us the order, 'Comrades, stand to!' But we can't do nothing if there's nothing to eat, Central Committee. The satellite towns is your support, father Central Committee, and there you go feeding that rotten whore Moscow... And even in Moscow you can't always find vodka to put some lead in your pencil."

* * *

Our Avdotya made her escape. And she saved her little bag too... Avdotya's lived a long time on this earth, she knows a thing or two. It's not the truth she seeks, it's groceries. But this day's not going to go according to plan. She called into a "delicatessen". Quiet, calm, the air's clean and the counters are neat and empty. Could at least have put something on them for appearance's sake. Even if it was only a bone for a dog. The sales-girl sits there with her cheek propped up in her hand. People come in, swear and spit. But our Avdotya went in and stood there, taking a pause for breath, then spoke.

"Have you got any nice fresh fillet steak, love? Or some nice tender sirloin?"

"I think you're in the wrong place, granny," the sales-girl answered. "It's not a delicatessen you need, it's an eye doctor... Can't you see what's on the counter?"

Our Avdotya didn't take offence.

"Thanks for the advice," she said.

Off she went to another delicatessen, and when she went in, — there was something there! She snatched a pair of kidneys from under the nose of some dimwit. The kidneys were lying on a dish in damp isolation, like anatomical specimens, and the dimwit was studying and sniffing them. Taking off his glasses and putting them back on again. Avdotya dashed across to the cash-desk and paid for the kidneys.

"That's not right," cried the intellectual, "I was first." "You were sniffing them, but the granny here paid," replied the retail trade worker.

"What about some more?"

"There aren't any more... Buy some of the specials, they're not in very often."

The intellectual took a look and couldn't make out what they were. He read the label — "Egg with caviare." He looked closely, and it was indeed a hard-boiled egg, not too fresh, cut in half. And the sulphurous surface was dotted with black sparrow's droppings.

"Where's the caviare?"

"That's as much as there should be. Thirty grammes. What d'you expect for that price?"

It's a price for which under that voluntarist Khruschev, on the eve of the historical October 1964 Party plenary session which marked a turning-point in the development of agriculture, you could buy two hundred grammes of fine caviare in any delicatessen. Russia moves on apace, as though there were dogs barking at its heels... But where are we going in such a hurry? Why not sit down and take time to draw breath and think, wipe the sweat from our brow? Just you try suggesting it. The political columnists will make you a laughing-stock.

* * *

So this is the life of Avdotya, the little old grocery-store granny without any personal history. She's adapted to it. She peers at the political commentators on her little television and regales herself with kidneys. The political commentator's face twists and warps and his voice roars distortedly, because her television's been

Bag in Hand

out of order for ages. But what can she do about it? They've forbidden the consumption of caviare and fresh-smoked sausage, but at least they still let you chew on kidneys. And there's other food that hasn't been totally requisitioned yet. Russia's abundance is unlimited. In one place they queue for Indian tea, in another they queue for Bulgarian eggs, in yet another they queue for Rumanian tomatoes. Just stand there for a while and you get them.

Our Avdotya went into the milk shop. That calm and peaceful food-product — milk, the non-alcoholic drink. Children drink it, and people on strict diets. Sometimes the queues in here are calm too. But not today, when they're selling prepacked Finnish butter...

Avdotya goes in and listens: the queue's buzzing like a circular saw that's hit a stone when it's running at full speed... The queue's face is hypertense, white with red blotches. A rosy blood-and-milk complexion... Avdotya pushes in backwards, into the Tatar's shop, where the manager is a Tatar and his wife is a sales attendant...

The Tatars are under seige by plundering hordes from the Ukrainian steppes... Makhno's anarchists... All in the same uniform — neck-scarves and double-breasted fur-trimmed plush jackets. Beefy scarlet hands, crimson faces and garlic breath...

But then just recently Russians, especially the policemen for some reason, have garlic breath too... Perhaps it's from the sausage, perhaps they're trying to kill the taste of the poor food with garlic?

The anarchists shout at each other:

"Teklia, ver's Tern?"

"Gonfa shompine wiz Gorpyna."

While the satelliters plunder the basic products, Makhno's warriors plunder the luxury items. They bring their sacks of pumpkin seeds or early pears to the market, stuff the sacks full of money, and then fill the sacks up with delicacies.

There's Gorpyna helping Teklia lift a sack full of champagne on to her shoulders. There's Tern clutching rucksacks bulging with bars and boxes of chocolate in both hands. It brings back memories of the old partisan gun-carts loaded with plundered landlords' property. But this is a different kind of pillage. Inspired not by Bakunin, but by Marx. Goods — money — goods...

The Soviet shop is an object lesson on the history and economy of the state — and on politics and morals and social relations...

"How much they giving?"
"Still won't be enough for everyone..."
"Two kilos each..."
"You in the queue?"
"Nah, I'm just standing here to take some air."
"What?"
"Shove off..."

The permanent cold war for hot-smoked sausage shows no signs of settling down. This is where the fighters for peace could have a real field day! This is where the foreign diplomats should study our problems. Pick up a string bag, stuff it with empty yoghurt and wine and vodka bottles, put on a dirty shirt, stand in front of the radiator for a while till you start sweating, then go off to the grocery store. You have to be able to shove with your elbows, glare viciously, and know just one word in Russian:

"Otvali" ("Shove off...")

You can add anything extra in your own language. Everyone gets the meaning anyway. But a foreigner in Russia is a privileged individual. He goes either to the "Beriozka" foreign currency shops or the Central Market. At the Central Market there is an abundance of high-quality foodstuffs and foreign cars. The country is capable of producing firm sun-ripened tomatoes and cool fragrant cucumbers, sweet dessert pears with succulent flesh and aromatic peaches so lovely that they are as good as flowers for decorating any festive table. The country is capable of covering counters with the delicate yellowish-white carcasses of geese, ducks, chickens and turkeys. Mounds of fresh meat. Chunks of lightly-salted, mouth-watering pork fat, spicy fish, full-fat off-white cream cheese, thick sourcream... Here at the Central Market it's still the NEP period, there's no onward march towards communism here, no overfulfilment of the plan, no grandiose space-flights or struggle for peace...

The Central Market is a good place...

* * *

But where's our Avdotya got to? We've completely lost sight of her... There she is in an itinerant queue — there are some like that. A shop-porter in a blue overall is dragging along a trolley, and on the trolley there are foreign cardboard boxes. No-one knows

Bag in Hand

what's in the boxes, but a queue forms anyway and runs after the trolley. New people keep on joining. Avdotya's somewhere in the first third of this long-distance queue... She should get some.. Avdotya's grey hair is soaking wet and itchy under her headscarf, her heart is in her mouth, her stomach is squashing her bladder, and there's a rasping ache from her liver somewhere in the small of her back. But she mustn't fall behind. Fall behind and you lose your place in the queue. The shop-porter is hangover and he wants to clear his head with a breath of fresh air, so he drags the trolley along without stopping. Someone in the queue, exhausted, calls out:

"Can't you stop for a while, we're tired, start selling the stuff..."

Then the woman from the retail organisation, following behind the trolley with her fat backside and short dirty overall, tells them:

"You make any fuss, and I won't sell anything."

The queue turned on the timid rebel and began sniping at him:

"If you're not happy, you can go home and cool off... What a fine gentleman — can't even stand a walk in the fresh air! They know better than us where they're supposed to sell the stuff. Maybe they've got instructions from their boss."

Our Avdotya runs on after the others. The drunken shop-porter deliberately swings this way and that. Over towards the tram-stop, then back towards the bus-stop... And the woman with the fat backside is laughing... She's been drinking too... They're just taunting everybody, the monsters...

Under the present state structure they share direct power over the people with the local policeman, the house-manager and the other public servants... Avdotya once arrived in the offices of the Moscow energy corporation, after some kind people told her how to find it, in tears. The kind young girls working there, their characters still unspoilt, asked her:

"Why're you crying, granny?"

"I've no paper left to pay the 'lectricity. They say they'll turn off the 'lectricity. What'll I do without 'lectricity? I can't cook and wash in the dark." And she held out her old payment book, all used up now, the one that a kind neighbour filled out for her.

"Oh, your payment book's finished? Here, take another one." And they gave her a nice new one, didn't even take a single kopeck for it. How Avdotya thanked them and wished them good health. And how much mockery she must have suffered in her life in various offices for her to be so afraid of all civil servants! These weren't just clerks, they were her providers.

Avdotya runs on, although she already has black spots in front of her eyes. The porter turns this way, the porter turns that way. And whichever way he turns, the queue follows him, like a tail. On one steep turn the engineer Fishelevich dropped out of the queue with a clanking of yoghurt bottles and a crunching of bones. Couldn't stand the pace. But the rest stick with it, even though they're almost out of energy. Then luckily the porter tried to be too clever, turned too sharply, and the cardboard boxes tumbled off right in the middle of the pavement... A few burst, and egg white and yolk came running out. The queue was delighted — they were going to get eggs. They felt better already. Something they needed, and they didn't need to run after it any more. The queue stood there, breathing heavily, resting while the porter and the woman with the fat backside conferred in obscene language. Volunteers were even found to carry the boxes from the middle of the pavement over to the wall of the building. Selling began...

The Russian heart and the Russified heart is easily appeased... difficulties and injuries are quickly forgotten — too quickly forgotten. Following the catastrophe the porter and the woman with the fat backside have decided in consultation that at the request of the people they will allow each purchaser ten whole eggs and ten cracked ones... And instead of calling them "table eggs," they will dub them "dietary eggs" and increase the price shown on the label. But at the same time they will give out polythene bags free of charge. Good. Our Avdotya took her ten whole eggs in one polythene bag, and her ten cracked ones in another, paid the new price, put everything in her little bag and went away happy. She called into the bakery and bought some bread — half a black loaf and a long white one. No queue for bread in Moscow yet. If ever there's a queue for bread, it'll mean the beginning of a new stage of advanced socialism. To advance the struggle against cosmopolitanism they'll ban the consumption of American, Canadian, Argentinian, etc. grain. For the time being this question remains in the province of peaceful co-existence. International flour bakes good

Bag in Hand

bread. A bit of meat to go with it would be good. Since she didn't get any nice young chicken, a little bit of meat would do nicely... And there's the meat shop, right in front of our Avdotya. The meat shop's buzzing, the meat shop's humming. That means they're selling. Our Avdotya goes inside.

The queue's by no means small, but there's no violence. Meat queues are usually some of the most violent. Maybe the smell transports people back to the times of our ancestors when the leaders of various caves fought each other for a prime cut of mammoth sirloin? A human being can turn wild as easy as drinking a glass of beer...

Those are the kind of thoughts that come to you in a Moscow meat queue, as your nostrils are assailed by the smell of tormented flesh. Our Avdotya began sniffing too, our toothless predator. She spotted something... That little piece lying over there... Not too big, not too small... Ah, if she just could get that one... Our Avdotya would pamper it like a child, wash it first in cold, cold water, and then in lukewarm water, clean out all the little bits of tough tissue and tendons, cut out the marrow-bone to make a bit of soup. And she'd use the soft meat for a nice matching set of cutlets, like twins. She could try begging the queue for that piece in the name of Christ the Lord. The queue didn't look vicious.

Just as she thought it, she took a closer look — and she froze... Standing there in the queue is Kudriashova, Avdotya's old enemy... Kudriashova is a hardened bread-winner, the backbone of a large family of voracious children, and our Avdotya has often beaten her to the goods... Kudriashova has sloping shoulders and hands like meat-hooks. Kudriashova can carry two bags that our Avdotya couldn't even lift for long distances, as long as the load consists of foodstuffs. And Kudriashova is a fine child-bearer. Her eldest is already in the army, and her youngest is still crawling. Kudriashova is a strong woman, well adapted to queues. She can take on the average male at fisticuffs on equal terms. But when it comes to grabbing — and as we know, that's sometimes what's needed in the retail sector — then our Avdotya is quicker and smarter than Kudriashova, just as a sparrow is quicker than a crow. She might easily grab a little head of cabbage or a wrapped piece of Tambov gammon out from under Kudriashova's hand.

"You just wait, you witch," Kudriashova threatens and abuses

Friedrich Gorenstein

her, "you just wait till I nudge you." "I'll call a policeman," Avdotya replies. "You and your nudging."

But she's still afraid: "Oh, she's going to nudge me. Oh, she's going to nudge me."

Now seems like the right moment to explain what this word "nudge" means. It comes from an old Slavonic form, the meaning of which is still preserved in a modern Ukrainian word. In modern Russian it translates as "to shove", but it's not quite that. A different intonation can change the meaning of a word, so that in usage, if not in grammar, there are actually two words. To shove means to push or move someone away from oneself. Sometimes someone who's shoved you will say sorry, beg your pardon. But if they "nudge" you, then there won't be any apology. Because when they nudge someone they try to make sure he gets smashed good and proper.

"Oh, she's going to nudge me," thinks our Avdotya, "she's going to nudge me." But the queue is calm, not at all bellicose, and Kudriashova is calm too. She glowers at Avdotya, but she doesn't say anything. What reason could there be for that? The reason's not the meat — it's the butcher.

An unusual butcher has appeared at this trade outlet. An intellectual butcher, looking more like a broad-boned professor of surgery with a white cap set on his greying hair, with his firmly moulded, well-fed face, wearing glasses. A butcher as merry and cynical as a surgeon, not gloomy and dirty like a butcher. For him a queue is an object of jolly mockery, not an occasion for neurotic altercation. He is above the queue. With his immense but clean hands he takes the pieces of meat and sets them on the meat tray in the display cabinet. And he replies to the murmuring in the queue when it demands quicker service with a faultless rendition from Pushkin's *Eugene Onegin*...

"What's going on?" grumbles a woman with a tired face, who's obviously not standing in her first queue of the day. "What's going on?.. You're put there to serve the customers."

"Chapter Two," replies the butcher: "The village where our Eugene suffered so Was really quite a charming little spot, Where a simple pleasure-seeker might well go And thank the heavens for his pleasant lot..."

Bag in Hand

A strange picture, and one which summons up strange thoughts. A picture which leads to unexpected conclusions. The first conclusion is that Pushkin should be recited to the meat queue by a butcher. This is actually the most important conclusion, well worth a few moment's reflection in the oppressive heat of the shop. The butcher jangles Pushkin's lyre with a cynical and vulgar hand, but nonetheless he soothes the savage beast. The people remain silent, in line with the final stage direction in Pushkin's play *Boris Godunov*. They stand there quiet, not actually listening to Pushkin, but hearing him. Just let some great Pushkin specialist or famous actor try reciting Pushkin to a meat queue. They'll be lucky if the response is no more than mockery. Viciously expressed hatred is more likely. No, culture must be brought to the people by the authorities. Then what kind of culture is it? What kind of Pushkin? We can answer that question by starting from a different angle. Answer a question with a question. Have you ever watched the sunrise? Not over luxuriant subtropical greenery that knows all about the sun and consciously lives by it and waits with academic assurance for it to rise. And not over a calm, grass-covered forest glade, which is itself a particle of sunlight, which believes in the sun and lives through the sunrise as an intimate experience of its own.

We're thinking of the sunrise over lifeless northern cliffs, where you ask yourself: what good is life to the dead? What good is the sun to the cold rocks? The rocks lie there calm and heavy and dull in the remoteness of night, covered with ice and snow, the stones greet the short grey day with indifference, accepting on their unfeeling breasts its barbed blasts of wind. But the sun does rise over them, a weak imitation of the hot, fructifying sun or the gentle, caressing sun that we know. A sun rises that would plunge the subtropical greenery or the forest glade into horrified anguish. And suddenly the cliffs are transformed. The rocks turn pink, moss and lichens appear, and an unprepossessing insect crawls out of a cleft to greet the brief holiday. It's probably not even aware of where the light has come from or why the wind has died down, why the indifference to cold is no more, or what this new feeling, or rather sensation, of warmth and peace really is. But let the southern sun, or even the gentle temperate sun, rise over the rocks of the north, and it would be a disaster. The cold rocks would split, the lichen would dry out, the unprepossessing insect would shrivel up and die. The cold north needs a cold sun.

* * *

...The butcher picks up a piece of meat in his huge white hands. A really fine, juicy piece. And a bone like loaf-sugar. Our Avdotya just can't believe her eyes. What happiness!

"Happy holiday!" she says, trying to flatter the butcher's feelings, so he won't change his mind.

"Thank you very much," answers the butcher. "Which holiday's that now? The Party holiday or the church holiday?"

The rumbling subsides. The people are in happy mood, even though the queue is packed in tight. And with merriment comes awareness.

"It's tough enough for us," someone says, "but what about the lonely old folk?"

Our Avdotya reaches out for the meat. The butcher doesn't give it to her. Avdotya is even a bit alarmed. But she needn't be.

"Let me put it in your bag for you," says the butcher.

The meat's in the bag. Avdotya, happy, has turned to leave, but the butcher calls after her:

"Thank you for your custom."

"God grant you good health," Avdotya replies.

Avdotya has gone outside and she walks along with a smile on her face. She goes round the corner, takes the piece of meat out of her bag, jogs it up and down like a child, kisses it. Some nice young chicken might be better, but Avdotya doesn't have any chicken, she didn't get any, and this meat is all her own. Our Avdotya's day started badly, but it's turned out well. While she's in luck she might as well make the best of it. Avdotya decides to visit a shop a long way away, one she rarely goes to. "Never mind, there's a little bench on the way, I'll sit down for a bit and then go on. Maybe I'll pick something up..."

Off goes our Avdotya. She walks, rests, walks on again. Suddenly she sees a fool coming towards her. She knows his face to look at, but not his name.

This fool was no longer young. He had a bad burn on his head, so he always wore a cap. This sharp-nosed fool travelled around on the public transport and cut silhouettes of people out of paper. They caught a good likeness, but they cost money. At one time the fool used to work as an artist in a tannery. Then one day, instead of the slogan "We shall fulfil the five year plan in four years," he wrote "We shall fulfil the five year plan in six years." What could he have been thinking of? But then, the fool's own brother, a colonel and a hero — medals, four-room flat, honoured veteran of the Great Patriotic War — suddenly announced one day in public that "Today, by order of the supreme Commander-in-Chief, comrade Stalin, snow fell in the city." And at that time not only was comrade Stalin no longer in this world, he wasn't even in the mausoleum. How could he have ordered the snow? They thought it was just a poor joke on the colonel's part, but when they looked closer they saw he was quite sincere, and there was an unhealthy gleam in his eyes. In short — bad genes. Maybe it's true and he is a real fool, but they do say that in some district quite a long way from his own, where people don't know him very well, the colonel's younger brother, the artist, approached the very jaws of a raging, bloodthirsty hours-long queue standing in the baking sun at a kiosk where they were selling early strawberries and declared: "In the name of the Supreme Soviet of the USSR I propose that you serve me three kilogrammes of strawberries." As he spoke he extended his right hand with the palm upwards. The palm was empty, but the people did as he asked, and he took his three kilogrammes of strawberries... There's a fine fool for you...

The fool sees our Avdotya and he says:

"Granny, they're selling Soviet sausage in store number fifteen... And there's no-one in there."

A man who happens to be walking beside her and overhears the fool's words, says:

"What kind of nonsense is that... All our sausage is Soviet, Jewish sausage is what we don't have here."

"It's nice sausage," answers the fool. "Smells good. Haven't seen any like it for ages."

"He's a bit.. y'know," our Avdotya whispers to the man, and taps a finger against her headscarf.

"Ah," says the anti-semite, and goes on his way. Store number fifteen is the one Avdotya was going to. She gets there. The shop is as long as a narrow hose and dirtier than dirt itself... Even for the Moscow suburbs it's far too dirty. A shop, you might say, just begging to be satirised in the *Moscow News*. The sales-assistants are all dirty, crumpled and unkempt, standing behind the counter as though they're just out of bed and they had vodka instead of coffee for breakfast. The cashier is drunk too, and she's facing a drunken customer. They babble at each other, but they can't come to any agreement. She's speaking Ryazan dialect, he's speaking Yaroslavl dialect. And all the shop-porters have tattoos on their bony arms and on their sunken alcohol-corroded chests... One has Stalin tucked away in his bosom, peeking out from behind a dirty undershirt as though from behind a curtain, another has a grinning eagle, a third has a maritime chest — a sailor with the inscription "Port Arthur."

Avdotya knew about this shop, and rarely came here. But here she is today. Avdotya goes in, looking around her, sees the picture described above and already feels like backing out. But then she glanced into the far corner, with the "Delicatessen" sign. She glanced, and she couldn't believe her eyes. The fool was telling the truth. Lying there on the counter was beautiful sausage, such as Avdotya hadn't even thought of in an age. Firm as dark-red marble, but you could see at a glance that it would taste juicy, with a white pattern of firm pork fat. A miracle, that's what it was. How had several cases of smoked, Party-standard, delicatessen sausage turned up here, as though they'd come straight out of the stocks in the Kremlin? And why hadn't the shop staff plundered it all themselves? They must have been really drunk to put it on sale to the public. And the label hanging there said "'Soviet' sausage". The fool hadn't lied. The price was no joke, but the other cheap stuff there was full of starch and garlic. Matveevna said that they put the meat of water-rats in sausage when they used their skins to make fur caps. But this was prime meat, pork and beef. And the meat smelt of Madeira... The closer Advotya came, the stronger the smell. If you sliced it fine and put it on bread, you could dine on it in fine style at breakfast and supper for a long time.

And there was once a time when Avdotya didn't take her supper alone. There was a boiling samovar of pure gold, and Fillipov's breadrolls. He was handsome. And Avdotya had a long tawny

Bag in Hand

braid. Nineteen twenty-five it was... No, twenty-three... Half a pound of sausage in a crackling paper bag. The sausage had a different name then, but it was the same one... When he brought it he'd say: "Try this, Avdotya Titovna. It's made with Madeira." And he used to bring a little bit of smoked sturgeon... "Try a bit," he used to say.

"Well then, old girl," the drunken unkempt sales-assistant behind the counter says to Avdotya, "you buying any sausage? Be another ten years before you can get sausage like that."

But Avdotya doesn't answer. There's a lump in her throat. "Which one d'you want?" asks the sales assistant. "This one?" And she lifts up a fine firm stick of smoked sausage. But Avdotya can't see, her eyes are full of tears.

"What you cryin' for?" asks the sales assistant. "Son-in-law thrown you out, has he?"

"I haven't got a son-in-law," Avdotya scarcely manages to answer, and she sobs and sobs.

"Must've had something stolen," suggested the shop-porter with the maritime chest. "You had something stolen, old girl?"

"Yes, stolen," Avdotya answers through her tears.

"D'you do it, Mikita?" — the question is for the one with Stalin peeping out from behind the curtain of his undershirt...

"Never even laid eyes on her," answers Mikita. "All you could steal from an old crow like that is her piles."

"Stolen," says Avdotya, and the tears keep on and on pouring down... It's a long time since she's cried like that.

"If you've had something stolen, go to the police, don't stop the shop working," says the sales assistant, and puts the stick of sausage on the scales to weigh it for the anti-semite.

The anti-semite has clearly come to his senses and come back, having decided to believe the fool. And more and more people keep turning up. The fool has obviously done a good job spreading the word about the Soviet sausage.

Soviet sausage deserves a special mention of its own. Sausage queues and orange queues form the main axis of the trade war between the state and the people. You and I have not stood in any real sausage or orange queues, because Avdotya avoids them. Our Avdotya is cunning, and so too are the satellite-towners. And

Friedrich Gorenstein

Makhno's Ukrainian anarchists are not often found there either. They stick more to the outlying districts, where the goods in short supply turn up. Then just who does stand and fight in those queues? The railway stations. And what exactly are the railway stations? They are the USSR. But the USSR only stands in line for oranges against its own will. Instead of pears and apples the USSR grows "Kalashnikov" automatic rifles in abundance, and the third world grows oranges. A natural exchange unrelated to Marx's *Capital*. The orange is a strange foreign product. It gives the USSR bitter acid indigestion. The orange is not a serious product, it doesn't go with vodka — only good for giving to children to chew on. But sausage is a different matter...

The sausage shops of Moscow are filled with the spirit of the railway stations, the stuffy air of the railway stations... In the Moscow sausage shops you have the feeling that any moment your head will be set spinning by a barked announcement:

"Attention, boarding is beginning for train number..."

And then the trains will set out directly from the Moscow sausage shops for the Urals, Tashkent, Novosibirsk, Kishinev... The railway station people are not violent. The satellite towns are cunning, but the stations are patient. Cunning is elastic, but patience is strong as iron...

Iron knows how to wait. And iron has its own reasons. It knows how far which products can be transported. After all, education has made great strides in the USSR. There's a high percentage of educated people in the queues. There are engineers standing there, physicists and chemists... Standing there and calculating... Meat and butter will travel as far as Gorky. But meat goes bad before it reaches Kazan, while sausage survives. You can take smoked foods, tea and tinned foods out beyond the Urals. And those oranges to amuse the kids. But there's nothing better than genuine smoked sausage. And the iron stands patiently in line. The USSR queues up for sausage. "Ah, sweetheart, a bit of you with a little bit of butter and some bread, and it's just like the good old times."

Then our Avdotya came to her senses. "I'm first," she yells, "I was the first in the queue."

Useless, they'd crossed her off the list. Avdotya got angry, she got really angry: "People nowadays are no better than scavengers,

Bag in Hand

people nowadays are just rotten swindlers." Our Avdotya got really carried away in her resentment. Her scarf slipped off her head. She bruised her fist on someone, she bruised her elbow on someone else. Avdotya even heaved and strained and tried to "nudge" someone. But then she got nudged herself. Some man nudged her with his backside, without even bothering to turn round. And his backside was a progressive, Young Communist League, reinforced concrete backside.

Avdotya comes to in hospital. She comes to and her first thought is for her little bag.

"Where's my bag?"

"What bag?" asks the nurse. "You'd do better to worry whether your bones will knit. Old bones are brittle."

But Avdotya mourns and can't be comforted.

"There was meat in it, and three tins of herrings, and bread, and two lots of eggs... But most of all I want the bag back..."

Getting treatment in the same hospital as Avdotya was the engineer Fishelevich, a low-paid cyberneticist. Hospital is like jail — people get to know each other quickly.

"Yury Semenovich."

"Avdotya Titovna."

"What's wrong with you, Avdotya Titovna?"

"I got nudged."

"What kind of illness is that?" Fishelevich asked ironically. "I, for instance, have a fracture of the right arm."

Avdotya took a close look.

"That's right," she said, "they shoved you out of the queue on the right hand side, I remember that. But don't you be upset. Going without eggs isn't nearly as bad as going without sausage."

But then one day the nurse said:

"Rodionova, there's a package for you."

Rodionova is our Avdotya's surname. Avdotya looked — it was her little bag... She looked again — it really was her little bag, she wasn't dreaming... No meat, of course, and no eggs, and only one of the three tins of herring. But someone had put in a bottle of yoghurt, a bag of honey-cakes and about a kilogramme of apples...

Then how Avdotya set about hugging her little bag, how she stroked and cuddled her Daisy-cow... And then she suddenly thought — who brought the package? Avdotya had no-one at all. She reached into the bag and there was a note in the bottom written in a crooked hand: "Eat and drink, granny, get well soon." And the signature was "Terenty." What Terenty?

Terenty was that shop-porter with the maritime tattoos, the one with "Port Arthur" on his chest.

Which goes to show that even in the very darkest of souls the spark of God's light is not entirely extinguished. And therein lies our only cause for hope.

April, 1981

© *Translation Andrew Bromfield, 1993*

First published in Russian in *Ogonyok*, 1991.

RUSSIAN BOOKER PRIZE 1992
the short list

LINES OF FATE, OR MILASHEVICH'S TRUNK
Mark Kharitonov

Lines of Fate takes as its subject the life and fate of Milashevich, a major, though forgotten, writer from Russia's past. This is reflected through the studies of a contemporary scholar who discovers that Milashevich's trunk contains much that will change his own life. In this work conventional literary structure is replaced by a combination of diverse literary styles, and the plot of the novel itself becomes the way it is written.

MARK KHARITONOV first gained fame as a writer in the 1970s with his novella *A Day in February*. He is also known as a translator of German literature.

NO PLACE
Friedrich Gorenstein

A brilliant and terrifying novel, *No Place* is based partly on autobiographical material (the arrest of Gorenstein's father in 1932 and his subsequent death in the Gulag) and continues the Dostoevskyan tradition of describing the desolating existence of a man who has no place in the world, but who must adapt both politically and psychologically to the extremes of post-Khrushchev Russia.

MONOGRAMME
Alexander Ivanchenko

The novel *Monogramme* describes the life and spiritual quest of a librarian in a small town in the Urals. Unusual in its thematic structure, which includes texts on meditation techniques and a Chinese legend, the work has had wide resonance among Russian readers.

ALEXANDER IVANCHENKO, a young writer who was born in the Urals, first gained attention among Russian readers for his 1988 novel *Self-Portrait with Dog*.

MANHOLE
Vladimir Makanin

Manhole is a tautly concentrated novella describing a post-apocalyptic Russian world in which society is divided between those who live above ground and those who live below. In many respects, this work provides the key metaphor for the polarisation of Russian society today.

THE TIME: NIGHT
Liudmila Petrushevskaya

The Time: Night is a corrosive novel about the tortured relations between mother and daughter, in which Petrushevskaya mordantly analyses the nature of contemporary Russian society as well as the nature of the family. The novel is due to come out from Virago Publishers this year.

LIUDMILA PETRUSHEVSKAYA is well-known as a major Russian playwright and a remarkable prose writer. She lives in Moscow.

FOUR STOUT HEARTS
Vladimir Sorokin

Four Stout Hearts is a masterful parody in novel form of the new conventions of Russian literature of the period of Glasnost, as well as the traditions of socialist realism. His frighteningly amoral heroes may excite disgust in the normal reader but at the same time there is a tender quality to their quest for a solution to life.

Excerpts from this novel were published in translation in *Glas*, No 2.

VLADIMIR SOROKIN is a young Moscow writer known in the West for his novel *The Queue* (Syntaxis, 1985, tr. Readers and Writers International 1988), and his absurdist stories (collection *Vladimir Sorokin*, Russlit, 1991).

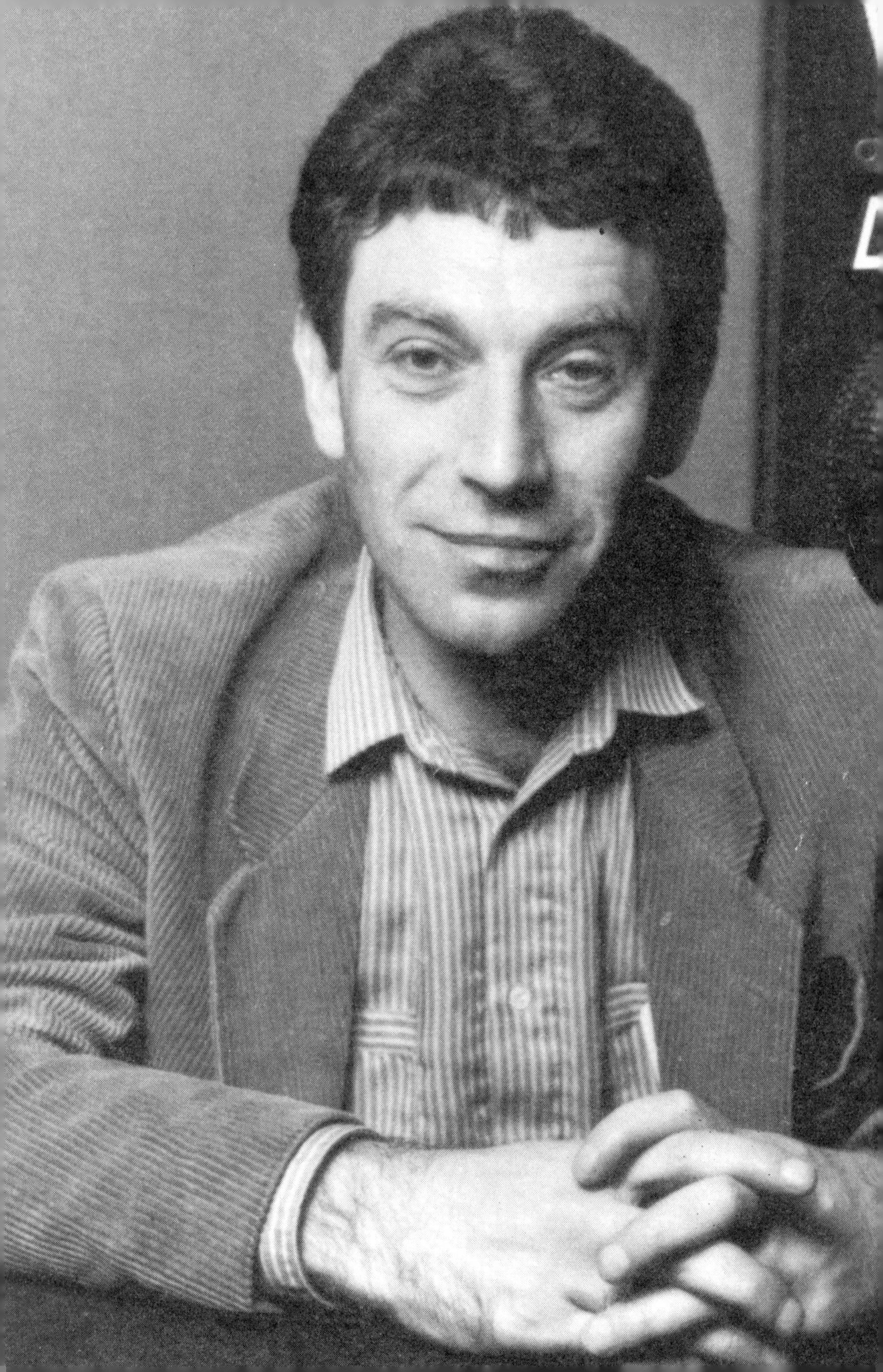

Zinovy ZINIK
MEA CULPA

At the far extremity of Africa nearest the Eastern coast of the Mediterranean, the sun, as it sinks into the setting West, obliterates everything in its path, the distance between objects as well. Eliding perspective, the homogeneity of this celestial incandescence makes the white cubes of hotels look like clouds, though there are none at this time of year, and the whitewashed native shanties look like slightly grubby flecks of foam. People and objects are reduced to their contours, turn into cut-outs, like one of those designs on a kimono transferred to human skin in the radioactive flash of Hiroshima. A palm tree is superimposed on the sea, an orange on a naked breast, the horizon fuses with a beach umbrella. The world is seen as a flat projection, a slide with a blindingly powerful lamp behind the lens. Absence of depth and distance sweeps the nudists scattered along the beach into a single orgiastic heap. In a show of modesty, you retreat beneath an awning, but staying in the shadows makes you a shadier character still. Though coming back out into the sun does nothing to whiten it. You just go pink. And not with embarrassment, either. Such is the moral dialectic of the beach. This is the East, where collectivism rules supreme and your western individualism is as thin as your return ticket to London. Not that you keep it on you. It's back in your room. Trousers (civilization) and body (nature) are no longer a single entity.

This flatness of landscape and muddling of perspective infects your view of past, present and future. How lucky the people of the desert, the people of the East are. The uniformity of the horizon means that distance is measured by time, and time by the changing tints of the horizon. Under a sun like that, the whole of existence merges into one long, drawn-out moment. This endlessness and immobility lie at the heart of the East with its enormous optimism so alien to the West's nostalgia for times past and the West's despair, provoked by constant departures, changes of geography, the metamorphosis of the near into the distant and vice versa — in short, by a constant sense of loss. The opposite is no less true. No one who feels exalted at the stirring times he has lived through and the distance he has covered can come to terms with the ahistoricity of lazing on the beach in the East, where all go naked before Time, like a nudist under the seaside sun, the medals of a heroic past locked in a strongbox and the keys tossed into the drifting sands.

After soaking up enough solar timelessness, I strolled back from the beach to the town square. Little restaurants and souvenir stands crowded round a concrete apron, ice cream and falafel vendors competed with the wailing pop of the music shops. The locals compensated for the absence of any perceptible temporal or spatial changes by artificially generating noise and movement. The restaurant owners' fussing around their empty tables, their scurrying from the bar to the doorway and back to attract custom, the way they almost dragged their customers in, formed perhaps the only point of similarity between the holidaymakers and the aboriginal population. Though even this was an illusion. In their anxiety to turn a profit, the restaurauteurs danced rather than scurried about their business. They performed a ritual ballet to lure the clientele, regardless of whether that clientele was in the vicinity or not. The concert went ahead with or without an audience. The tourists surged back and forth across the square, shying nervously away at every move to draw them into one or another establishment, sensing that this ritual native dance in the square had a hidden purpose — to clean them out, rip them off and, possibly, poison them into the bargain.

I was sitting one day in my favourite Arab cafe in a corner of the square, watching as if at the theatre these various antics going on and smiling condescendingly the while. It was an unprepossessing cafe. The tables were plastic and you had to ask specially if you wanted a paper serviette. But the place served a remarkable humus and you couldn't get a better coffee even in East Jerusalem. Its scruffiness — tables spilling out on the street — saved it from being inundated by tourists. I would sit over a coffee, waiting for the newsvendor to open up after the siesta. I'd drop by every day, on my way back from the beach, to pick up a copy of the *Herald Tribune*. In these surroundings the familiar English constructions began to sound incoherent, and gave a weird feeling of pleasure precisely because of that incoherence. Government crises and stock market crashes, political scandals and generation gaps, the right to choose your place of residence and the interconnection of time, civic conscience and the end of an affair, these were all a mirage — what else could they be in a country of eternally blue skies? They were all as illusory as, say, the diversity of faces in the crowd I sat watching in the square.

What multifariousness, you might think, what a kaleidoscope of faces, clothes and behaviour. But if you looked closely, you found astonishingly repetitive stereotypes: high cheekbones, thick lips, albino pallor, freckles, and that's it — that exhausted the whole gamut. The extravagant variety of their clothes could soon be classified by the stripe of the various countries and nationalities. And while it might be hard to assess a person's precise ethnic origin, the passport he held could be guessed at a glance. If not his current one, then his true one, the one he started out with. It crossed my mind I might even see a face horribly reminiscent of Mikhail Sergeyevich Grets. How on earth could they have got here — those powerful balding temples, etched as if by sweat? Or those uniquely Russian massive lobal bumps, which identify the denizen of Soviet public libraries? Or the broad, stooping, bull-like neck and shoulders that come from years of bending to talk in the library smoking-room, back pressed into a corner, speaking from behind the hand, trying to catch what the other person's saying through the smoke? Or those blatantly Soviet hornrims that have been slipping down his nose these past forty years, so that the index finger, in forever pushing them back up, has almost grown into his forehead in a gesture of eternal reflection, an everlasting posing of choices?

This type was more of an anthropological specimen, apparently, than a specific socio-historical one. The physiological similarity between Grets and an overweight tourist in a Panama hat was astonishing. I had not even completed this formulation in my mind before a completely different thought began to seep through the convolutions of my brain. This type, who had the hunted look of any starving new arrival, was steadily moving in my direction and with every step, with every shuffle of his rubber-soled shoes, a somewhat unexpected conclusion was being beaten into my temples as loudly and strongly as the pounding of my heart. The resemblance between the person approaching me and Mikhail Sergeyevich Grets was not simply surprising — the resemblance between them was perfect, so perfect that this person and Mikhail Sergeyevich

Grets were identical. In other words, the person bearing down on me was none other than Mikhail Sergeyevich Grets himself.

In Moscow people of his own generation had been giving him a wide berth as far back as Khrushchev's legendary Thaw in the late fifties. He plagued Moscow gatherings during the samizdat sixties, forever calling everyone out into the streets to immolate themselves as human torches. In the seventies, he was the one forever denouncing Jewish emigrants as rats leaving a sinking ship. He wanted them to remain, Russian frogs croaking the truth in a Soviet swamp. He didn't so much produce elaborate syllogisms and outmoded paradoxes, as reproduce them. He was a tape machine for recording public opinion, one with a mighty powerful amplifier. He bored his friends by announcing as amazing discoveries things they had learned long ago from bitter personal experience. Callow youths and neurotic adolescents were the only people he could depend on to accept his role as martyr and latter-day Socrates, parroting after him the tired old samizdat slogans about crystal palaces built on the blood of infants, revolutionary utopias ending up as totalitarian nightmares, passive silence being no less criminal than active informing. They simply could not remain silent. They were utterly fixated, huddled in conspiratorial knots, while their intolerance was a mirror image of the bolsheviks'. I found it all repulsive, which made me an outsider and forced me to adopt a course of resolute isolation.

I knew perfectly well, of course, what Grets meant when he launched into his muddled declarations about being guilty of complicity in the dreadful things that were going on. He belonged to the generation that discovered too late — a century after the event — Dostoevsky's once-banned novel, *The Possessed*. He was horrified to recognise one of the heroes in himself. Unlike his generation, tainted Dostoyevskian characters that they were, we felt rather like ashamed readers of *The Possessed*. At a certain point, the book became hateful to both groups and we slammed it shut. And so, we had both found ourselves in exile. Though instead of beginning a new life, he embarked on a repeat of the same old story, making new enemies here to keep up the old effort to prove his own rightness back there.

Deliberations on the totalitarian paradise built on the blood of infants and on silence being criminal in that atmosphere of complicity were swapped for a more historiographical version of the old question "Who is to blame?", in an emigre version this time. Had the Bolsheviks landed from Mars in dialectical tripods? Or was Soviet power merely the dialectical consummation of the slavish trinity of "Orthodoxy. Autocracy. People"? He felt his departure into emigration was a public protest against Soviet serfdom and regarded all the regime's steps down the road of liberal reform as a threat to his own heroic past, present and future in emigration. If everything was so liberal over there now, what had been the point in emigrating?

I used to bump into him every so often on the highways and byways of the Russian community abroad: at premieres, conferences, in private homes. Besides, his wife came from a wealthy Greek family which patronised the arts and literature, especially Russian literature. And where money and grants are to be had, people gather. Whenever we met, he would take my arm and pin me in a corner as if we were back in the old library smoking-room, then start interpreting the latest trends in Europe, which proved, in his dazzling expose, to be nothing less than the same old bolshevism dressed up in new clothes. I had a vision of him waving as he recognised me, putting his arm round my shoulder, sitting down at my table, leaning towards me earnestly and launching into his latest conspiracy theory, utterly fascinating to him, deadly boring to the rest of us.

The very thought struck me in the temple, pierced the trifacial nerve and seared my eyeball like a blinding ray of mediterranean sun reflected from Grets's hornrims. My first reaction was to run and to hell with the bill. But at that moment the crowd parted, as if on purpose, and I sank back into my chair. A corridor cleared between us, four duellists' paces long. A sudden movement and his eye would trap me in the lens of his glasses. And with me this beautiful, sun-drenched world, naive as a primitivist painting. No more the suntanned female knee at the next table, blurring into the pile of oranges on the bar, behind which a swan floated across a tacky reproduction lake, tangling with a white sail out at sea in the corner of the back window. No longer the illusion of leading the simple life far from our apocalyptic tumbles and eschatological leaps, I was only kidding myself. No matter what the sun did here,

Mea Culpa

collapsing human destinies and distances, in this setting a Russian intellectual like Grets (be he Tatar, Jew or Russian) would be still more clinging, unavoidable, insistent, like the shadow of a cloud sliding over the sun in England. I was pinned by the apex of that shadow to my place at the table, hoping the cloud would slip away over the horizon. If I sat without moving a muscle, the sharp eye of this snake that had come slithering out of the bushes of Russian spirituality might pass over me, this Westernising rationalist rodent.

But no, the ideologically sharpened pupils of this Russian bookworm and Pharisee fixed directly on me, I slumped. Like a bed-ridden invalid, I half raised myself, supporting myself on the table with one hand and giving him a feeble, if ostensibly friendly, wave with the other.

No reaction. His beady, unwinking eyes continued to eat me up. Not a muscle moved in his face. He was looking straight at me without, however, seeming to see me. "Maybe he's gone blind these last few years?" In a panic I was trying to remember whether he'd always worn glasses and what kind they were, though at the same time I was well aware that if he was blind he wouldn't need glasses. His hypnotic glare petrified me, literally. Sweat poured down my face. Reproach was written in his silence, in the clenched line of his mouth and his unwavering stare. It was the wordless reproach of a prophet, the unspoken reproach and disparaging mien of an oracle foretelling world catastrophe, an imminent ice age called totalitarianism, from which ice age I had so heedlessly fled to this tropic clime of flat ideas and uncomplicated journeys. I looked round for what I thought might be the last time, taking in this place which had no real meaning and was, therefore, paradise to me. From the moment Grets appeared on the scene, this uninhabited islet was threatened with transformation into a Soviet communal flat dense with all the usual ideological squabbles.

My eyes lit on a menu hung up behind me in the doorway; I suddenly realised what it was he had been staring at so fixedly. Like in many such small eating places, the menu had been scribbled up on a blackboard. Middle-aged Grets had the look of a schoolboy nailed by the teacher's question to the board on which a classmate has scrawled some obscure formula. He obviously didn't know the answer. The menu was half in Arabic, half in illiterate and spidery

English, the prices and dishes all out of sync. I watched Grets move his lips, mouthing repetitively to penetrate the meaning of the hieroglyphs on the board. The greater his concentration on the mysteries of the menu, the more forcibly it was borne in on me how terribly selective human vision is. It fails to absorb even objects that fall within its field; it obeys the laws of subjective idealism. Man sees only what he wants to see. Mikhail Sergeyevich Grets was horribly hungry. And thus he failed to see even his ideological opponents, myself included. He saw menus; the various menus of the various eating places. For all my variety, I was not on a menu and so he did not see me. He was looking over my head.

Very cautiously, trying not draw his attention, I slid off my chair and sidled crouching away from the tables. I never for a second took my eyes off Grets. There was only one avenue of retreat, up some stairs to a first floor arcade of shops and restaurants. From this moment my mind was beset by ideological dilemmas. I was thinking like a partisan behind enemy lines, like a strategist trying to thwart an enemy blockade. This gallery served one useful purpose at least. Up there I had an excellent vantage point on Grets' every move. I pictured myself with a spyglass, following his movements from eating place to eating place, from window to window. Eventually he stopped at a postcard rack outside a cafe where the *Herald Tribune* was usually on sale to an English-speaking "intellectual" clientele.

He stood there, turning the stand, examining the postcards, and I got mad at myself for watching him. Why was I interrupting my postprandial cup of coffee and perusal of the IHT for that old fart? Surely I could dig down to that vein of inner hardness that would deliver me from this hypocrisy and let me give him the standard brush off, "lovely to see you, but some other time perhaps"? Why did I have to hide from him, like some truant schoolboy hiding from his parents? At that moment he looked up and scanned the upper storey, focussing for a second, so I thought, on the staircase where I was standing. My knees went wobbly again and my heart sank, like a schoolboy's heart before exams. Had he spotted me? Surely not! With his short sight! But why short sight? Why not long? How did I know? Was I his optician or something?! By now even madder at myself, and at these existential dilemmas,

Mea Culpa

I drew myself demonstratively up to full height, held my head high and clattered loudly down the stairs, only to grab nervously at the handrail and skulk behind the passers-by when I saw Grets approach the tables of "my" establishment.

Once again he was dumbly examining the unyielding menu. Then, glancing around furtively in a very Russian manner (meanwhile in my anxiety I had dived behind yet another passing back), he sat down at a table and began mopping the sweat from his brow. Did this mean he knew a good place when he saw one? What was it about this place, a place that hardly looked different to a dozen others, that made him choose it? The appearance of the place and the dishes displayed in the glass cabinet were more likely to put off a person like Mikhail Sergeyevich Grets, who regardless of climate, craved only his Russian borsch and meat balls with kissel for desert. The only possible explanation was that he'd seen me sitting there. And since I was a well known connoisseur of such matters, the fact that I had chosen this establishment meant it must be the place to eat. That was Grets's remorseless logic. Unless, of course, he was guided by some other logic, the logic, for example, of a chance decision.

However it was, he didn't stay there long. Clutching a copy of the IHT in my sweaty paw, rather like the proverbial dog with a paper between its teeth, I wove through the crowd to the edge of the magic concrete square that marked the restaurant's territory. Suddenly, a few feet away a face began to swim, like a hallucination, through the kaleidoscope of repetitive human types, the face of Russian conscience, the face that I felt was the obverse of mine, imprinted with Russian lack of scruple. Once again I felt he must have seen me, but I didn't let on. "You ought to say hello," chorussed my inner voice, my outer sense of dignity, my conscience that had emigrated from the Soviet Union with me, and my civic voice that had been stripped of citizenship. Our faces came bobbing closer, unacknowledged by each other thus far, unrecognised amidst the other foreign faces. In the press of bodies retreat was impossible.

My lips were opening, my larynx taut, my shoulder muscles, tensed to reach my hand out to him, but when we were once again separated by those four duellists' paces in the crowd that had momentarily parted, I chickened out. I couldn't figure out what it was he was looking at. It seemed he was looking straight at me, yet past me, as if he were looking straight through me. I was struck once again by the impression that he was blind. We were advancing on each other in the midday sun as if we were in pitch darkness or playing a game of blind man's buff.

At the last moment I couldn't bear it. My legs diverted me down a narrow gap between buildings, a blind sidestreet squeezed between the flanks of restaurants and encumbered with garbage bins. My furtive dash ended with me slipping on a piece of rotten cabbage, or something of that sort. Trying to keep my balance, I put my hand out to the slimy walls, smeared myself with some filth oozing down from overhead and landed in a heap of garbage from an overturned bin. Still clutching the IHT, my hand skidded over stinking asphalt spread with a liberal coating of either sheep or cat shit. I swore, slung the paper in a bin and went straight back to my hotel on the seafront, the Hotel Neptune.

I couldn't say precisely how many hours I lay in the bath in an attempt to lather away the memory of the embarrassing meeting and subsequent tumble in the mire. From time to time I took a swig of smokey Jameson's bought at the Heathrow duty free. My skin prickled with moisture. Either it was sweat provoked by the memory of my blunder or just drops of condensation running down from my forehead into my eyes. My eyes, in turn, were red either from whiskey and steam or from tears of remorse. I cursed my selfishness and misanthropy. How the hell had we landed up in the same Middle Eastern hole, where you were bound to run into each other at some point? Anywhere else — New York, Paris or Jerusalem — I would immediately have given myself the job of guide, showed him where to go, what to see and where to stay. I felt embarrassed at the thought that here he was, an old man, at a loose end somewhere he didn't know with an ageing wife, who could barely stay on her feet, and trying to decipher the menus in the restaurants. I had thrown them to the wolves. He had noticed me. Of course he had. Three encounters were quite enough. He'd seen I didn't want to see him, and so had pretended not to notice me. And no amount of rationalising along the lines of being blind to familiar faces in exotic locations or of vision being selective depending on one's intentions and desires would alter the fact.

Mea Culpa

But for all my sense of guilt at what had happened, I knew I couldn't have acted otherwise. I hadn't dragged myself all the way from England to spend a week nattering endlessly in the emigre equivalent of a communal kitchen with the most boring neighbour possible. Suddenly this pleasant, quite comfortable, yet unpretentious resort struck me as being symbolic of the narrowness and hopelessness of emigre life. Not just emigre life. Why had I been obliged back in Moscow to reckon with, talk to, meet and part company with, and then meet again this stupid, droning demagogue? Why had the existence of a common political enemy compelled us Russians to pretend we were as good as related to one another?

I suddenly felt I hated Mikhail Sergeyevich Grets. Not because he belonged to a different generation or because I had no time for his ideas, but simply I couldn't stand, never had been able to stand the way he spat when he talked, his filthy nails, his sweaty bald patch and pot belly. Under different historical circumstances, in a different civilization, one glance would have told us we were mutually incompatible, and we would never meet again. In the Russian emigration, however, we spent nearly twenty years concealing straightforward personal dislike under a cloak of fundamental differences in ideological stance and of the power of the generation gap.

The sharp aroma of whiskey in the bathroom swept me back on swirling clouds of steam to London. It would be misty back there now, in the evenings especially, when every tree in the parks grew a halo and seemed even more independent and detached from the outside world on its patch of lawn. And a light in a distant window gleaming through the mist or the thread of a neon light altered perspective by its visible proximity, so heightening the feeling of space and at the same time of the hypnotic accessibility of objects on the horizon. I reached for the bottle. It was empty.

This was the point where I ought to have stopped, but I was drawn outside, back to England, as if the very waters of the Channel lapped outside my room in the Hotel Neptune. Outside, though, the little town was bathed in the warm Southern night. I moved unconsciously from bar to bar towards the centre, towards that same small square where I had encountered Grets. I was drawn there the way a murderer is driven back to the scene of his crime by the urge

to correct a poorly constructed story. In the light of the lamps, overhead spotlights and fat funereal candles on restaurant tables, the two-storey complex of cafes and discos reminded me of the stalls, boxes and balconies of a gigantic theatre. The light on the faces made them look like theatrical masks. In an outburst of drunken sincerity and emotion, I wanted to tear the mask off this world that pretended to be so two-dimensional and simple in the daylight, but with the onset of darkness was transformed into a cunning shadow play. I, who had in the hardness of my heart virtually condemned my old acquaintance to death out of revulsion, now tried to make amends for my heartlessness by hurling imprecations at the mechanistic artificiality of our civilisation, at our alienation in general.
I wanted to tear away the iron mask of civilisation and snuggle up to the warm, yielding body of nature.

Instead, I attached myself to the warm, yielding body of an American tourist. I met her in one of the bars after I had launched brazenly into a Russian rendition of an aria from either *The Flederwidow* or *The Merrymaus*, "to wear a mask is ever my fate." I heard an American drawl: "Jesus, this place is just crawling with Russians!" I was about to dispute the point, but had to admit that she was absolutely right — the place was crawling with them, and with Americans, too, for that matter. I told her she was right, and because the place was crawling with both Russians and Americans there was nothing for it but to drink Bloody Maries, made from Russian vodka and American tomato juice. She said that was her name. Mary. That was the last thing either of us said. We soon found the Bloody bit of the Mary to be superfluous and started drinking vodka neat without any bloody tomatoes or other such Americanisms. We rounded off this festival of international friendship in my hotel room, where we spent the night mixing juices of quite another sort with a special frenzy. This was communication beyond considerations of ideology and generation. Early next morning she had vanished without trace.

Actually, I'm wrong. Nothing disappears without trace, be it a stain on somebody else's sheets or on your own reputation. The sun, as I've said before, elides the distance between objects. Fate, like a cunning storyteller, brings together in the one denouement utterly disparate events and circumstances. And this has to be paid for by a loss of opportunities, the way sunburn is the price of a tan.

Mea Culpa

After our fatal encounter on the African coast, I realised I could never accept an invitation from the Grets household to go and write at their villa in Greece. The Grets's had inherited it from Mrs. Grets's family, the Popandopoulos's. Sofya Konstantinovna was, as I think I've mentioned, the daughter of a Greek millionaire from Theodosia. He spent half his life in Russia, was a connoisseur of Russian literature and art, dabbled as a collector and knew Diaghilev and Benois. He had left a modest bequest — enough to set up a bursary — to help needy Russian emigre intellectuals. It was sufficient to pay travel expenses and full board (from one to three months) in a luxurious house with marble columns (modelled on the Parthenon, of course) on Crete. Cretin that I was, after being awarded that year's bursary, I felt I had to turn it down. I couldn't bring myself to look at Grets's face oozing faith in humankind every morning at the breakfast table. Nor could I bear the memory of him looking lost as he stared at me with unseeing eyes under the African sun. My amorality did not allow for inconsistency when it came to questions of moral principle.

This was why when an envelope was delivered to my London address containing an official invitation and requesting a formal reply, there was nothing for it but to compose a lengthy refusal, in which after thanking the Popandopoulos Fund effusively for the honour it had bestowed upon me I explained that on this occasion I simply could not avail myself of Mr. and Mrs. Grets's hospitality.
I had signed a contract with French radio that required my presence in Paris. (I had, indeed, signed a contract for a radio adaptation of my novel, but my presence in Paris was the last thing that was wanted.) At the end of the letter I expressed the hope that I would be able to take up their generous offer at a future date and that we would meet in the not-too-distant future. Yours very etc, etc... A few days later I received a reply by express mail from Mikhail Sergeyevich Grets. The text follows without further commentary.

"*Mea culpa*, Zinovy, *mea maxima culpa*. I anticipated you would refuse, hoped that this cup of shame might pass from me. But no! I am an old fool and I have to confess that I have received my just deserts, *mea culpa*!

My dear boy, the look of silent reproach in your eyes as you sat at your table, and when you were in the crowd and up on that gallery, will stay with me the rest of my life. Like a fool, I pretended not to see you, the very person with whom I have always enjoyed exchanging a few words, swapping views (sic!) on current events. And I besmirched myself not once, but thrice; thrice pretended that I did not know you, denied you thrice on that damned pocket handkerchief of a square.

How many times, dear boy, have I taken up my pen to apologise for my monstrously childish behaviour, hoped, old fool that I am, to bump into you at one of our emigre talk-ins. I would explain myself at some conference or other. I thought I could smooth this silly episode over. All the time I was hoping against hope that I'd got away with it, that you hadn't seen me, and that if you had, you hadn't recognised me. One can do that, you know, see without noticing.

But when we received your courteous refusal to take up the Popandopoulos bursary, I knew the game was up. It was you, dear boy, gentleman that you are, who made me realise how deeply wounding my loutish behaviour was. But it's so unnecessary. I know I'm a boor and utterly stiff-necked and that my behaviour was unforgivable, but I do assure you, dear boy, that Sofya and I love you dearly and hold you in the highest regard.

I apologise abjectly and unreservedly. *Mea culpa*! My apologies — *ad absurdum*. It was my mendacity, depravity and the insatiability of my lusts. Would you believe me if I told you I was being unfaithful to my devoted companion, my fellow warrior on the ideological front and medical orderly in the trenches of the emigration, in short — to my wife, Sofya Konstantinovna? I love Sofie with all my soul, mind and civic conscience. But my heart, dear boy, began a desperate race with my greying hair. And the devil beneath my ribs drove me to that African resort where our paths so unfortunately chanced to cross.

The American girl you undoubtedly noticed at my side during our fateful encounter was the cause of my unforgivable snub. I funked it. With your excellent English, you were bound to engage her in small talk and, quite unconsciously, let slip that I was married and that would mark the ignominious end to my brief affair. I met her at a

Mea Culpa

human rights conference. She fell in love with me for what I'd been through, and I embroidered the more lurid details. Humiliating as it is, dear boy, to have to go into all this, but the fact of the matter is I was scared stiff. If you had started talking, that would have been the end of my legend. And so, dear boy, I started that silly schoolboy game. As soon as I saw you at the table I began putting a telescope to a blind eye and behaving as though you weren't there. Shameful, utterly, utterly shameful!

Except that it was a complete mental aberration, I cannot explain this sexual escapade at my age. Should you still harbour any grudging sentiments towards me, my dear, perhaps I can put them to rest with the information that nothing in this life goes unpunished. After the incident with you, the young American lady and I quarrelled violently. She insisted she only wanted a cafe frappe, while at my age I need three square meals a day. She slammed the door on me and vanished without even saying good-bye. Probably she was picked up by some young yahoo. Not even probably. I know for certain she was, because I managed to find the hotel where she spent that night (the Neptune, down on the seafront, you may remember it) and the porter told me she didn't spend the night alone. Slut! Still, *mea culpa*.

  Ever yours,
  Mikh. Serg. Grets.

Translated by Frank Williams

First published in Russian in Syntax №18, Paris, 1988

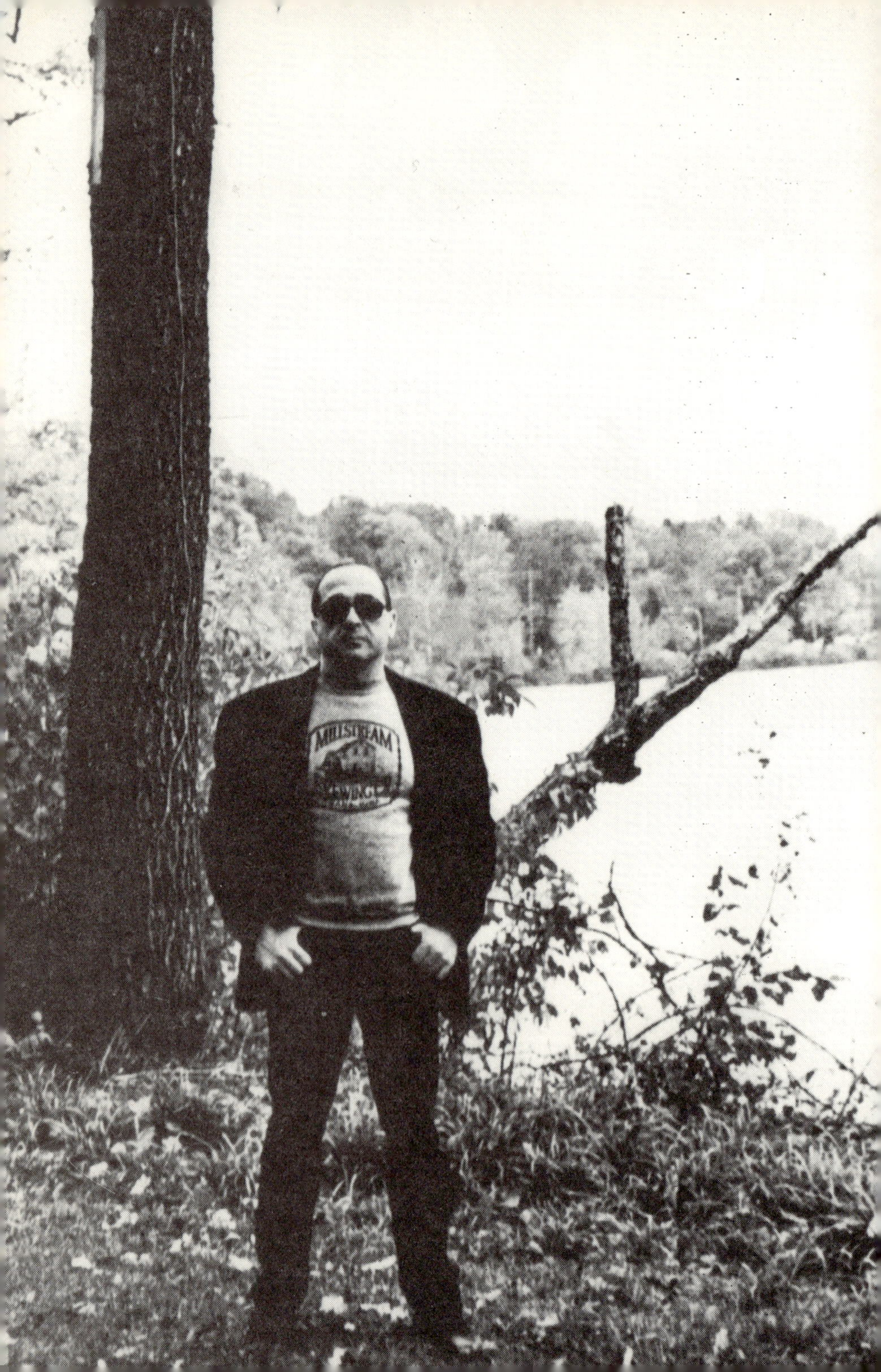
MILLSTREAM

Yuri
MILOSLAVSKY

THE DEATH OF MANON
ON EXILE

The Death of Manon

When they knifed Shamil on the Tyurenka the cops didn't come anywhere near the place for a week, instead (in threes) people from Gorky Park, and Pushkin and Lermontov streets, with muslin mourning bands round their collars came searching for the murderer.

They threw a bottle of vodka on Shamil's coffin, and a pack of Dzhebel cigarettes.

Shamil didn't smoke Dzhebels, I'm sure. One Sunday he was going past the Dynamo restaurant with his girlfriend Zorka, Ukhan and I were standing by the fence. Shamil sent Ukhan to the Dynamo to get a pack of Feminas from the doorman (extralong Bulgarian cigarettes with a gold tip; red box with some gal smoking). Shamil gave a cigarette to Zorka, let up one himself, and handed me one. I tossed my stub behind me, though it was only half smoked, and took a Femina.

Ukhan asked, "What about me?"
"Tough shit!" Zorka smirked.

They knifed Shamil after the dance at Artem Park. Zorka yelled at the top of her lungs, not understanding what she was saying:

Shamily, Vladily
Who did you in?
Yell me, oh, tell me
Why didn't you kill him.

Vladily Shamily
What was your fate?
Tell me, oh, tell me
But now it's too late.

The Death of Manon

Well, no one thought to ask me.

Everybody knew Shamil was murdered, but why Manon had hanged himself — that was something no one knew.

Manon was thirty-five.

There was a woodburning stove in my late aunt's apartment — they never put in central heating, or hooked up the gas line. The brown rings heated up slowly, cemented in from underneath. Each ring had three filaments. First the rings would darken, without changing color. Then the middle rings would swell scarlet, glow bright grey. But only when the heat was highest would the outer rings turn a deep cherry. And that was it for them — and that was the color Manon was: his neck, his ears his cheeks, his hair — all the same color, no distinctions.

Manon didn't do anything — he didn't want to. He'd stand by the gates of his house number fifty four in that bright blue coat: he snatched it off an actor from the Kiev Drama Theater, so he still looked like some dude out of the Sputnik era, a village thug with patch pockets.

Now you've got to have a black coat, fitted, tailored, with lapels like on a suit jacket, with three buttons and slanted slash pockets, no vents.

In winter you can wear a "Moscow" jacket with a high collar.

Spring-summer: a pinkish or lightgray raincoat with belt and epaulets — from the Friendship factory in China. But Manon would stand there in that Kiev actor's coat, and his loafers didn't even have pointed toes.

"My toes've got frost bite," Manon was saying. "They hurt, they hurt, they wanna flirt. You've got this buddy. And your buddy decides to treat himself to labels like 'Maid in Thighland,' and our Leo will help his buddy. Right Leo?"

And Manon stretched out his hand and grabbed hold of the passing Leo Kantorovich — the one who can get you Italian loafers with hollow aluminum heels. Manon sort of embraced Leo pressing his palms on Leo shoulders — and Leo's eyes filled with tears, he smiled and tried to embrace Manon too — you do it to me, I do it to you — but he couldn't get his chamois-gloved hand up to Manon's shoulder. And Manon pressed down on him and sang:

Yuri Miloslavsky

> *Ya gotta have money to get a good lay*
> *I've thought alot about that one*
> *I figured that stealing was the easiest way*
> *To dress like someone who had some.*

That happened once in a blue moon.

Manon would stand by number 54 and not say a thing; no one knew how things were going for him — they didn't ask. You have to be careful about that — talking with Manon. It was hard for him to approach you, your language, your life; he'd dump you in a minute. And he'd start fooling around in that special way of his: he'd lock his fingers together and smash his fists into the shoulder of the guy he was talking with. His interlocutor would run off, Manon would guffaw, but keep on hanging around. He wouldn't say another thing. Once in a while, guys his age would come over from other sides of town — one guy from each neighborhood. They'd stand in a quiet bunch, smoke, and spit. And when they'd left, there'd be a puddle of spit and phlegm with Russian cig stubs in it — no one smoked western cigarettes in this group.

I didn't know what Manon was up to. Skull from the Park would start in, "That Manon is something!... Professor!" Any time you met him he'd be bragging. "I went boozing with him yesterday." Once Skull came over to our neighborhood to play chess with redhead Mishka Abrasimov. Skull saw Manon from the other side of the street, all the way from number 54, and yelled, "Hey Manon! How ya doin', you fucker!" This was meant with due respect, even fear — but Manon turned and faced us, looked us up and down and said, "Come here, jerk."

Skull started to cross the street and go over to Manon. He walked over and came up to him. Manon said something to him (we couldn't hear it), and then Skull laid down at his feet, face up, and opened his mouth. Manon unbuttoned his fly and pissed in his mouth. Then he stepped on Skull's stomach and jumped on him. Skull went like this, "ugh — ugh!" We heard that, and we were about to scatter while Skull was sobbing, "How can you treat your friend like that? Your best friend!" Well, with that word "friend" Manon kicked Skull in the teeth. Skull didn't get up from the pavement, his hands gripped his face, and he rolled over on his sto-

The Death of Manon

mach. Manon wanted to do something even worse to Skull, but some neighbors were leaning out of the windows and shouting, "Call Nadka! Call Nadka!" Nadka was Manon's invalid mother. So they led her over to the neighbor's window — Manon's was blocked up with plywood — and she yelled, "Son, son, come home, son. I'm awful scared, I can hear your daddy." She wasn't fooling, and she wasn't trying to help Skull, she hadn't the vaguest about him — she'd been hearing her husband's voice — Manon's dad — who they say was rubbed out by cops right by the building. She and her son Manon were drunk at the time and didn't even come out... It was only a year later when Nadka started hearing a voice she hadn't heard then. "You cunt, I'm dead!" That Nadka decided she wanted to save her husband. But Manon wouldn't let her jump out the window — he kept her in the room with her leg tied to a table. So the neighbors had untied her and taken her over to their place, and she was yelling to Manon that the two of them should try to save his old man. Manon was scared that the neighbors wouldn't keep her away from the window. He screamed, "Don't move Nadka!" and raced up to the apartment. Skull got up, twisted up his big gut, pressed his forehead against the wall of number 54 and puked out Manon's piss.

But that happened once in a blue moon, because Manon hardly ever reacted to outsiders. All his meetings were taking place inside himself, he'd talk with them himself — I myself saw it one time I passed close to him. He was having a chat with someone inside himself, laughing and arguing, barely audible. And he'd sort of shake his fists and wave his hands, convincing the other guy.

Manon had a golden ring on his right index finger. He'd started wearing it a long time ago, before his fingers swelled up — so you could tell what they must have looked like ten years ago. But now he couldn't soap that ring off, and I think he forgot that he had the thing on him. Otherwise he'd have sold it for three bottles of booze. He wouldn't have bothered to haggle with Leo Kantorovich, who was a gold scarp.

People think that a drunk will kill for booze. It's not true. I've seen corpses and murderers — and at the very instant those titles are conferred — when they're still together. I heard the sound of the knife that Revena jabbed into a patrolman — the knife stuck motionless between his ribs. The blade was only about eight inches, but the sound of the stab split into three as it slashed the clothes, pierced the skin, and slid through the rib cage.

The patrolmen drank more at headquarters than Revena did, they had plenty of booze as gifts and confiscations. Every nightshift, every patrolman would rake in around a liter and a half, but for Revena, every drop cost money. He worked the morning shift at the "Miner's Light" factory, but in the evening he'd mug a few, spending almost a quarter of his pay. He didn't kill the patrolman because he was drunk, but over his sister — his sister Katya had TB, chronic, had done well in school.

I'm looking out the window now, and I can see Katya. She's wearing a green cardigan. But then I see all the dead like that — walking the streets at night, hurrying to my place.

The patrolmen caught Katya when she was coming home from a craft club where they taught her how to make green cardigans. They felt her up and decided she was okay, took her back to the station and gang-banged her until blood ran from her mouth. Then they threw her out of the station in a snowdrift, green cardigan and all.

I'd tell one more story, only they're all the same anyway: the patrolman's last breath reeked of alcohol, the last puke out of his mouth was sardines, vodka, and blood. And then Revena and I got up some money for a shot-bottle.

Every killing I've seen was unrelated to booze. Well, sure, both of them were smashed — the killer and the killee. They could have changed places — the killer drank to the point where he didn't know he'd killed someone; the person he killed, to the point where he didn't know it was his last drink.

Manon drank so much he couldn't kill anyone. Someone who drinks that much becomes sort of friendly and confused; he'll ask people for strange little odd sums — nine kopecks, twenty-seven kopecks. Sums we find strange — but the alky keeps his own accounts, financial and spiritual — and those accounts are sad and fussy. The twenty-seven kopecks get clubbed together with the two two-kopeck pieces he got from the phone. That's thirty-one. So you just need nineteen, and that's a glass of wine at "Pop and Liquor." In a few hours you'll get the price of another glass together.

The Death of Manon

Perhaps I'm mistaken, but what all the killers I know have isn't the power of anger, but an ability to carry things through, they could make a decision. But a drunk is no decision-maker.

So, Manon stopped making decisions and didn't kill anyone — because he was drinking.

At first he drank at home with his Mother Nadka. But Nadka stopped drinking pretty soon — she just wasn't up to it. Her man was down at her window screaming, dying, and she couldn't even help him. Her son didn't hear the screams and wouldn't believe her. He wouldn't take the plywood off the windows, or let her out on the street. Nadka got tired: she'd sit under the table, naked, tied to the cross bar; and that's where she ate and slept. She'd almost decided not to sleep at all; she was ashamed to have been so loaded when her old man died, but she couldn't help it, and she trained herself to catch his death cries in her sleep. So now he couldn't complain: "Your husband's being killed, and you've fallen asleep." After all, he couldn't know that she was asleep, since Nadka could hear his voice.

Manon would drag his mother out from under the table, sit her on a stool, and set a green glass in front of her — though it was no fun for him to drink to the constant refrain, "O son, my dear, he's out there screaming, let me loose, I'll just take a look. I won't do anything, I'll be good, I'm just a damned whore..."

Manon paid as little attention as he could; he'd sing:

> *Pot bellied, snot picking*
> *Fucked-up — a real gas.*
> *Sticks his nose up your behind*
> *And tongues your pimply ass*

And his mother would keep on bugging him while he got more and more noisy.

He'd drink at home until the new neighbors from downstairs would come to curse him out about the noise. Manon was sitting at the table alone, Nadka in her place, accidentally untied. "Son, dearest, he's really out there screaming..."

The new neighbors were wearing T-shirts and crew cuts, they

didn't know who Manon was. They just threw the door opened and bellowed, "You shit, what the fuck are you making all this noise for?! We've gotta get to work tomorrow, morning shift, you shitty sponger."

"Nadka, sic!!" said Manon.

And Nadka jumped out from under the table at the head neighbor, ripped off his T-shirt and hung on his shoulders, sinking her toothless gums into his Adam's apple.

The neighbors retreated to their own floor, to sleep until the morning shift, but Manon went off to drink in the courtyard with guys he hardly knew who wandered by. He didn't want any interference, or anyone to stop him from singing about the fat snotpicker. The year before, he would have eaten the neighbors alive, kicked the shit out of them, but now he drank and couldn't kill over booze.

Once we were sitting in the Cafe Youth — Vic from the Machine-Tool Technical College and our chicks. At Cafe Youth they served coffee with liquor — the coffee in white pots and the liquor in a little carafe, just like in Riga, Tallinn, and Vilnius. We treated our chicks to this Baltic drink — trying to take advantage of them — and smoked one cig after another.

And then Manon appeared on the yellow plastic circular staircase — the cafe was in the basement — in his heavy coat, a white silk scarf, a cloth cap down to his eyes and no gloves. He came halfway down the steps, stopped and looked around. Other people look around a few seconds, but he took at least a minute, and no one in the cafe recognized him except me and Vic. Just a few people who were sitting at triangular tables facing the entrance vaguely noticed his arrival, assumed it was the bouncer's mistake. Manon just looked on and was about to leave, but I pressed through to him and tugged at his sleeve. Manon started, then turned his eyes towards me and gave me a drawn out smile. "What's up, kid?" I dragged him over to our three cornered table, though it didn't really seat four. He came, didn't ask any questions; but he bumped into some athlete's table — a boxer apparently.

An exchange of looks.

Tall, tow-haired, a gaze of polished stone, the silver badge of a "Soviet Master Athlete," and Manon's whistling past, free of everything that kept the young athlete living comfortably in the world and forced him to wear the badge on his ribbed sweater. Athlete and chair moved closer to the table to let the man through while Vic brought a fifth chair to our foursome.

We ordered another round, and gave all the liquor to Manon: including his fifth shot, it was one hundred and twenty-five grams. Manon poured all the shots together — in the carafe, there were no glasses — and sort of chewed it rather than drank it, tried to strain the thick reddish liquid through his teeth, to hold it as long as possible, to separate the sugar, the dye — and whatever else there is in liquor — from the alcohol — drunk and fine. He finished chewing around on it and then started to speak. He spoke to the girls, to their feet in light colored stockings, their hair-dos piled up on the backs of their childish heads, their stiff "Hungarotex" dresses. Like any other guy, Manon wanted the girls to see his power and to give in to him because of that power. Manon started telling how he gave himself an ulcer when he was in prison: "You take a long thread with a knot at the end, you tie it to your last lower tooth, and swallow it..."

He was looking at Vic and me — not at the girls, but it was really meant for them, so that they dropped their lower incisors in delight, raised their ink-blue lashes at this plight of his, which not one of those hoots from the hospital could tell from a real one, and froze from the measured locutions of the terrible tale.

Manon's sleeves knocked over a couple of shot glasses without his hands noticing; Manon was almost lying on the table, and now he was looking somewhere over toward the far wall, contemplating his own fate.

But he came out of it in about ten minutes. When he'd knocked back everything he hadn't already put away, Manon got up from the triangular table and grabbed Vic by the tie. "You drunken faggot, you shitty bastard!" He slapped me across the face and again fell to contemplating the girls — but he didn't do anything. They just got a blast of air from the flaps of his blue Kiev overcoat, that's how fast he walked out and left.

A day later it started to blizzard, with strong ground-winds and bluish ice on the drifts, where some water left from before

Yuri Miloslavsky

crashed down from the gutters. Parents sent me out for bread: a 20-kopeck loaf of white, three rolls, and a round of black — we eat a lot of bread.

Mishka Abrasimov was standing by the store — his neck uncovered, no hat, in a faded pink raincoat — he didn't have a "Moscow" jacket with a high collar, which would have been more seasonal. Mishka Abrasimov was poor, and bitter about his poverty. The ground wind got up his pants, and the upper wind got down his open collar.

Later they gave him eight years for armed robbery with a scalpel, and broke both his legs before the trial. But in this particular blizzard his legs were intact and numb with cold.

"Gimme a smoke!" I cupped my hands and gave him a light as well as a smoke.

"Manon hanged himself," said Mishka.

"What?!"

"Don't what me, you piece of shit. They took him away yesterday. Nadka called the neighbors. She bawled all night until they came — they thought she was just hysterical. He tied her hand and foot, blindfolded her with a kerchief, and hanged himself in their room. There was a hook there for the curtain rod. Drunk as a skunk. But when was he ever sober..."

"And her?"

"Nadka?" How should I know? Maybe they took her away too."

Katya, Revena's sister is walking along the unlit street. And so are my grandpa and grandma, leaning on each other: they don't fight anymore, but then, they don't speak either. And Manon is walking next to them, looking for his mother Nadka.

Translated by David Lapeza
Translation edited by Tomislav Longinovic

From: *For the Noise of the Horseman and Bowman*, short stories, 1978-1982
Ann Arbor: Ardis, 1984

On Exile
Aquae et ignis interdictio

In my language the word "exile" has such a carousing air about it, with blizzards and fate in its modulations: "*Proshchaite*, farewell, for we should meet no more..." And so, your musquash-capped head hitting the ground in a last-time bow, you pull fastidiously away from the hand of the escorting undercover agent, ascend the gangway with a measured step, linger on the platform for a moment, taking in a final glance, and the thing drones sorrowfully, casts off the rope, gives a shudder, rises up, and rushes impetuously — fading away into the irrevocable distance. And all this is so marvellous that there's nothing I can do but, turning my back towards the visages of suffering, excrete — wide-open sheaf, full pressure — a substance yellow and acrid, as does the hopoe bird defending its nest.

"EXILE, in a broad sense, the condition of a person unable to live in his native land due to government decree, personal circumstances or choice," reads the once authoritative Great Encyclopaedia, published in St. Petersburg at the end of the century before the present one. "The Romans," the Encyclopaedia continues, "did not consider exile a punishment... A person found guilty of a crime might remove to another land; to prevent the return of such an exile a banishment verdict, *interdictio aquae et ignis*, was issued, i.e. he was to be cut off from the communal fire and water. If the exile nevertheless chose to return, it was permitted to kill him."

For citizens of a great number of countries in modern times, under the influence of an avalanche of progress, exile has become a supreme reward, a kind of lucrative life-long trip abroad that is to be sought at all cost. Tens of millions of people, it is claimed, dream of becoming exiles; in any case, tens of thousands of politicians, newsmen and government officials are nicely earning a living helping — or hindering — the realization of that dream. The exiles demand unhindered, speedy and comfortable exile, special conditions for their integration in their new lands; exiles who made exile a profession are appointed to high-paying jobs as government experts on the problems of exile, are heading the exile associations, contribute to the exile media, receive decorations and pensions; exile-losers (there are not all that many of them, though) demand immediate government aid, threatening to return to the country that exiled them, thus exerting a bad propaganda influence on would-be exiles.

Like a Laocoon bound by a bull tapeworm, the exile is unable, even for a moment, to rid himself of his curious incongruities; he exposes the abominations of the exiling regime, gabbling weightily about the truly important and responsible work which he was entrusted prior to exile by the same hideous regime. Without ever having seen, even from afar, anything like free elections, even those of a village head or a person responsible for the cleanness of the hallway in a block of flats, the exile lambasts the society that gave him refuge for its inability to stand up for the defense of democratic freedoms. A partisan of a strong rule, he prefers, however, to vegetate on lands belonging to governments of liberal persuasion, despite local disorderliness, flourishing homosexuality and drug abuse, inspired, undoubtedly, by a network of totalitarian/communist agents.

And finally, the exile is extremely noisy.

On a sunny day in the street of a small town somewhere in Texas two cowboy buddies sit down by the hitching post. Suddenly, crushing chickens and raising clouds of dust and straw, a sinister rider gallops past in a roar of gunshots and thundering hoofbeats.

"Just wonder, Harry, who that might be," one of the cowboys drawls lazily.

"It's Never-Catch-'Im Joe."

"Oh!" exclaims the Simple Simon and then enquires respectfully: "But who's after him?"

"Well, no one..." comes the calm reply.

I'm being unfair to this thickset, corpulent, a bit disturbed being, having grown into such an inveterate liar that one would be ill advised to ask him the time of day, incurably out of his conscience, warped, vain and unhappy.

But that's the way we exiles are.

On Exile

And that's the mildest of what could be said of us, unless we mention the indispensable kicks "for the road". These are often delivered in a scornful, half-hearted, offhand fashion: "Get outa here"; sometimes — with the vexed nervousness of a man trying to rid himself of an obnoxious wife who doesn't want him to go to a bachelors' party: "Fuck off, you goddamned bitch!" The rarest are the resounding ones, bestowed with the sense of purpose: "Get lost, you slime, or you'll get what's coming to you..." Having flitted off to a respectable distance, we snap back: "Just wait, you'll wish you hadn't been so short-sighted, but it'll be too late then; and for me, I'll be back — if not in body, then in spirit."

It's clear, however, that nobody will be sorry about anyone, and there won't be anything, or anybody, to come back to, for the gap in a vacated space soon begins to shift away somehow, and gets filled with healing balm from within. It would be ridiculous to lay the blame for this process on the cruel administration; even more ridiculous would be attempts to bully it by threatening to show it in its true colors, disclose the full truth... Even if we imagine that someone other than the narrator/champion of truth himself shows up to express interest in this pitiful inside information, the exile's intrinsic untrustworthiness, and refusal to acknowledge defeat (and the exile is just that — a defeat, not a victory!) will soon alienate even the more sympathetic listener — assuming, naturally, that querying exiles is not part of his job...

It's time now to lay aside sarcastic witticisms and forgive, or, at least, feel shame. All that I've said so far belongs to journalism; extending one's limbs from the pulpit, a commissar's epileptoid righteousness pushing its way into the Sanctuary itself. One has to hurry, for otherwise the tax collectors and adulteresses will enter the Kingdom of Heaven before me, and I'd like to worm my way into their number — and not be hopelessly late. Left home almost fifteen years ago — and still learned nothing.

And what about the anguish of an exile — the yearning for the lost land of birth, once defined by that great Russian expert, or even more than that, our spokesman on exile affairs, Marina Tsvetayeva, as the "dark fascination exposed long ago"? This anguish is easy to summon up, especially if exile has turned out to be a financial success: in a decent restaurant one orders a plate of ethnic hors d'oeuvres and a bottle of folkloristic drink. It takes less than fifteen minutes for the sweet grief to enter the exile's heart.

"The wind doesn't bring me *here* (the emphasis mine) weeping/sounds of Russian trumpets of war." These lines from Joseph Brodsky's ode contain in a condensed form an answer to the question: what does the writer do with exile? He demythologizes it, degrades it to the ranks, and puts it into its place — an honorable, lawful place, but no more than that. From there — here, where I am at present, sounds never reach. I know that I'm here, and am ever ready to admit it; and, if desired, I can provide the curious with a semiotic road map of the place, on which the symbols carry not the basic, but only an auxiliary meaning, since I'm not trying to pass off as a map what is only a landscape in oils on the theme "Nevermore."

"Now let's take the opposite," comes the question. "How does the exile, being cut off from the fire and water available to the rest of his compatriots, influence the writer?"

This rather polite question merits, however, an intelligible answer.

As for myself, I don't regret a single day. Exile has allowed me to look aslant, as it were, at the loss; to perceive it simultaneously in an inaccessible distance — and in one's own gut. It has led me to take delight in the word crumbs I would surely have scorned in more favorable circumstances. It could even be said, with only a bit of exaggeration, perhaps, that exile has put some sense into my head...

And then the night falls, finding me midway between St. Elias monastery and Bethlehem. I am lying in one of the flats of a four-storey house shoddily built upon a whitish rocky ground. This land, called Palestine, the Holy Land, the Promised Land, etc., was lately taken from exiles by other exiles, through force and cunning. The evil freshly done has had no time to settle, dismiss its case under the statute of limitations, fall under the amnesty of Redemption, which, as the opinion of the profane goes, is just a step from here. And so all Palestine reeks of uncollected rubbish; the phosphorescent carcasses of dogs and cats crushed by the motor cars are scattered along the roads; being run over again, they raise their small heads, show their teeth and hiss. Living here is a shame and abomination, but I got used to that.

Around two in the morning a piercing scream of fright, my own, maybe, or one from the outside, wakes all of me up at once, completely; and at such a treatment of a man — prostrated, guilty, with exposed, vulnerable balls — I, hurt, give a sob and start asking: "Lord Jesus Christ, Son of God, have mercy on me, a sinner!"

This nighttime bombing raid on the soul, this night robbery — or night interrogation, when they drag one down the stairs, face down — lasts until the tormentors come upon something silly, tongue-tied, drunk with cheap wine, begging for a wash — but hard to vanquish, most likely thanks to its viscosity, thickness and unsightly form.

This spherical defense, behind which there's some subtle spiritual flesh, I would let myself call the sense of motherland. Not in the imperial-patriotic sense, of course: we're talking about the tiny, thoroughly real and tangible area, the spot where my feet, getting larger with age, are placed. At first fitted with knitted, dull-blue woolen baby bootikins, later — in strapped sandals, then — in black wrinkled shoes made in Kharkov shoe factory No. 5, and so on, up to the outre French boots with then popular platform soles that my first wife bought me a day before the flight.

Leonid Latynin, *Sleeper at Harvest Time, Stavr and Sara*, Glas Publishers, Moscow, 1993, 12 illustrations by Timur Iskhakov

A blend of historical narrative, myth and antiutopia, dominated by the theme of sacrifice.

The protagonist is the son of the pagan priestess and a bear. They are all involved in dramatic developments of Russian history beginning with the tenth century and culminating in the downfall of Moscow and Jerusalem in the 21st century.

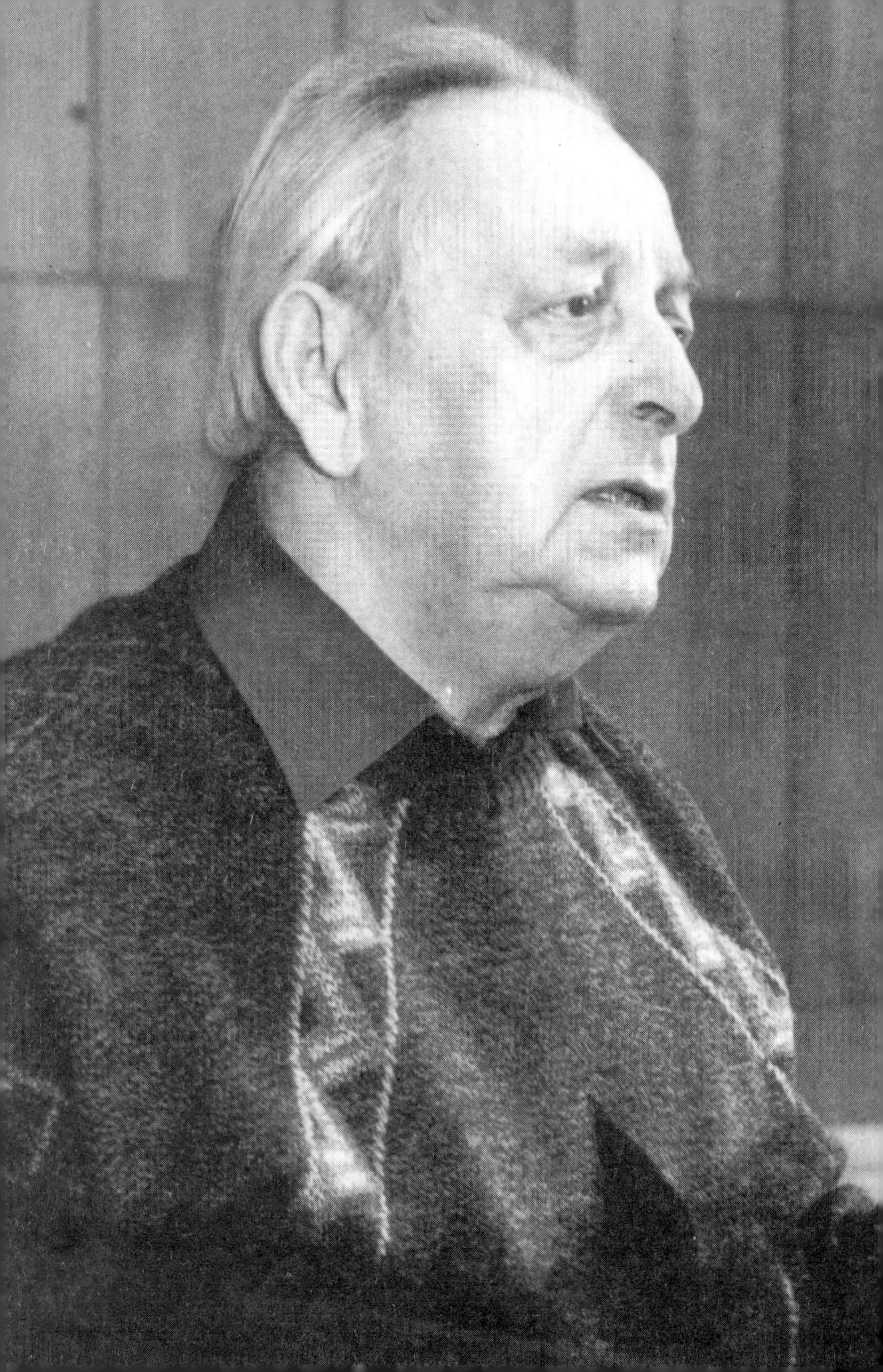

＃ Lev RAZGON

THE PRESIDENT'S WIFE

A Saturday night in summer. The evening was wearing on and I should have been on my way by now. I usually spent my brief weekends at Vozhael, and was used to walking the thirty kilometres from our prison camp to the administrative headquarters there, and making the same journey back twenty-four hours later. In winter the road was packed down hard and smooth as asphalt, the cold air was exhilarating, and I had little difficulty putting the distance, almost a full marathon, briskly behind me. In summer the surface was pounded into fine, shifting sand by the wheels of lorries and the going was much tougher. I would seize any opportunity of a lift.

A likely looking vehicle was standing outside the sentry post. It was a small, cross-country "Kozlik," a Soviet version of the jeep. For all its toy-like appearance it was capable of speeding me to Vozhael in just over an hour. Some top brass from the medical section had arrived in it a few hours earlier: the head of our medical department had brought over a colonel who was deputy Chief Medical Officer for the whole of the Gulag system. Why not try cadging a life with them? After all, I was a free man now and, in theory at least, the equal of any of them.

The brass came out of the sentry post and moved towards their jeep. I went over to our doctor. "Comrade Major! If you have a spare seat in your vehicle may I ask you to take me to Vozhael?"

I was counting on the Major's reputation as a fair-minded administrator, and was not disappointed. The tall Colonel, with green tabs on his collar and the medical serpent emblazoned on his uniform, treated me with studied politeness. I got in the back beside him and the jeep set off, bumping along the sandy road. The two officers continued a conversation evidently begun back in the camp.

The President's Wife

Unlike our Major, whose entire career since graduation had been spent working in the camps, the Colonel was new to this department of the state. After studying at the Academy of Military Medicine he had served exclusively in the Army. Needless to say, there was nothing in the conversation of these two senior officers to give me any clue as to why the Colonel now found himself serving in the Gulag.

Of the two men the Colonel was the more talkative, describing life at the front and interesting people he had met. One of his subordinates had made a particularly strong impression. The Colonel had been commanding officer of a divisional medical corps. His senior surgeon was the son-in-law of Mikhail Kalinin, first President of Soviet Russia and a close associate of Lenin, and subsequently Stalin. This circumstance produced a number of very tangible benefits for the divisional medical corps, and also resulted in my travelling companion's being introduced to Kalinin himself. He went on official business with his senior surgeon to Moscow, and was invited out to Kalinin's dacha, where he wined and dined without formality with the Head of the Soviet State.

The Colonel's voice trembled with emotion as he described how charming Kalinin had been, how unassuming he was, how steadfast in his beliefs, and spoke of the high regard in which he was held throughout the Soviet Union. Then he moved on to sing the praises of the son-in-law and to say how much he regretted their ways had parted. He told the Major that his former subordinate was now working as divisional surgeon in such-and-such a place.

At this point I most unwisely interrupted to say that in fact Kalinin's son-in-law was currently the chief surgeon on one of the fronts, and working in quite a different town. The Colonel said nothing for a moment, then turned to enquire with icy politeness,

"Forgive my asking, but what is the source of your information?"

His tone was so cutting that I answered very levelly,

"His wife, Lydia Mikhailovna, told me."

The Colonel was silent for quite some time, evidently assimilating this unexpected nugget of information received from a man whose past was manifestly murky. Finally he could contain himself no longer.

"Forgive me again, but when did Lydia Mikhailovna tell you this?"

I had all but burnt my bridges.

"A couple of weeks ago..."

The Colonel was now silent for even longer. His face registered hectic, but evidently fruitless, mental activity. Perplexed, but consumed with curiosity, he was obliged to turn to me again.

"Do forgive me if I seem to be prying... But where did Lydia Mikhailovna talk to you?"

God almighty! Why had I ever got involved in this? And with our Major sitting in the front seat! God knows what might come of this idiotic conversation, but it was too late to think about that now.

"We were talking in Vozhael."

This time the Colonel reacted instantly.

"No, this really is quite beyond me! What on earth could Lydia Mikhailovna be doing in Vozhael? What could possibly have brought her here?"

I was silent as the tomb. What could I possibly say? For all I knew the Colonel wasn't supposed to be told things that were common knowledge in Vozhael.

"Major, perhaps you can enlighten me. What could Lydia Mikhailovna be doing in Vozhael?"

The Major answered very coolly,

"She came to visit one of the prisoners."

"What do you mean, man? What prisoner could she possibly have been visiting?"

"Her mother. Mme. Kalinin is one of our prisoners here at the camp regional headquarters."

I've seen plenty in my time, but seldom have I seen anyone as shocked as the Colonel. He clasped his head in his hands and buried his face in his knees. He rocked from side to side as if he were having a fit, babbling hysterically and incoherently, words pouring uncontrollably out of him.

"For heaven's sake! This is beyond comprehension. It's beyond belief. The wife of Kalinin! The wife of the Grand Old Man of the Soviet Union! No matter what she did or what crime she committed... to put the wife of Kalinin in a common prison, a common prison camp! Lord above, this is scandalous! Terrible! When was

The President's Wife

this done? How could it be done? Is it possible? What did the President have to say about it? No, I don't believe it! It can't be true!"

The Colonel drew himself up as if about to rise from his seat.

"I wish to pay my respects to her, Major! You must introduce me to her!"

I was angry with myself for ever getting involved in this conversation. I found neither the cause of the Colonel's hysterics nor his hysteria itself any laughing matter, but I did find it hard to keep a straight face at the idiotic mouthings of a man who was, after all, the deputy Chief Medical Officer of the State Directorate of Labour Camps. I had a fleeting vision of the ever-meticulous President's wife, sitting in her tiny room in the bath-house at the camp headquarters scrupulously scraping nits from the grey, newly-washed, prison-issue knickers with her piece of glass just as the Colonel arrived to pay his respects...

To give the Colonel his due, his violent reaction was a natural response to what he had heard. Even the most hardened had difficulty in coming to terms with the fact that Yekaterina Ivanovna Kalinin, the wife of a leading and much respected figure in the Communist Party, indeed the Head of State of the USSR, was a common prisoner in a common or garden labour camp. The intelligence had the potential to shock people a good deal more conversant with the ways of the world than this greenhorn military medic.

Even my girlfriend Rika had reacted analogously. It was through her I had first discovered that Mme. Kalinin was in our camp.

One time when she was staying over with me she told me she had become great friends with an old woman who had recently arrived from another camp. Her file stated that she was to be employed only on gang labour supervised by the prison guards, but the doctors at headquarters had recategorised her as unfit for heavy labour. It had proved possible to fix her up with a job at the bath-house picking nits out of the underwear before it was issued to the prisoners who were washing there. Yekaterina Ivanovna lived in the linen room, able at last to rest from the many years she had spent on hard labour. Rika would go to see her every day after finishing work in the camp office and take her some of the better food supplied to non-convicts. She enjoyed just sitting and talking to a charming, intelligent old lady. Rika told me she wasn't Russian. She evidently came from one of the Baltic states but had become totally russified years ago. She didn't look like an ordinary working woman, although she had once mentioned working in a factory many, many years ago. Her surname was wholly Russian...

"What is that?" I asked.

"Kalinin."

"She can only be Mikhail Kalinin's wife."

Rika did not throw a fit like the Colonel, but categorically refused to believe me. It was out of the question! And anyway the two of them were so close that Yekaterina Ivanovna could never have kept something like that from her. Besides, everybody would be bound to know.

For my part I was almost certain it was true. I did not know Yekaterina Ivanovna personally, but she had been on friendly terms with my in-laws. In the summer of 1937, when we began to find a void forming around us as all our numerous friends and acquaintances vanished and the telephone stopped ringing, Yekaterina Ivanovna was one of the very few people to continue to enquire after the health of my wife Oksana, getting her supplies from the Kremlin dispensary of medicines unavailable to ordinary mortals. Towards the end of 1937 this source of help dried up, and we learned that Yekaterina Ivanovna had been arrested.

In all honesty, neither the Colonel nor Rika should have been so thrown by the knowledge that the wife of a member of the Politburo was in jail. If members of the Politburo were themselves liable to be arrested and shot without ado, why should their wives enjoy special immunity?

We already knew that Stalin, for all his enthusiasm for modern technology, found it hard to part with old ways. He saw to it that many of his henchmen had close relatives arrested and indeed, as I recall, that applied to every member of his inner circle without exception. One of Kaganovich's brothers was executed, while another chose to shoot himself; Stakh Ganetsky, who was married to Shvernik's only daughter and actually lived in his house, was arrested and shot; the parents-in-law of Voroshilov's son were arrested, and they tried to arrest his wife; Molotov's wife, who held a leading position in the Party in her own right, was arrested... The list could go on. It was not really so surprising, then, that Kalinin's wife should also have been detained.

Kalinin himself had long since ceased to be a force to be reckoned with. Even before my own arrest they had came for his oldest and closest friend, Alexander Shotman. The two of them had been workers together at the Putilov factories in St Petersburg.

I was a friend of Shotman's son and he filled me in on some of the details of what was a story fairly typical for those days. Not only was Shotman a friend of Kalinin's, a Bolshevik from the earliest days who had been close to Lenin, but as a member of the Central Executive Committee of Soviets he theoretically enjoyed parliamentary immunity. At the very least his arrest should have needed the formal sanction of Kalinin himself as Chairman of the Executive Committee.

In fact, however, they simply arrived at the Shotmans' apartment during the night, put to him the same question they asked of all the old Bolsheviks: "Do you have weapons or documents relating to Lenin?", and took the old man away. Shotman's wife could hardly bring herself to wait until morning before ringing Kalinin. He was delighted to hear from her, and began to croon down the telephone:

"How wonderful to hear from you at least, even if Alexander hasn't found time to phone an old friend for the best part of a week. Fancy abandoning me at a time like this. Tell me, how is his rheumatism? How are the children?"

Shotman's wife interrupted the cheerful banter:

"Misha! Surely you know they took Alexander away last night!"

How many such calls must Kalinin have had.

Rika was unconvinced by my arguments, so I suggested that next time she saw Yekaterina Ivanovna she should give her my regards and ask whether she had any news of the whereabouts of the Shotmans or how they were faring. The very next day there was a telephone call for me from the regional centre, and I heard Rika's voice cracked with emotion:

"You were right! It's just as you said!"

She later described her dramatic conversation with Yekaterina Ivanovna in the bath-house. She had hesitantly passed on my message as instructed. For all her Estonian restraint, Yekaterina Ivanovna had turned pale. Rika burst into tears and asked her straight out,

"Can this be happening! Are you really...?"

Mme. Kalinin flung her arms around Rika's neck, and they both wept the tears women weep the whole world over, even women as self-possessed and experienced in the ways of the world as the wife of the Soviet President.

The arrangements for her arrest had been banal rather than theatrical. She had simply been phoned from the Kremlin couturier's, where she was having a dress made, and asked to come in for a fitting. When she arrived they were already waiting for her.

I have mentioned Yekaterina Ivanovna's typical Estonian taciturnity and her years in the underground as the wife of a professional revolutionary. She was a long-standing revolutionary in her own right and did not readily talk about the things that had happened since that phone call from her dressmaker, but we knew she had had a hard time of it. She had had half the Soviet criminal code thrown at her, including the dreaded clause 58.8, terrorism. The file was crossed through, which indicated that she was to be given hard labour and kept under guard at all times. For the greater part of her ten-year sentence Yekaterina Ivanovna was set to the most gruelling work women could be forced to do in the camps. Fortunately she was a robust woman accustomed to hard work from an early age and she survived. It was only when her previous camp was disbanded during the war and she came to us that a way was found of fixing her up with one of the cushier jobs.

During the last year of the war things began to change for the better for Mme. Kalinin. Evidently Kalinin, unlike other "close comrades-in-arms" of Stalin, kept interceding on behalf of his wife throughout her time in prison. Molotov, for example, never uttered a squeak about his wife. When his daughter was joining the Party she stated that her father was Molotov and she had no mother. At all events, during that last year of the war Yekaterina Ivanovna began to receive regular visits from her daughters, Julia and Lydia. When one of them came to the settlement they would be allocated a room which was stylishly furnished and even had carpets. They were, after all, the President's daughters, and the President's criminal wife was allowed to live with one or other of them for a whole three days without the supervision of the camp guards.

The first time Lydia came to visit, Yekaterina Ivanovna invited me, through Rika, to pay a social call. It was the first time I had met her. I sat there, drinking fine wine all the way from Moscow, a taste I had long forgotten, dining on improbable delicacies, and listening to the tales of someone freshly arrived from the capital.

Even I quailed to hear how often Kalinin had begged Stalin to have mercy on his life-long partner and release her so that they could at least be together for a time before he died. Eventually, when victory over Germany was assured, he caught Stalin in a sentimental mood and, weary of his aged colleague's tears, the Leader decided to kick over the traces and let the old bat go free as soon as the war was over! Now Kalinin and his family were waiting for the war to end with perhaps even greater trepidation and impatience than the rest of the country. It was during one of these visits that I received the intelligence about the whereabouts of Kalinin's son-in-law which was so to disturb the mental equilibrium of the deputy Chief Medical Officer of the State Directorate of Labour Camps.

After the three day period of socialisation with her daughter Prisoner Kalinin was returned to the camp, there again to take up the means of production allotted her, to wit, "one piece of glass, nits for the scraping off of."

When some future novelist is immortalising the acts of Stalin and comes to describe the great man's exalted feelings at his successful prosecution of the war, let him not forget to mention that in this moment of glory Stalin did not overlook even so insignificant a detail as his promise to Kalinin. Almost exactly one month after the end of the war a telegram arrived ordering the release of Yekaterina Ivanovna. Admittedly the telegram omitted to mention the grounds for her release, so that there was no reason for the camp administration not to issue her with one of customary poisoned passports for ex-convicts which would have deprived her of the right to visit Moscow, and 270 other towns besides. An urgent request for clarification was sent to Moscow and the camp commandant, wreathed in smiles and overflowing with the milk of human kindness, invited Yekaterina Ivanovna to come and stay with him in the interim. She chose, however, to spend those last days with Rika. A short time later a limousine laden with the camp's top brass drew up outside Rika's humble hut. They proceeded to lug out the suitcases of their former ward and Mme Kalinin, with Rika to see her off, departed for the railway station.

In autumn 1945 I was in Moscow and went to visit Yekaterina Ivanovna on several occasions. It was a trying experience for a number of reasons. She was living with her daughter in the apartment block where my wife Oksana had spent most of her short life and where I too had lived. Indeed, Lydia Kalinin lived directly below what had once been our flat, and to cross the courtyard and again automatically glance up at those windows pained me greatly.

Yekaterina Ivanovna was always glad when I visited her. She couldn't bring herself to go and live with her husband in the Kremlin, and Mikhail Ivanovich himself recognised that this could be inadvisable. It was obvious that by this time he himself no longer had any illusions about the realities of the situation. When Rika was in Moscow she saw a great deal of Yekaterina Ivanovna and they would go to the theatre together. Back in Vozhael she received many pleasant letters from her.

It is not difficult to understand why Yekaterina Ivanovna was reluctant to live in the Kremlin. She was frightened of bumping into Stalin by chance, unlikely though that was. In the event, she was unable to avoid it.

Kalinin was already terminally ill when he was permitted to see his wife again. He died only a year later, in the summer of 1946. At that time we were still living in the Ustvym labour camp. We reacted with very mixed feelings to the rhetoric gushing from the radio and press about how deeply the deceased had been loved by the Party, the Soviet people and Comrade Stalin himself. Even more bizarre was to read in the papers a telegram of condolence from the Queen of England to a woman who only a year earlier had been picking nits out of underwear in a prison camp. But most terrible of all was to see the newspaper and magazine photographs of Kalinin's funeral, with Yekaterina Ivanovna following the coffin, and Stalin and his entire retinue walking beside her.

So she did bump into Stalin again, forced to act out a charade so diabolically improbable that it would seem out of place in one of Shakespeare's chronicle plays. It would have been terribly heartless to enquire into what she was feeling during that encounter, but I would have done so had I ever met her again. Rika and I had only a brief interval of freedom, and when we returned to Moscow in the 1950s Yekaterina Ivanovna was no longer there.

I was once introduced to Julia Kalinin at a publisher's. She had written a book for children about her father. I told her we had met before.
"Of course. I thought your face was familiar. We met on holiday at Barvikha, was it, or at The Pines?"
"No, we weren't on holiday. It was at a place called Vozhael."
I saw her eyes glisten with compassion and dismay, just as they had at our meeting in Vozhael.

Translated by Arch Tait and Rachel Osorio

"MEDIUM" SAVES RUSSIAN PHILOSOPHY

From the **History of Russian Philosophical** Thought series was first conceived as a book supplement to **Voprosy Philosophii** journal and due to be published by Pravda, the country's largest publishing concern owned by the CPSU Central Committee. Having lost their owner and changed their name, the publishers refused to honor their previous obligations and threw out the philosophical series from their publishing plans, although several volumes have already been prepared for print.

The Moscow Philosophical Foundation and **Voprosy Philosophii** journal were fortunate to find a new publisher, Medium, a non-profit publishing house specialising in books representing the best in Russian and Western intellectual thought.

To come out in 1993:
Ivan Ilyin, **Works,** in 2 vols
Vol 1. **The Philosophy of Right. The Philosophy of Morality.**
The concepts of right and force. Regeneration of Hegelianism. Fichte's philosophy as a religion of conscience. Hegel's philosophy on the concreteness of God and man. On the overcoming of evil by force.
Vol 2. **The Religious Essence of Philosophy**
On good manners. The religious essence of philosophy The road to spiritual renovation. The singing heart. The book of quiet meditations.

Evgeny Trubetskoi,
The World Views of Vladimir Solovyov, in 2 vols.

Alexei Khomyakov, **Works,** in 2 vols.
Vol 1. **Historiosophy.**
Semiramis. A study of the veracity of historical ideas. About philosophical writing. About the old and the new. About architecture. Certain features in the life of caliphs. Answer to Granovsky's article. Notes on the "Lay of the Host of Igor"
Vol. 2. **Theological Works.**

Communal Living

A Crowded Place

by Boris Yampolsky

He met her one autumn evening outside the cinema — a slight figure in a nylon blouse and a high-fitting plaid skirt with a fringe at the hem, and a white funnel shaped hat perched on her head. Her eyes were heavily mascara'd.

There were no tickets, as usual, and it was raining.

He said, "You haven't got a spare ticket?"

She grinned.

"How about you?"

And so they met.

She said her name was Stella, and he made up a name for himself, just in case — Dima.

They chatted about Jean Maurais, and she said she preferred Marc Bernes.

"Shall we go somewhere?" he said.

So they went to the "Mars" cafe.

They had two big vodkas each, some soup and boiled tongue, which the menu claimed was entrecote steak. He had a black coffee, and she asked for the house speciality ice-cream, in the shape of a tower dotted with preserved strawberries and little biscuits.

"Are you really called Stella, or did you just invent a pretty name for yourself?"

"That's a military secret," she said, and he had the impression she was making fun of him.

It got to be midnight. There was a light drizzle, and the leaves were falling along the road.

He walked her home to Taganka square, to a quiet, deserted side street, into a big courtyard with a lot of staircase entrances veiled in darkness. They went into one of them to say goodnight.

He kissed her, and she responded with some enthusiasm.

"Perhaps I could come in for a minute?" he asked.

He felt strangely unsure of himself.

Communal Living

"For a minute, only a minute," he whispered.

She unlocked the door and said "We've got to be very quiet," and took his hand and led him in darkness down a long corridor. He kept stumbling over boxes and panels on the floor, and getting slapped in the face with wet rags which he realized must be washing dangling from clothes lines. There was a smell of gas and washing powder, the lively, gipsy squalor of a communal flat.

A door squeaked open, and they went into a dark room. "Don't move," she said, and as he stood there she made a bed on the floor, working by feel alone.

Outside it rained and rained....

"Ciao," she said, as she fell asleep.

At daybreak, when he usually woke up for his first cigarette of the day, he opened his eyes and was scared out of his wits. In the grey, lifeless half light of an autumn morning, he discovered he was lying on the floor of a big room crammed with people.

There was one lad squatting in his underpants doing exercises with dumb-bells and behind him another one who could have been his double sitting on a folding chair shaving in a mirror propped up on a stool, and yet another sitting at a table digging in to his breakfast.

Under the window there was a big, old-fashioned wooden bed with an old man lying there reading a paper.

He got the idea that the old man might set the lads on to him, and they'd start beating him up with the dumb-bells, maybe even slash him with the razor, and he swiftly closed his eyes again and pretended to be asleep.

Then he thought it must all have been a dream. He cautiously opened his eyelids again and saw, as if it was in a movie, the lad who'd been brandishing the dumb-bells, now fully dressed, sitting on the folding chair shaving himself.

The one who'd been shaving before was sitting at the table working away with a spoon, and the third, who by this time had finished his breakfast, was standing at the dressing table doing up his tie. The old man was still reading his newspaper.

Last night's Stella was lying beside him, sleeping as peacefully as a child.

Communal Living

He closed his eyes again in pretended sleep, and still couldn't make his mind up whether or not it was all a dream.

After a while he looked warily round him again. This time the lads had gone.

Then a little boy with a skipping rope appeared, a baby in a pram in the corner started to cry until an elderly woman shoved a dummy in his mouth. He started to suck it and stopped bawling.

And the old man looked over his newspaper with wide-awake eyes, and he had the impression he'd been sitting there all night like that, staring at him in the darkness.

In the end he thought "Oh, the hell with it," jumped out of bed, and started doing his exercises in his turn. The old man silently observed his performance. The little boy went on skipping. The woman dandled the baby.

It was quite light by now, and sunny. Factory hooters were sounding nearby.

He gently woke the girl.

"I'm on the evening shift," she whispered without opening her eyes. She smiled and went back to sleep.

The old man got out of bed. He was fully dressed in a donkey jacket and white felt boots, and when he stood up he was revealed to be a sturdy big-nosed old chap as bald as a mushroom, with deep-set eagle eyes.

"Well, what about it?" he demanded severely.

The guest produced some money, and the boy was despatched to some Uncle Agafon. He grabbed his scooter and shot off down the corridor, from where he shortly reappeared with a sealed half-liter bottle. The woman produced a pan of fried-up potatoes and some herring. They sat down to eat.

"Just to keep out the cold," said the old man, knocking out the cork. He ate and drank with gusto and thoroughly enjoyed himself, breathing in the joys of this unexpected feast day.

When they had finished up the bottle and the potatoes, the old man said to the woman, "Well, come on, let's push off. They've got young people's things to do." And he grabbed the newspaper and went off, with the woman and the child in tow.

The girl went on sleeping.

What relation was she to them? Daughter, niece, or just a tenant? That he simply didn't know.

Translated by Gordon Clough

A Marriage Of Convenience

by Ksenia Klimova and Elena Salina

"A good thing you came," said Sergei, drawing me into the dark depths of a communal flat cluttered with the junk of ages. "It's time I had a decent meal, too."

Somehow, Sergei always managed to get the wrong end of the stick. The one good thing about communal flats, everybody knows, is that they are all situated in the centre of Moscow. But the view from Sergei's window was onto the heavy traffic of the Outer Ring Motorway, and, moreover, onto that ten-kilometre narrow stretch of it which is notorious for its head-on car crashes and the almost total death-rate of those motorists involved in them. Nor could the window be rightfully called his own: he had got this room out of a complex "chain exchange" engineered by some operative who kept saying, "It's just a matter of greasing a few palms, and everybody will be happy." When the operation was eventually finished, everybody was happy — with the exception of Sergei, who found himself sharing this room with an old lady, who, after the proper palm had been greased, was pronounced to be his grandmother. She had been expected to die before the operation was completed, but proved to possess an aristocratically tenacious hold on life. To give her her due, she also possessed an equally aristocratic probity. She apologized to Sergei in French with a shrug, offered him tea, and promised to burden him with her presence as little as possible. She was as good as her word, too, though nobody knew where she spent all those hours when she was away from home, waiting for death to catch up with her.

"What does he mean by a decent meal?" I wondered. I had thought we were going to the tennis court, which Sergei's firm rented for an unknown purpose since Sergei was the only one who

Communal Living

ever played tennis there, except for me who tagged along in the hope of learning at least the ABCs of the aristocratic game.

"You could at least have warned me that you expect to be paid for the tennis lessons with food," I grumbled.

"Sorry, no tennis today. I'm thinking of getting married. This evening I'm going to negotiate."

Luckily we had by then reached his room, and I had the old lady's settee to faint on. This bum, this workaholic, for whom any effort outside work was a bother, was thinking of getting married! Unbelievable. OK, I could imagine him bringing a wife into this den of his, but calling the girl on the telephone, taking her out, making a declaration of love — no, he just wouldn't be able to go to all that bother.

I discovered that there actually was something to eat in the place — my function was simply to cook it. Sergei finds cooking an excruciating drudgery. Even boiling noodles is too much for him, involving as it does the pouring of water into a pan, lighting the gas stove, taking the pan off the heat and then sieving the noodles.

So I decided to cook him lunch just out of curiosity. On a full stomach he was prepared to enlighten me:

"There's nothing for it but to get married," he pronounced in the tone of a Podkolesin[*]. "It's marry, or die. Earning money is one thing, but standing in food queues, cooking... I made meat jelly once. It's supposed never to go off but after two weeks it acquired the consistency of glue, and began to stink, too. And it's not only the question of cooking either. A married person feels less vulnerable. My foster grandmother, roommate that is, is also thinking of getting married. Another resident in this room. Between them they'll get rid of me in no time. I've met the prospective husband — a racketeer if ever I saw one."

"And does your future wife have somewhere to live then?"

"Absolutely! This very room. She's my former wife, you see. That same Valentina whom I divorced five years ago."

"But why the hell should you marry your own wife all over again?"

---

[*] The hero of Gogol's play "Marriage", who just could not muster up the courage to take the plunge.

Communal Living

"Oh, there are plenty of good reasons. All you women have kinks, but at least I know hers and she knows mine. It costs a lot these days to get a new passport when you take your husband's name, and she's already got mine. And do you know how much wedding rings are? We've still got the ones we bought last time. And generally this is a bad moment to start on any new ventures, plough up the virgin lands, so to speak. There've been all these beauty contests, and women expect a lot. Why, a bunch of roses would leave a horrible gap in my budget. Let alone a honeymoon... Where can you afford to take your young bride to give her something to remember? And my ex may still remember all the good things we had during out first honeymoon. The trip down the Yenisei... Almost a cruise."

"I see. What about love?"

He looked at me commiseratingly, as much as to say: What are you talking about? What love? The main thing is to survive.

"You know my pal Yuri?" he asked. "He's making a lot from his business trips abroad, so he thought he could afford a new wife. And do you know what this new wife has gone and done? After love had paled a little, she invited over some of her burglar pals. They picked the apartment clean. Even carried off the computer he borrowed from the firm. So he lost his job too."

So when Sergei left for his "negotiations", I went along, and even made the sign of the cross over him.

And get married they did. When the photographer at the registry office tried to bully them into posing for a "newly weds" picture, they showed him their old ones, saying they were even better, because they were younger then. Valentina, a thin nervous woman, looked content.

Translated by Raissa Bobrova
From: *Stolitsa* №52, 1992

Communal Living

By Alexander Terekhov

Basically, I've got to agree that communal living is socialism's harsh legacy and of course, there was nothing like it before the Bolshevik revolution. But the happiest time of my life was when I lived in a communal flat.

"Why don't you move in tonight?" suggested the man who had the room before me as he tried to avoid looking me in the eye. You've got eight meters all to yourself and the neighbor's a real cracker. You won't regret it, I can tell you."

I moved in that night, instructions fully memorized: top lock, two turns, bottom lock a bit of a push and then one turn and down to the sixth door on the left. I fumbled my way through the darkness, weighed down by bundles and parcels and then crashed out on the bare mattress in my room.

Not that I could sleep though in my new surroundings. All through the night I kept waking up. I would wake up, turn over and think "great!" Then I'd be asleep again.

And next minute, I'd wake up thinking about the sort of person who ends up in a communal flat. They've always come from somewhere much worse, either off the streets, straight out of the army or prison or from a doss house, so you can understand their joy once they get there.

And then I'd go off again only to be woken up once more in the dark with the feeling that I owe all the best in me to communal living. My roots are here and my best roots at that. It's a source of all the very best in this country: the commune, the communist working weekends, communist awareness... And then I would doze off again.

Next minute I was wide awake. I just lay there scratching my belly, and started to think about the things I would soon need to get — a table, a chair, a wife, a lamp... Then I glanced at my watch and gasped: it was already lunch time. So why the hell was it so

Communal Living

dark? Aha, it turned out that my window was completely blocked by the wall of the warehouse next door. So that's why the son-of-a-bitch wanted me to move in at night. Oh, what the hell, anyway.

The post-woman was like a poultry maid feeding her chicks as she distributed the mail among the post-boxes — she knew everything about us just by the newspapers and magazines we subscribed to, and the letters and postal orders we received. And we knew each other inside out, right down to the color of each other's underwear and who had what for dinner.

My neighbor was forever just about to get married. Her mute mother was banished to the kitchen each time it seemed like a proposal was on the cards. Her fiance would sit in the room playing the accordion and singing away to himself, "Oh such brave lads are we, are we, such brave lads are we...!" He cut a lively figure as he sat there stamping his foot in time to the music. The morning after, he would come out of her room, still in his pyjamas, and with an assumed air of importance call his office.

Everyone was listening to his every word. No one missed a thing in that flat. We could tell who the door was for by the number of rings and all of us knew the long single ring of a stranger — the local policeman or the plumber. Everyone kept a mental register of the others' comings and goings, whether they were trips to the kitchen or the loo. Only the old man who had just moved here from the country couldn't get used to city amenities and would always go behind the nearest fence in the yard where the kids from the nursery had planted some dill. His wife thrived on scandal and whenever she had a chance she would pounce on some poor soul and accuse them:

"Why are you always thieving my papers? What? Me a bitch? That daughter of yours is a bitch!"

Another favorite habit of hers was to wander up and down the corridor late in the evening.

"So whose hair is that in the bath?" she would ask, a hint of a threat in her voice.

Life there was fraught with tragedy, poverty and vileness but it was a great life, the same as life anywhere else in this country. Everyone knew everyone else's business so that only our souls remained undisclosed. There are times when I mourn the passing of this era.

Communal Living

It was the happiest time of our lives because there was always something to look forward to then: everyone dreamed of getting a flat of their own. The time would come... When we have a few more kids... And everyone did leave. Not all at once of course, but one by one, with a sort of shameful pleasure. You would be going off and they would still be there — left behind. There would have been no sense of happiness if everyone had left at the same time, because one person's happiness is always at the expense of another's.

Happiness comes to an end when you get stuck somewhere and, try as you might, you remain stuck there. Then in your defeat you can only become the stain on another's happiness. In these new times there will be more happiness and with this more suffering too. Expectations, tears, applications — they won't get you anywhere, and you will only get whatever you can scrap out for yourself. If you're born in a communal flat, you will probably die there. It works the same way if you're born in a palace. Too bad this comes to light much too late when we've all been shaped for a different life.

But on the other hand — what a gift! No one can ever take away the joy of dreams already dreamed.

Even when I'm an old man puffing away like an old steam-engine, I'll never forget the worst horror in my life... It was about one in the morning and I hadn't hung my wash bowl properly on the wall. It came crashing down on top of the toilet, smashing it to pieces. I had a real battle with the water as I first tried to mop it up, then tried to catch it in a bucket and finally sealed the main valve. But I knew that at six in the morning the whole world would wake up and want to know what the hell had been going on. I was just about ready to end it all, but instead spent the night searching the town high and low and finally managed to find myself a plumber who had had more than a skinful.

I hauled him and his toolbox back under one arm and the new cistern under the other with as much love and care as though it were a crystal treasure chest carrying diamond jewels or a prince's crib. I kept lighting the plumber's cigarettes and fussed around him, and he did manage to fix the cistern. When he left I tried it to see if it was working. It was. I went into the kitchen, swigged some water from the kettle and looked out of the window. Suddenly, I just knew that I would never feel this happy ever again. Funny, eh?

Communal Living

In the Russian Federation, 5,425,500 people live in communal flats.
The waiting list holds 9,964,100 families.

Translated by Sandra Stott

Pitch Black Void

by Alexander Terekhov

No one will tell you anything good about the Moscow metro. "This year there's been a mass invasion of rats. That's why there's been so many train delays — the engine-driver has to brake when a solid mass of rats rolls across the rails. If you try and drive through them, the rats get rolled up onto the wheels. They like it in the metro — there's plenty of water and refuse, too, even scraps of meat: criminals often dump corpses in the tunnels — they throw them out from the last trains..."

"You see, they had to take the trash cans out of the metro — they're afraid of explosives. There's no way they can nab the terrorists; you expect an accident every minute."

"Once the escalator broke through, and under it there was water, so many people drowned. The only ones to survive were those who managed to hang onto the lamp stands..."

"And now they've started to kidnap people. In a crowd they'd poke 'em with a needle and drag 'em along as if they were drunk.

"The metro is like a whirlpool — you can disappear here without a trace."

Those are probably exaggerations, but the truth about the metro isn't particularly cheery.

A mine-field is spread out under the feet of millions of Muscovites. It could paralyze the capital. The Moscow metro strike committee threatened a warning strike. Through clenched teeth, the strike committee admitted to the public that the metro is no longer safe.

From a leaflet: "At present a difficult if not grave situation has developed with respect to passenger safety... The organization of passenger transport has essentially gone out of control..."

The metro went cold underground like an immovable crossbar that will be raised only with the rest of the country.
 We used to love our metro so much. What happened to our love?
 To find out what happened we need the night. Night is love's time.
 Night is a pause; it is the bliss of the Miserly Knight. To descend beneath the marble arches and with slow fingers fondle the sacred, leisurely turn down to the left tunnel through the walkway, down the escalator, from a radial onto the circle line, pushing through, to feel on the face the sad draught from the empty halls, to wander aimlessly through the abandoned rooms, touching, sighing, weeping and forgetting where you are right now.
 Fewer and fewer are shuffling through the underground crosswalks. The rustling of bright shiny autos on the blackened asphalt, like falling autumnal foliage, grows more and more rare. Night falls with its hairy paunch over the heads of the buildings. The insatiable underground octopus of the metro gathers together a quiet national assembly. It calls night owls in yellow vests who know not the light of day into the deep marble dens to serve the first wonderful love of socialism. A love built without any foreign aid, in the midst of ironic smirking from abroad, built on the bones of eight centuries. It calls them to serve the best underground in the world, the Moscow metro!
 The metro coughs into the damp handkerchiefs of the streets, freeing its lungs from the remains of that dog-tired people so unworthy of this first love.
 "The last to drag in are the ministerial grocery stores salesmen. From the restaurants comes a typsy crowd. Not like the ordinary Russian drunk, but dignified. Some guy's walking around right up to closing time. The oddball type. He examines each woman carefully. He'd step onto the escalator and cross himself. And we notice that he often goes up with different ladies. Once when he didn't show up we even missed him. From the Arbat, I wouldn't even call them people. They go around naked. I can un-

derstand girls, but she's a size 58, and her back and legs are all showing — yuck! And then the Afghan vets on their way to some celebration, jumped right through the turnstiles, broke all the lamps! But then there's the big events when we close down — perfect order, everyone with a pass, all military.

"At Revolution Square the deaf get together, yeah, those, you know, the deaf-mutes. They used to get together at the Novokuznetsky station, now they hang out here till late hawking duds, selling porno stuff and playing shell games. At night it's dangerous; thugs can harass and intimidate you. They'll strip a drunk in the last car. Or: "Caution, the doors are closing," one of 'em will hold the door just a second and snap off your fur hat — snitch! and he's gone; you try and find him. It seems like even the police could clean your pockets, let alone punch you or say something rude... The bag ladies from the train station ask to let them spend the night."

With one last short jolt the escalator jerks to a stop, and you can suffocate on the silence. The trains are rushing off to the depot, and the weak echo of their hurrying howl floats up from below. The yawning guard locks the doors — it's over. The life of the underground homestead begins.

In the stone bunker under the vestibule two old women wrap washed bandages around their hands. They're escalator operators. Their job is the most dangerous. Narrow dirty gutters lead down, all the way down to the very bottom... At night, the operators have to wipe down every step. They wipe them down with a mythical washing solution that is really just stinky, hand-corroding kerosine. According to regulations it's supposed to be turned completely off, in reality they let it run slowly, drawing their hands through the smacking steel gears. To get through all the steps once takes three hours. They are majestic and meek — like aged Madonnas.

"The machine... Well, it has feelings, you know. You treat her rough and she'll drag you down fast. She'll catch a corner of your clothes and hang onto it. Does anybody ever trip up? Yeah, if they're inexperienced or too tired out. I had four years of schooling. Young folk come, they try it for a while and leave. You can't sleep — the boss'll show up and cut you down to size, take your bonus away. They used to get you for reading even. You're sitting at night, and you start to see things, like someone's in the machine room. You step out to take a look: no one's there, except 380 volts. Anything can happen here, you know, I mean the Kremlin's right next door."

The escalators have been here since the beginning. They've held up pretty well... In the metro the skeleton of the past is best preserved; it's like in the Mausoleum. It's hard to do repairs — you open everything up and then what are you going to replace it with?"

Behind the lemon colored shades in the ticket-collector's window coins are jumping like a ringing whirlpool into the change machine. One hundred rubles, that's 666 fifteen-kopek pieces and two five-kopek pieces. SChMO — stands for Senior Change Machine Operator. She is Aleksandra Nikolaevna Volkova; her collar is white polka dots on a light blue; she's been at it for a quarter century. Her professional ailment is lower back pain. She started as a ticket checker, she tore tickets to make them "invalid from now on."

Dear Aleksandra Nikolaevna, invalid from now on...

"And for the metro they chose only tall, good looking girls... Sometimes we'd be standing at the control point, each more beautiful than the next, all dressed in uniform. They were strict about the uniforms: regulation overcoats with epaulettes, little berets, modest sports shoes. Stockings were required — no bare legs. There was a tunic dress, too, but we tried to hang on to that. We'd pull something black on under the overcoat, not too colorful so it wouldn't show through the openings. How clean it was! In the morning a nurse and the duty master would take over the station; they would take a swab of cotton or gauze and check the dust. Or they'd use their fingers — the index finger for the railings, the thumb for the sculptures, the middle finger for the benches..."

She puts on the kettle and assures me:

"We're all past retirement age. When we leave you'll have no metro... When it got really cold we warmed things up with our own bodies."

I walk down the strangely stationary steps between the round lamps that look like puffy pussey willow buds with a fiery little wire worm within. A forlorn figure in a winter cap and repairman's orange vest drags himself up the adjacent path with the humility of a pilgrim crawling into holy places. He doesn't even hope for a

Communal Living

burst of kindness from the station master who could with her power bring the escalator to life and with an angel's omnipotence lift up towards the draughty vestibule a soul that has left its duties of labor. You're happy to meet a human being, as if you were in the desert. He is sad, although the aroma of our heroics of labor, the smell of hangover that he drags behind him like an unfolded parachute, suggests that his melancholy is serene.

The station master, Ira, sullenly takes down notes from the velvety voice of the intercom. Surrounded by old telephones with heavy-headed receivers like dumbbells, she sits under the shadow of the extendable hook used to fish off the tracks things lost by passengers: glasses, keys, money, combs, shoes, lighters. Next to the hook — a sample "lost-and-found" form. "Identification card for special privileges in Irodiad Ivanovich Stulev's name. If this document is discovered confiscate and send to our office." In the pauses of the night you forget what era you're in.

"Some of our people are afraid of the intercom," concluded Ira with an intercom announcement. "Is our station kind of gloomy?"

I nod my head, donning a vest with crosses made out of a "light reflecting polymer material" and look like a Knight Templar on his way to the Crusades. The instructions read, "In case of the soiling of the vest it may be washed out at home."

"No hot meals," Ira counts on her fingers. "All of a sudden some passenger decides to drink a beer in the tunnel, or they start fighting... So it's up to me to warn the train crews, get a policeman into the engine-driver's cab to catch the guy. They barely managed to pull him out of the walkway between the tunnels. And the police walk around behind us pointing out scraps of paper, but as soon as there's a fight — they're nowhere to be found. Someone took the pistol from the sculpture of the sailor, and one of the partisans just needs a push and it'll fall. The hygienist arrives and you got a real circus on your hands. What kind of cleanliness are you gonna find there...? I once found a note in the station: "Lyuba, I waited and waited and waited for you, but couldn't wait any longer," she concludes, smiling happily and dreamily.

On the empty platform, in the shelter of the fierce-looking statues, hefty workers from the overhaul repair crew are battling it

Communal Living

out at cards. Their speciality is menial, back-breaking work. Theirs is the hardest lot in the metro.

With a quiet grumble a small freight car rolls in — a motor loader model 908DM, full up with tarry sleepers. The crew gets up slowly to load up. Foreman Savelev, a stern man with grey hair, takes a long silent expressionless look at my new little vest and asks lazily under his nose:

"You comin?"

The freight car flies into the ribbed throat of the tunnel and the dusty wind blows into the open door — foreman Savelev flicks his ashes out of it; in the car they're spitting sunflower shells, sleeping or standing blankly with the eyes of pilgrims at a team huddled together on their spread out jerseys, conserving heat on the windy platform. A little further, at the very end, with the immobility of a snowmaiden, sits a lonely female figure in black motorcycle glasses — the motorman's assistant; she'll wave if anything happens...

Like short apparitions the marble banks of the stations fly by. Once again we pierce the sparse bracelets of light in the endless black sleeve. The light is strung together behind us into a radiant sun. We don't notice the few passers-by, squeezing up against the wall. There is no time at night — there are people who sleep every day and work every night. People who for a quarter century haven't worked in the light of day, and, if they're lucky enough to make it to retirement, if some injury doesn't get them, even then they'll pine for the mute enormity of the lifeless stations, for the blackness and the emptiness — how much they are like us all... No point trying to understand them when we can't understand ourselves. The tunnel — without sky or earth — is like a confessional.

The woman holds up her hand — our stop. The motor loader cuts its speed. The ribs of the tubing go by ever slower, quieter, just barely moving — stop.

The crew sits silently, not moving off their jerseys, like Greeks who have arrived to fight for the beautiful Helen and learnt that the first man to touch the shores of Troy will die.

The woman makes her way to the driver's booth and pulls off her glasses, making herself comfortable on the bench: the two hours that the crew is going to be changing sleepers are her own...

Communal Living

I stick my head out of the booth and try to make out on the rough arches the figures of time: 25 meters of ground overhead, the Pokrovsky line was commissioned in 1938, iron tubing overhead — the cast iron age.

And suddenly the tunnel is wrapped in garlands of yellow light — it's over, the pressure is off, as if the gigantic live rail had gone dead. You can work now, and everyone stirs as if the pressure had been released through human bodies. People jump down, and a booming lingering groan of seventy kilo sleepers follows suit.

"Black, like they're from Angola," the foreman comments on the sleepers.

"It has been universally recognized that no other country has an underground system as beautiful and technically perfect and comfortable as Moscow's. Stalin's care for the people can be felt here at every step." I. Novikov, head of the L.M. Kaganovich metro line.

The previous night the rotted pieces of sleepers had been cut out and a jack hammer had chopped out from the concrete grainy graves for the new ones. Sledge hammers pound the plates from the rails. The crew overcounted by one the number of sleepers needed and is now carrying, walking in step, the extra one, like a coffin, back to the now fairly distant motor loader.

The opening is scheduled for the second week of March.
The architectural layout of the stations and vestibules of the second line is unquestionably a great step forward, a new stage in the architectural expression of the greatness of the Stalin era.

In the first days of March 1938, next to the Revolution Square station another event took place, equally worthy of the greatness of the Stalin era — the trials of the "anti-Soviet right-wing Trotskyist block."

"To the firing squad with the miserable fascists!" "No mercy for the trainters!" "Shoot every last one of the villains!"

"There's no place on our Soviet soil for these bloody executioners and traitors!"

The tunnels are like a desert. Once in a while you run into rats

Communal Living

and mice. Closer to the street, sparrows and pigeons. Sometimes, very rarely, a cat, like an abominable snowman.

"So... this is our work", the foreman Savelev gestures with his hand; beneath the blows of the sledgehammer a barbed evil spark winks briefly. "All the tools — crowbars, axes and sledgehammers."

Beneath the sleepers oozes slow black water.

"These boys are bison. Right now it's kids' stuff — only forty sleepers in all. But when twelve guys have to change four hundred meters of rail in one night — that's three and a half tons on each guy. People don't take a job like this when they have something better to do. Only for the sake of their kids. There's no one to take care of 'em in the daytime. He comes home from work — takes the kid to school or kindergarten. He wakes up; brings the kid home. You come home Saturday morning, you can't go to bed. Stick it out, then maybe you'll be lucky — you'll fall asleep at night. Here it's strict — no boozing whatsoever."

Modernized cars will serve the Pokruvsky line. The cars are painted a light blue and are comfortably equipped. The Pokrovsky line will open for service March 13.

The night of March 12 the accused Bukharin was allowed a last word.

At four o'clock in the morning on the 13th of March they began to read the sentence. They finished around four thirty. The majority of the accused got the firing squad.

At six in the morning the first train set off. Along the tracks.

On March 14 the papers reported the following:

"*Great excitement reigned yesterday in the metro. Many Muscovites arrived long before the opening of service in order to be the first to ride the new line and look at the stations Revolution Square and Kursky... Passengers at the Revolution Square station took lengthy stops in front of the sculptures... The newly opened line's service personnel, mostly young people, handled their responsibilities admirably.*"

On the night of March 15 1938 the sentence was carried out.

Communal Living

I toss a coin among the black sleepers and the sparkling wires of track trailing off into the cold darkness, although I don't really want to come back here. But I won't forget it either. I'm headed in the direction of Revolution square, keeping to the side which you must keep to if you want to make it. The light reflecting crosses burn on my back and chest.

"The court's sentence calls on us to make new conquests!"

Eighty statues at Revolution Station as a symbol of the eighty years we've lived and have still to live?

And I walked along like someone superfluous, an alien glob, gobbled down by the bare gullet of the tunnel, where there is only wind and people — the last hostages of Stalin's insomnia. I walked through this underground country from one sector to another returning to my own time; and everything that was around me...

Four embarrassed men jumped to their feet in the dark pretending to be working, in the best tradition of the army, leaning themselves on their shovel handles, examining the passer-by with cautious curiosity...

In the wretched cave, behind the little door, in the uneven puddles of light people swarmed, dodging the water dripping from the ceiling, dressed in work jerseys. One of them, confused, not daring to breath in my direction, moved unsteadily toward the wall, supported himself.

These were the miserable rep-mechs, the repair mechanics, the dirtiest and wettest job. They mend things that aren't worth mending anymore. They grow numb from cold in the ventilation pipes which, contrary to common sense but in fulfilment of regulations, force cold air into the metro in the winter. In the summer they force heat into the street. Every night. On Saturday you won't be able to fall asleep if you don't get drunk.

The track inspectors push their cart along the tracks. Esteemed Anna Alexeevna moves alongside her line. She's a track inspector. Twenty-three years of underground nights for the sake of her children. In her right hand is a lantern, in her left a hammer. At the joints there are six bolts. The solid bolts ring loud and clear. In her plastic bag she has her work log, a cup and her lunch, all the things go into a bag and onto the cart — there's nowhere to leave

Communal Living

anything. You can have a cup of tea at the Arbat station or you can ask any station master for one, depending on who it is... She might just run you off.

There's one bad thing — going in the first train is dangerous. You better sit in the first car to be closer to the driver... if something happens...

At first like just another wreath of light, then a whitish spot, then as a white funnel the station appeared ahead. Majestic, unusually large, light, filled with silence and calm, covering up the melancholy songs of the tunnel with a merry harsh happiness. Your foot steps on the contract track (quiet for the time being), and you are already on the platform where the floor washing machine operator is pulling the machine to and fro. It's a MUM, labelled "mummy" by the people. And she'll finish soon, fix her kerchief and have her say, too:

"They used to give out five or six pieces of soap a month. And half a bucket of soda! And now? One piece — one! For three — three! — months. There isn't even any sackcloth for the mops. The cooperatives are a real plague: so much paper from the pies they're selling all over town. My machines... number 30 leaks water, and 41 you can't budge!"

Behind her back is the entrance to the tunnel where night is hiding, and morning, what of morning — it's not for waking up; it's the beginning of sleep. When you know the value of night you don't believe in the morning. Pauses disrupt life, and what is left when we know too much about ourselves?

From the accused Bukharin's last words:

"For, when you ask yourself: if you die, in the name of what are you dying? And then the pitch black void shows itself with striking clarity."

On to the center of the station where the cast iron people stand. A peasant woman, bending over obese chickens, somebody's kind hand has placed a cigarette in her hand; a miner in boots who has never gone on strike; a sleepless engineer, his crumpled scroll laid out on his knees like a napkin; an implacable sailor; the sinewy hands of the partisan in bast shoes; bushy headed little girls over a globe placing their fingers over the wonderful motherland; a woman with a rifle and a woman with a parachute, feet in knitted socks; an agronomist in a smart cap who sits like an iron on the treads of a tractor with a thick fistful of dusty grain in his hand.

Open, astonishingly unfamiliar faces, hand grenades, pistols, breech locks, burning the color of egg yolk from being touched — the hands of their grandchildren passing by have touched them so often. It's as if they are summoning the enchanted generation to stand up, go up the steep escalators, go out in dead columns into the squares, slam shut the bolts on the tunnels, return clarity to a time gone astray, a time that reaches its greedy hands down into the underground constellation, a time replete with strikes, thefts, dirt, emptiness...

But first love... All its heart-rending power is in its eternal place in the springtime confusion of downpours, in the intoxicating expanses of April. This love defies all-devouring time, is not doomed to turn into dust, and remains in your every breath, in the avalanche of memories and the abyss of despair like a saviour angel and serpent of temptation. It gives you a chance to justify yourself when you realize in the middle of autumn that life is over... And God forbid that you should meet this first love later, face to face, and see the surrender to time and wordly temptations, the repulsive wilting and previously impossible corporealness, see everything that deprives you of April's torments and the childish-naive faith that she is there somewhere, alive, you're just not fated to meet up.

This would cross her right out, tear, rip her out of your heart, rip her from the secret hideouts of your inner world where, since childhood, reside the victorious swing of the Winter Palace's gates, the roaring lava of the Red Cavalry, the tall blast furnaces and brave smiles, the bitter victory during the Great War and the conquered virgin lands, Siberia and the first, very first day when mother brought you — and you were in ill-fitting stockings — to the monument in the center of town and said, "And this is..."

And what's left then? What will you die for?

Two women — "custodians" — are washing the sculptures with mops. One of them smiles at me:

"The new stations are all chalk and tiles; if a train goes by the tiles crumble... Take the Arbat, it's spotless. I've been here for twenty five years already. Five nights a week. The husband was

Communal Living

livid at first, but now, when it's almost time to retire — it doesn't make any difference. Life's all over, eh..."

She leans over the bucket and snorts:

"We were washing the drainage... I say, "Hey Tamara, look here, a rat!" and the rat scoots into the drainage gutter and I'm spraying down there! The rat jumped out like nobody's business — I almost had a heart attack. I even once dreamed about work — we were washing some drainage or other. Look, see, now what with the water, my fingers don't bend — life's all over, all over..."

She walks off into the tunnel and makes her request before she goes:

"Be sure to write about the trash cans — you see they took the trash cans away and now they throw litter right on the tracks," she adds with feeling. "It's no good without the trash cans."

The last service train goes by leaving behind a soft hum; the light licks the walls with chalky tongues — it's always midday here; there's no night; on the benches huddle tired men who have already understood the old lie of the arrow which calls out "Exit to the City"; there is no exit; you can be merciless to your legs and count out the two hundred steps to the top, and the guard will open the spring night that has been won from the winter, a night with the rare shadows of the early workers or the night lovers. And you will be jerked out, stepping into a puddle — there's ice underfoot — it's a joy to crunch ice...

Today you are among those who go along empty streets, nod into a cup of tea, send off children and grown-ups to school and work, brush their teeth with their eyes closed, unplug the television bubbling over with the current congress, draw the blinds with a metallic rustling and let into their bodies redeeming sleep. In order to wake up and with calm despair see how the melancholy midday struggles through the dusty windows with its blind, cold light.

Translated by Nathan Longan

Originally published in *Ogonyok* magazine, this essay is included in the collection of Terekhov's stories published by *Glas*.

POETRY

Marina TSVETAYEVA

Gleb ARSENYEV

Olga SEDAKOVA

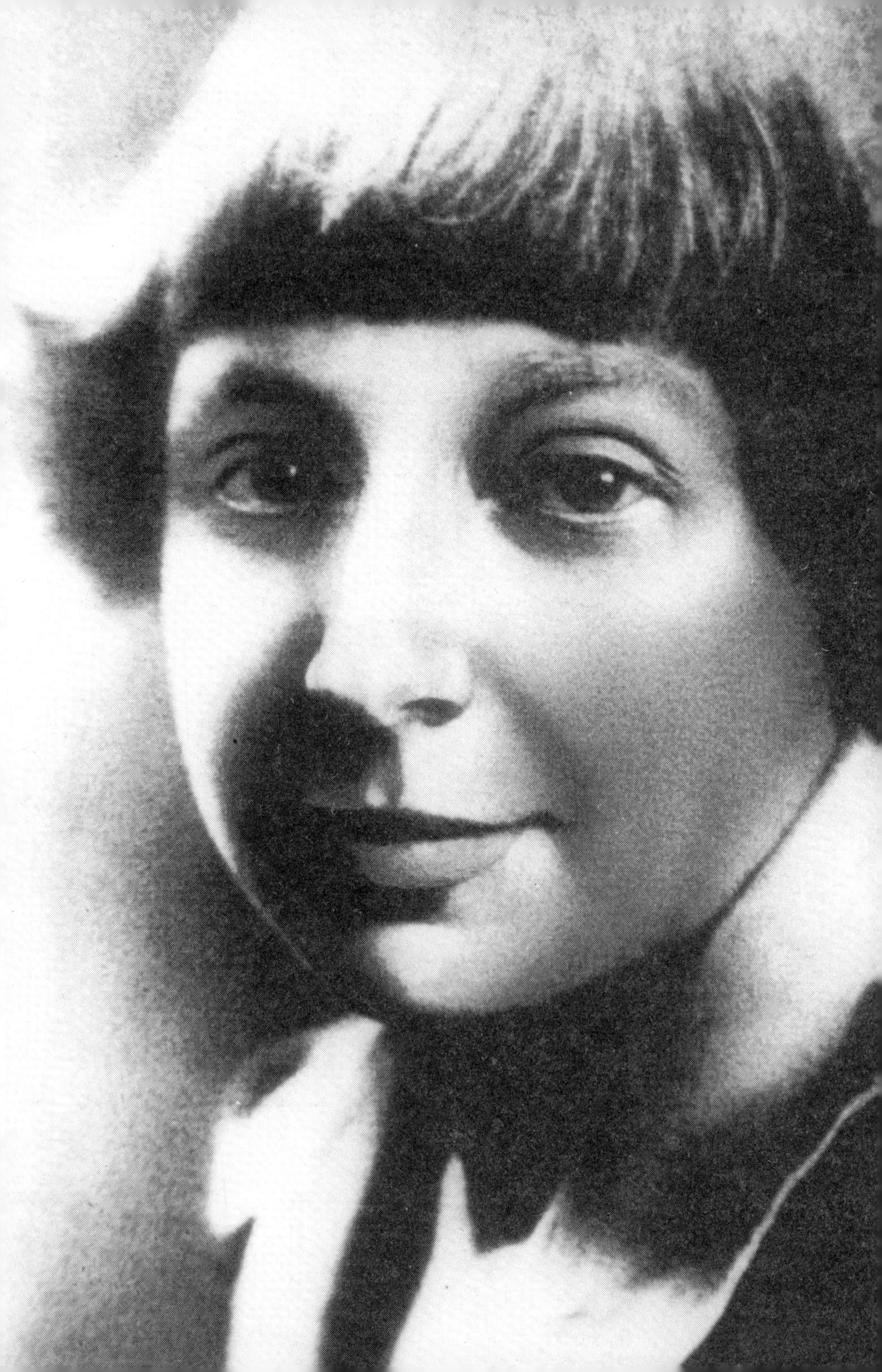

Marina Tsvetayeva

* * *

By the fireside, by the fireside
I pass the nights away,
Rocking my little son,
Rocking him all the time.

Better you'd floated down the Nile
In an ark, my baby.
Your dear father has forgotten
About his beautiful son.

As I guard the royal slumber,
Both my knees go numb.
Night is over... Another night
Comes to take its place.

So Hagar in her wilderness
Whispers to Ishmael,
"Your dear father has forgotten
About his beautiful son!"

You'll grow up, poor little tsar,
To know your father's glory.
You will learn that royal amusements
Cannot last forever.

In a dismal hour, another woman,
Sitting by the fire, shall say,
"Your dear father has forgotten
About his beautiful son!"

> 2 February 1917. Candlemas.

Marina Tsvetayeva

* * *

August
     asters
August
     astral
August
     bunches
Of grapes and russet
Rowanberries
August!

Like a child you play
August
With your ponderous, benign
Imperial apple.
As by hand, you stroke the heart
With your imperial name:
August! Heart!

Month of late kisses,
Late roses and late lightning!
Of starry showers.
August! Month
Of starry showers!

               7 February 1917

* * *

I saw the New Year in alone.
Rich, I was poor.
Inspired, I was despised.
There were so many clasped
hands somewhere, and so much vintage wine.
But inspired, I was despised.
Lonely, I was alone!
Like the moon, alone in the window's eye.

               31 December 1917

Psyche

1

No pretender, I came home,
And no handmaiden, I need no bread.
I am your passion, your sunday,
Your seventh day, your seventh heaven.
There, on Earth, they gave me a copper coin,
Hung millstones round my neck.
Beloved, do you not know me?
I am your swallow, your Psyche!

2

Take these, my gentle one, the rags
That once were tender flesh.
I have worn them out and torn them up.
All I have left is a air of wings.
Clothe me in your magnificence,
Have mercy, give me salvation.
As for those wretched, rotting rags,
Take them into the vestry.

           13 May 1918

* * *

I've slit my veins: unstanchable,
Irredeemable, the life gushes forth.
Put down bowls and plates!
Every plate will be too small,
Every bowl too flat.
              Over the brim and beyond
Into the black earth, to feed the rushes.
Irrevocable, unstanchable,
Irredeemable, the poetry gushes forth.

           6 January 1934

Marina Tsvetayeva

To Akhmatova

1

O muse of lamentation, fairest of muses!
O mischievous offspring of the white night!
You send a blizzard down on the land of Russia,
And your wails pierce our flesh like arrows.

We avoid them, and a muffled
Millennial oh! swears fealty to you, Anna
Akhmatova! That name is an enormous sigh
Falling into nameless depths.

We have been crowned because you and I
Both tread the same earth, and the same sky is above us!
Anyone stricken by your fatal destiny,
Lies down, already immortal, on the deathbed.

Now in my singing city the cupolas blaze,
And the blind vagrant glorifies the Saviour...
And I bestow on you my city of bells,
Akhmatova!, and my own heart as bounty.

                19 June 1916

2

I stand here, clutching my head.
Oh, these human intrigues!
Clutching my head, I sing
In the late dawn.

Oh, a tumultuous wave
Has lifted me on to its crest!
I sing of you, our one and only,
Even as the moon in the sky!

Marina Tsvetayeva

That, soaring on a raven's heart,
You pierced the clouds.
Hook-nosed one, whose wrath is fatal,
Whose mercy is fatal too.

That above my crimson Kremlin
I also spread out my night.
That my throat is constricted
By singing languor, as by a leather strap.

Oh, I am happy! Never did the dawn
Burn with a purer flame.
Oh, I am happy that, proffering you as a gift,
I go away, a beggar.

That you, the one whose voice —- O depth! O gloom! —-
Has made me hold my breath,
I was the first to call
the Muse of Tsarksoye Selo.

          22 June 1916

Translated by Alex Miller

POETIC PORTRAIT series
Volume One: MARINA TSVETAYEVA
For the centenary of her birth
Compiled and with an introduction by Olga Revzina
Glas Publishers, 1992, Moscow
The following volumes are currently being compiled:
EVGENY BARATYNSKY, ZINAIDA GIPPIUS,
IGOR SEVERYANIN,
NIKOLAI GUMILYOV, AFANASY FET,
LEONID LATYNIN

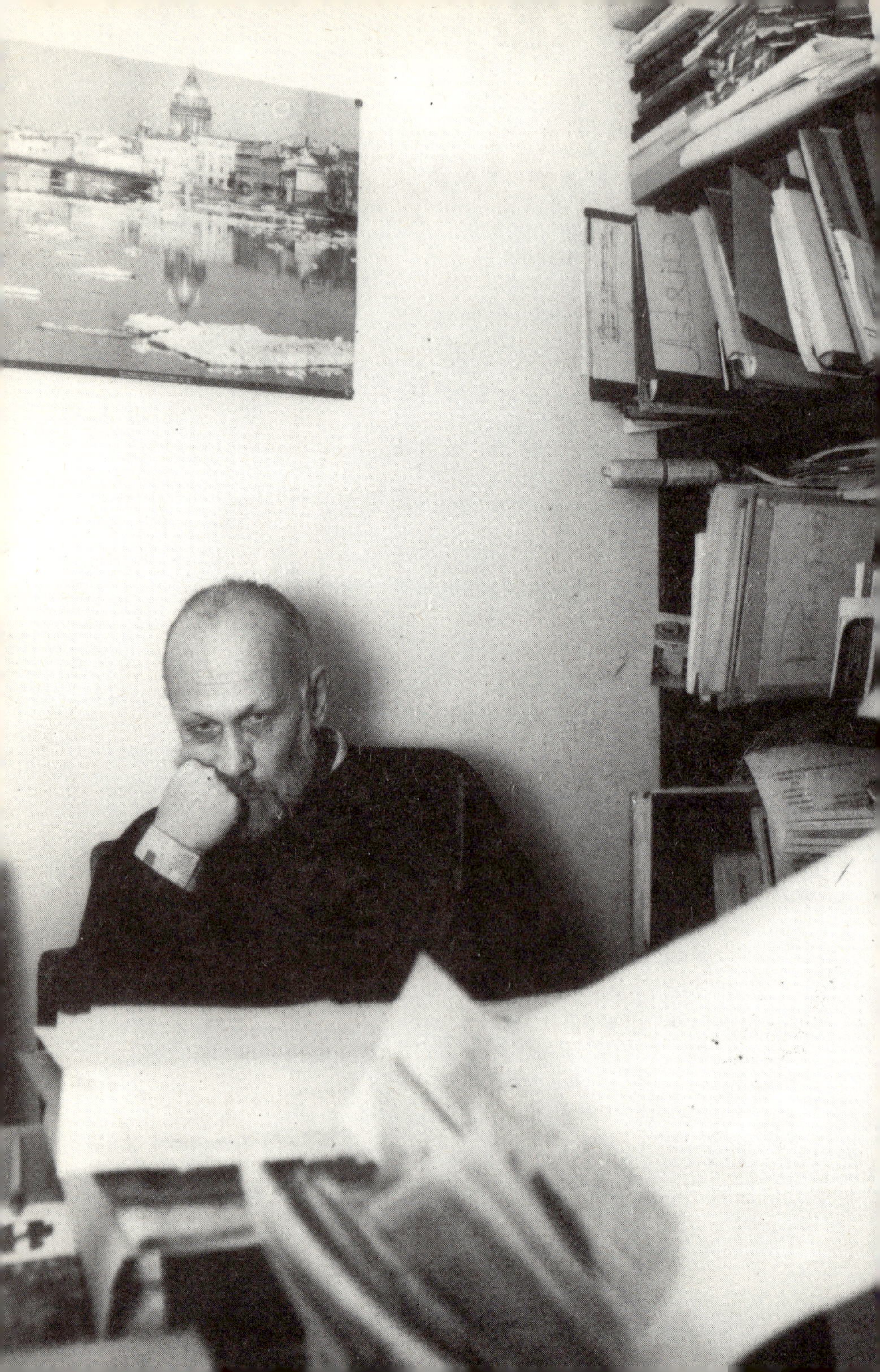

Gleb Arsenyev

The Soul

The soul
dreams the dark pleasures
of indulgent beads
the desired drizzle
an eye of bewilderment
and clement whispers
on both sides
the path is clear.
   *

Fluttering in the dark
a time will come for the soul
when the faces on icons
cooler and darker
when God has forgiven you
and words submit miraculously
to their parchment simplicity.
   *

I awake
but inside me
heavier than cement or salt
sadness and fatigue
ahead lies Anansi's spidery day
but I want to hide in the corner
not run anyone's errands
not be the glue between anyone's rib beams

I remind myself
it's a trifling sin
but in answer comes Origen's
"sin exists where there is plurality"

Hearing this phrase that emanates from no eternal abyss
I smothered it.

Gleb Arsenyev

*

I live on alms
beside the honeysuckle
of dusty voices
praying mutely
for shelter
a choir-voice
swollen
with the spittle of a raspy wheeze
I welcome this most esteemed clamor

the one to whom Xantippe speaks
has played the fool once more.

*

It's the dread of fear
pain in expectation of pain
whispers bounding
in a chosen silence
it's possible joy
outline of a smile
the sticky evidence
and "Save us, Lord" of spring
it's a lunatic sensitivity
to the despondency of grief
fingers wormwood bitter
from a blinding miracle
it's silent rockfalls
landsliding steps
it's pockmarks warmed
where fire doesn't blaze.

*

As if from a wash house
scrubbed in the seven seas
wrung out and dried
starched and ironed.
obtrusive honor
free will

the clean washed souls
will lick off the dirt and sweat.

The Runway

He's ready to jump
ready to leap
over there
where the white owl of the wind
plays with the rind of seconds.
*

A bolt of seething darkness
sent the sun's ball flying
into our galactic province
cooling the torrid gloom
twenty prosperous joys
are still running along the creaking
starry floorboards.
*

From the upper world
milk and honey
from the lower
blood and tears
slowly and surely
happily and gravely

Where's the channel?
we'll pour out the river
and lower the raft
just let the body of our shadow
fall from the white cliff.
*

From under the cloudy slope
three sobbing sobs
fell to the ground
for Thomas
seeds of tears

Gleb Arsenyev

facets in the rifle-sight
a torch of murmuring signet rings
heady drunks
sobbing.

   *

Like a ball
the circular wind
a snow storm
and some darkness
choked on a cry
and the evening hour
unrecognized till now
in us
there had never been a trace

   *

February
in the ranks of months
you stand last
as in days of yore
please return to us
the feast of purification
fetters of tears
for those departed to eternity's home
bitter waters
and unsweet earth
in your unredeemed name
we play hide and seek.

   *

Wind and lilac in the window
swooning candles in the house
the black, coarse cloth of night
spreads lushly

it's time to sleep
until white-winged morn
time to sleep
on sweet dreams

of goose down
and cocks' crow

it's difficult
for somnolent dawn
to sweep away the bruise of moon
with a brush of clouds.

*

The mourner
in dark violet
with white trim
warms herself on the paling
swaying cautiously
her wing-fan dulls
the caraway scented cool
the music offers no forgiveness
no bollard
knight music

*

That way, toward the blissfully smiling one
march doomed yaks and dreams
the dancing water is there
the singing apples

*

Separably inseparably
United unfusable
the frosty week
a snowfall sieve
fate and the visitor are invisible
the peeling of promises goes unheard
the river freezes and the voice
the twilight both are beggared
the nettle of battling hours stings
the orange hooves
of white horses
cleave the hammered toll.

Gleb Arsenyev

*

Unflowing
but honey it will be
words not fruitless
the dizzying flight will slow

The sweet night
has spread
its snowflakes
one in each pocket
but the fan
of sticky hexahedrons

believing
in the garden
where he himself
a rare and random waving
in exchange for morning
diminished the caterpillar
whiter than any grinding
water and millstone
betrothed in frost.

*

Reading
you begin to laugh
the price of sugar has dropped
wreathed sweetly in envy
in tarred envy
on bonfires of despair
on currant spikes
dogrose and blackthorn
dear God
toss me a life-preserver
against the wingfall.

*

You're closer
than the sleepy artery on you neck
a scent of freshly quarried risk

in the mouths' open trenches
closer than the seething minutes
your eyes whiter than rice
when the adam's apple of fire
pulverizes the trachea's ammunition belt.

   *

In the subway station it's cold as marble
the whirring trains are chilly
the subway sucks a minty lozenge
amusing itself with the pneumatic's
futile game

the jaws of the tunnel are tender

like a five copeck Kon Tiki
on Easter Island.

A Vision

O visitor of supreme kindness
twilight's cupped hand is shallow
its shadow takes leave
of a somnolent double
a river of ashes bills and coos
there's an eyeball of coal in the oven
the gaze of ashen adolescents
is clearly visible to me
fiery vineyard
please don't splash

   *

On soot-black iron
a face streaked yellow with fatigue
takes pity
beyond our backs
the coming eons
are entrusted to us

these sloping realms
sliding from the dish
like the head of Olofern.

*

The shadow's taste
and its smell
the ribbed brocade of music
and green grass
the sun's iodine
the sweet newborn
a spadix of dust
and the soul's rain
glissando at the source
my crossroads
the seven paths of the serpent
crawling toward death
beyond the wicker gate of the Garden of Eden.

*

I am warmed by the grace
of children's smiles
sweeter than the dream
of my own grace
in it even death is beautiful.

*

> ...when I die, I'll be happy.
> E. Baratynsky

Dreadful
the whiteness of paper
the brain's cloak rots
chronic are the sores
someone else's old rags
will keep me warm
this uneternal evening.

*

You're right Petronius
the body of speech is bone dry
it's sickly and prickly

on the stubble of illness
the lucid act
is no cure
only the mice of thought
swarm nimbly
and perhaps it's not asking too much
to become less and flatter than a point
blackening like the grains of a poppy
silently sharpened.

Why Stars Fall

This eternal gift
pattern of a game played by those
whose even yields to odd
whose shadow is cleaved by the sword.

My Dog

He approaches
lays his head on my lap and breathes
sniffing from his oval dog's world
at my silent conversation with hidden friends
he whines but I can't explain
that tears are winged prayers
that I am drunk on foreboding and the God of Catullus
that like water I am filled to the brim
of Einstein's cylindrical world.

Translated by Thomas Epstein

Reprinted by permission of the author from *Literary Review*, international journal of contemporary writing, Spring 1991, Fairleigh Dickinson University

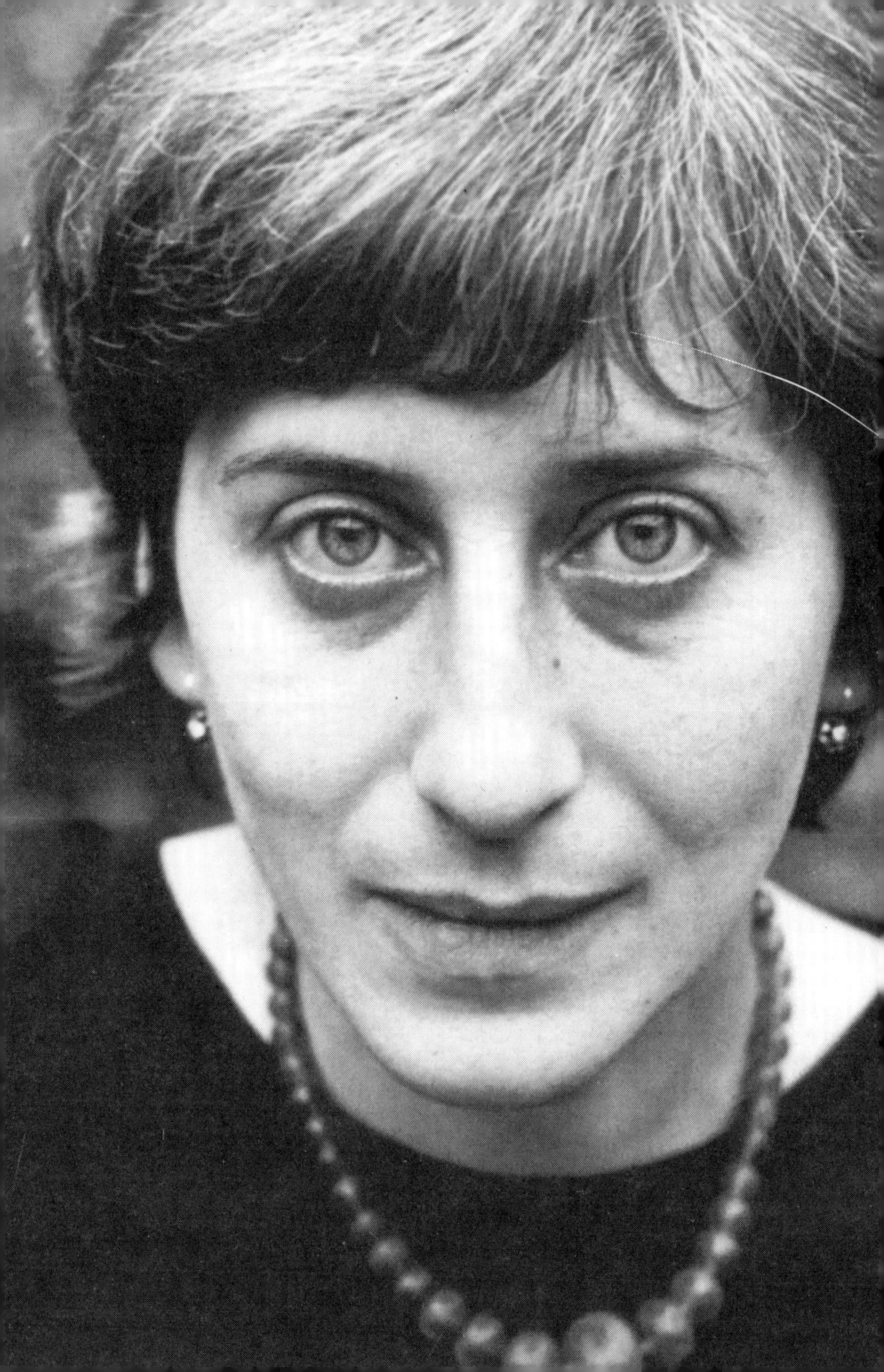

Olga Sedakova

1
A great thing is a refuge for herself.
a broad deep pond or Trappist's far-off cell,
a mythic fish that swims the hidden depths,
a righteous man, reading his Book of Hours
concerning the day that has no evening;
a vessel holding her own beauty in.

2
And as the ocean swims inside a shell —
a valve in the heart of time, a trap as well,
walking on velvet paws, a marvel in a bag,
a treasure hidden in a sleeping draught,
so in my mind, inside this creaking house,
she goes, and holds her magic lantern up...

3
But tell me, don't you think the verse above
is crammed too full? All right, it's well enough
for one who feels the pull, outside his dreams,
of images aslant with silvery gleams,
carrying us on pointed fins to where
we and all we have known are dust, no more.

4
The light (for let me note in brackets this)
is something we could call a mystery,
speaking at will of God knows what,
whilst speech, like a sunbeam's dancing motes,
spins slowly as the eddied fragments spin,
but means — the transparency of things.

5
A great thing is a refuge for herself,
a place where beasts can leap and the birds peck
music for food. But panting on the heels

of day comes night. And he who sees it fall
puts down his work, soon as the stars appear
with their magnetic pull, and ready tears.

6
It's odd how old one's eyes have got!
for they see only what they can't,
and nothing else. Even so from one's hands,
sometimes, a cup may fall. My friends!
what we have kept, like life, will slide away,
and a star we cannot know rise in the sky.

7
Poems, it seems to me, are grown for all,
as Serbian nut-trees grow along the walls
of monasteries, that keep a scoop of honey,
a well, with stars floating like ice in springtime,
so for a moment someone in the world
sees fragile life, like the spring stars that whirl:

8
— O, that is all: I knew that I was doomed,
and that my reason cried for lack of food;
trapped like a mouse in chilly vaults, it pined;
I knew no-one felt pity for a friend, —
all is in flight, and all is drunk on joy,
for "things must pass", as Horace used to say...

9
Why hurry, life, why chivvy on the hour?
You'll soon have time to sew my mouth right up,
stitching with iron threads. So humour me,
deign, then, to give my *sententia* a try:
"A great thing is a refuge for herself":
she sings when singing us to rest.

10
— they say, most beautifully. Now
at noontide, beauty's night-time door

Olga Sedakova

is open wide, and high up in the hills
the constellatory fire, both monk and angel,
reads by the light of its own candle-ends
the exemplary lives of guilty men.

11
A great thing is a loss to end all loss:
a glimpse of Mediolanian paradise;
its hearing is attuned; on the tuned string
fear strums away; dust is an animate thing,
and like a flame-tugged butterfly, it cries,
"I will not be the thing that I will be!"

12
The future rolls into the spacious house,
the secret cistern, forcing its way at last...

Translated by Catriona Kelley
from: *Anthology of Russian Women Writing. 1777-1992.* Oxford University Press, 1993.

EARTH

When in the East the nocturnal deep breaks into flames,
the Earth begins to gleam, as it returns

the abundance of the gentle light, freely given,
                        now no longer needed,
To things that answer to all things — to them there is no answer.

And who can answer that in this our vale of tears —
can simple greatness of heart? The greatness of fields,

which against no raid, and not against the plough
would ever dream of mounting a defence; one after one

they all — who rob that Earth, who trample her, who plunge
their ploughshares deep into her heart —
                      like dream upon dream they vanish

far, far away, in the sea, where all things look alike, like birds.
And Earth, not looking, sees and says: "May God forgive him!"

to them as they leave.
Thus, I recall, the cloistress in the Sacred Caves
bands to all pilgrims a candle as they go down to the Elders,

as for a tiny child as it sets off to that awesome place
where God's glory reigns — and woe to him whose life
                                    gives him no joy! —

where one can hear the heavens breathe, and fathom
                                    why they breathe...
"May God save you!" she says as they leave,
                            but they do not hear her.

Perhaps, going down on your knees is dying after all?
And I, who will be earth, gaze at the Earth, amazed:

purity that's purer than the first purity!
                      From the realm of bitterness
I ask about the reasons for protection and forgiveness.

I ask: "Are you, insane one, really content
to swallow insults and share out rewards for time without end?

Why are they dear to you, how did they find favour with you?"

"They did, because I am", she says. "Because all of us have been."

Translated by Peter Henry

THE FIGURE OF A WOMAN

                        Having turned away,
She stands in a large
            and voluminous shawl. It seems there's a poplar
next to her. It seems that way. There's no poplar.
But she would be willing to turn into one
Just like in the legend —

If only not to hear:
- What do you see there?
- What do I see, you lunatic people?
I see the wide open sea — That's easy to guess...
The sea and that's all.
                Or is that too little,
for me to eternally grieve, while your curiosity's piqued?

MISTRESS AND SERVANT

A woman looks into a mirror: what she sees can't be seen;
It's unlikely that anything's there.
                On the other hand, why then is she
admiring one thing and figuring out how to fix something else
with one trick or another? why study herself?
It's clear something's there. Something that needs
                        an affectionate balm,
pendants and beads.
                The servant stands silent
awaiting a wish that she'll never fulfill.
Yes, we never understood each other. That's understandable.
It wasn't hard. Something else was harder. We knew
all about everyone. All, to the end, to its
final and tender infinity.
Not wishing, not thinking — we knew.
Not listening — knew
and considered their wish in our minds, the wish that they
never had time to make known or to think about even. Of course.
For we've all got but one single wish. And there's nothing besides
that wish.

Translated by Andrew Wachtel

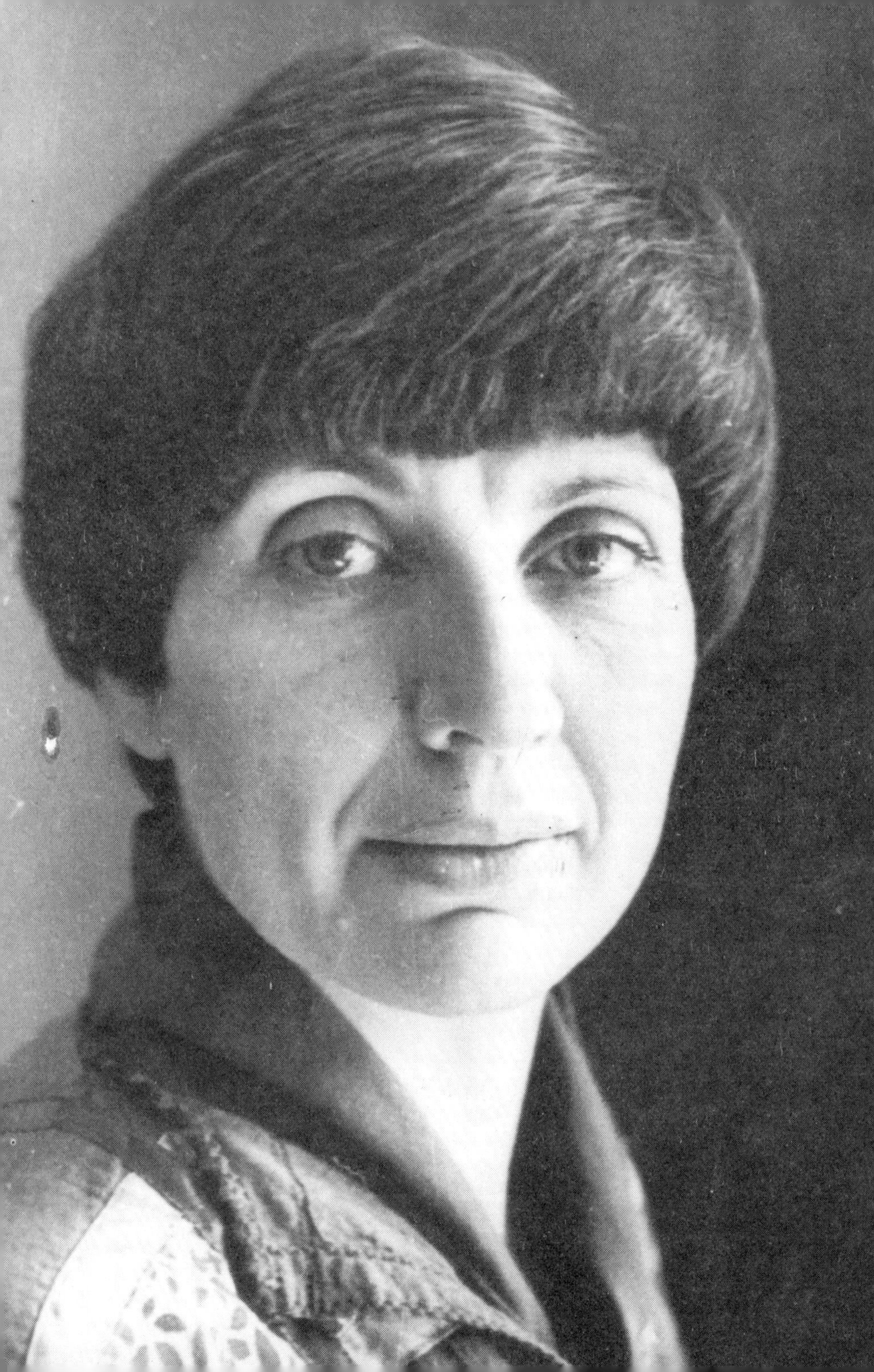

Alla LATYNINA

LITERARY PRIZE AND LITERARY PROCESS

The Booker Russian Novel prize has been set up to reward contemporary Russian authors, to stimulate wider knowledge of modern Russian fiction in the Western world, to encourage translations and to increase sales of the books.

The Prize is worth 10,000 sterling and is awarded annually. It is sponsored by Booker plc and Tetra Pak International SA. It is administered by Booker in the UK and by the British Council in Russia.

The Prize Management Committee is appointed by Booker and is responsible for the appointment of judges (including a chairman) every year, for the appointment of nominators, for the rules of the prize and for the arrangements for the presentation ceremony in liaison with the British Council.

Sir Michael Caine, chairman of Booker plc, is chairman of the Management Committee. Alla Latynina was Chairman of the Russian Booker Prize jury in its first year.

Q. Now that the winner has been announced and the heated debate in the press has subsided, do you think that the Prize was a success? Have you changed your mind about the current literary scene after reading some fifty novels?

A. Without any doubt the Russian Booker Prize eventually did succeed. In the beginning there was little public attention — it was all so new to us. But the announcement of the short list was a turning point. In my view, the success of the prize is clear evidence that there is a need for a nongovernment independent literary prize.

According to critic Andrei Nemzer, who first attacked the jury for not disclosing the whole list of nominations, the short list faithfully reflected the current literary scene in Russia.

Q. At the press conference on October 27, you announced the short list in alphabetical order without disclosing the preferences of the jury members. Can you tell us now who voted for whom? What considerations guided you in your choice?

A. We were mainly guided by considerations of the literary merits of the works nominated, although the author's image also mattered. Makanin's *Manhole* and Petrushevskaya's *The Time: Night* are not fully-fledged novels. They are short novels or novellas. But the jury decided that without these two authors any picture of contemporary Russian writing would not be complete.

Q. Many believed that Makanin and Petrushevskaya were the most likely candidates for the prize.

A. Makanin and Petrushevskaya were the most famous names on the short list. Their literary careers are very different. Makanin developed as an author during the 1970s and early 1980s — the period of "stagnation", as it is known today. It was the time of particularly acute conflict between the politicised "men of the '60s" and the Soviet regime: Voinovich, Aksyonov, Maximov, Vladimov and many others were forced to emigrate to escape persecution.

They claimed that in the Soviet Union a writer has either to lie or come into conflict with the authorities. Indeed, the literature of that time rejected non-conformists, with a few fortunate exceptions: Trifonov, Bitov, Anatoly Kim, to name a few. Vladimir Makanin found an ecological niche for himself — he depicted the joyless existence of intellectuals, stuffed full with the wrong kind of education under Brezhnev. That same Soviet semi-intelligentsia devoured his books which looked at problems they knew only too well. In the initial years of perestroika Makanin fell silent, waiting for the avalanche of politicised anti-Stalinist prose to die down, and then he published two short novels which were unlike those he had been writing before. *Manhole* is a blend of anti-utopia and the grotesque. Many critics agree that its scenes of a Moscow ravaged by civil war are nothing new, whereas the central metaphor of the Manhole appears to them highly significant.

The protagonist of *Manhole*, Klyucharev, who has appeared earlier in Makanin's other stories*, penetrates an underground city of plenty through a narrow manhole. What makes him invariably return to the devastated Moscow above ground?

Q. Is this a metaphor for the old argument carried on between the two sections of Russian intelligentsia — the emigres and those back home?

A. This is the most obvious interpretation. Makanin's novel is certainly a contribution to the ongoing argument about the role of the emigre. Indirectly it gives an answer to the question — what makes most of us stay in our impoverished homeland. But the metaphor of the manhole is much broader than that, embracing as it does the relationship between desire and duty, freedom and responsibility. But I do not find in *Manhole* the rich substance and wealth of visual detail of his early stories. The jury agreed unanimously that Makanin is a major writer and should be on the short list but only three considered *Manhole* worthy of the prize. According to the rules it is the novel and not the author that receives the prize.

On the other hand, Petrushevskaya's *The Time: Night* is her greatest achievement so far, apart from the plays which I like better than her stories. Petrushevskaya's legend of a writer cruelly suppressed under Brezhnev worked in her favour. True, the kind of suppression she sustained was relatively mild compared to what the dissidents had to go through. During the 1980s Petrushevskaya won huge underground fame and became an idol of the

---

* See GLAS №4, "Klyucharev and Alimushkin"

non-conformist intelligentsia. Her grim plays and stories are condensed portrayals of everyday Soviet horrors, creating a halo of a martyr around her name. In recent years this halo has been fading visibly as more and more critics observed that "the hellish nightmares and anguish she depicts are probably nothing more than a tried and tested literary device."

The Russian public shows some sign of tiring of endless pictures of the seamy side of life. Three or four years ago it was considered very brave to speak of people as dirty beasts — it was a rebellion against official Soviet ideology which proclaimed that under socialism "all people are comrades and brothers". With the downfall of this ideology finding fault with human nature is no longer an act of courage but rather a nuisance. It takes more courage nowadays to bring out the best in people.

When the short list was discussed Petrushevskaya had the full support of the jury but when it came to choosing the winner only Ellendea Proffer (Ardis Publishers USA) nominated her for first place. Still from all the finalists Petrushevskaya was closest to victory.

Q. Many people considered Gorenstein's *No Place* the most significant work on the short list.

A. In my view, his other novel, *The Psalm*, is really his magnum opus. *No Place* is a monumental novel and one which follows the tradition of the philosophical-political novel. It brings to mind Dostoyevsky. In fact many critics commented on the similarity of Gorenstein's hero to Dostoyevsky's "underground man". Even the collisions of the plot in *No Place* were borrowed from Dostoyevsky's *The Devils*. *No Place* is perhaps what Dostoyevsky would have written today, at this very different stage of political devilry. All the jury members included this novel in the short list but no one suggested him as the winner.

Q. What about Ivanchenko? Did he have any chance of wining?

A. Ivanchenko is an interesting writer, a young author with great creative potential. In his novel *Monogramme* he makes an interesting attempt to unite a portrayal of the nightmarish Soviet history with the heroine's Buddhist meditations. I am afraid he hasn't quite succeeded in blending the two. The novel is uneven. Its historical scenes are vivid and read well while the musings on various passages from Buddhist texts are not always logical. Most of the jury singled out his novel for the short list but he had little chance of winning the prize.

Q. Was Sorokin* included in the short list to demonstrate the jury's broadmindedness?

A. Yes. I am not one of his fans. I resent being dragged through shit, and I don't think that descriptions of an absurdist ritual of eating pus and amputated genitals is the right way to shock a reader into art appreciation. I am convinced that there is a limit to ugliness and horror beyond which the writer's imagination should not take the reader. Literature of the ugly does not assimilate new areas, as some people think, but is a blind alley for culture. Perhaps Sorokin aimed precisely to chart the limits of this blind alley.

Q. Why then was he included in the short list?

A. Most of the jury insisted that there should be an avant-garde novel in the short list. I never nominated this novel, but neither did I object to it. It certainly marks an important stage in the development of Russian literature. In all fairness one should admit that Sorokin has an outstanding gift for literary portrayal.

Q. As they speculated about the winner, the press made almost no mention of Kharitonov. Their preferences were divided between Petrushevskaya and Makanin. A few minutes before the winner was announced a TV news programme said it was going to be Petrushevskaya. What happened?

A. I am glad nothing leaked out — all the jury members observed the rules of the game. Not that it was classified information, but rules are made to be observed, especially in the case of the Booker Prize with its strong element of sportsmanship.

I am not surprised they could not figure out the winner. Most critics are mesmerised by names. Makanin and Petrushevskaya, as well as Gorenstein are very well known, while Kharitonov isn't. One business newspaper ran the headline the next day: "Obscure Author Wins World Fame". *Lines of Fate* is a complex and sophisticated novel, somewhat heavy reading for the layman, perhaps more interesting for a literary scholar than the general reader. In fact, none of the short-listed works address the general reader. That is, if by the general reader we understand the reader of cheap thrillers and whodunnits. But for the serious reader Kharitonov is no less accessible than Gorenstein or Makanin. In Russia huge printings of Akhmatova, Pasternak, Mandelstam and Platonov sell out in a matter of days, and the "general reader" hunts for Kafka and Herman Hesse. The Russian "general reader" will certainly have no trouble understanding Kharitonov's post-modernist prose and will not be perplexed with the novel's unusual structure, where the action develops not from event to event but from commentary to commentary. The author takes his reader on an exciting literary journey to reconstruct the life of a forgotten Russian author and philosopher from his notes scribbled on sweet wrappings. Kharitonov's novel is intellectual but not elitist. I see Kharitonov's victory as symbolic because it is probably the first time that a writer is judged on the strength of his literary merit alone, that an award is given to a completely apolitical work.

Q. Do you think that in the case of Makanin and Petrushevskaya there were other considerations apart from the purely literary?

A. Obviously. There is such a thing as reputation. Makanin made a name

---

* See GLAS №2, "A Business Proposition" and "Four Stout Hearts" for himself under Brezhnev and maintained it during perestroika In one way or another he succeeded in adapting to the conditions of censorship under Brezhnev. The dissidents were unable to adapt to such conditions and were persecuted. Under perestroika all forms of opposition to the Soviet regime were rewarded, from the political opposition of Solzhenitsin to the artistic opposition of Petrushevskaya.

Only one type of literary behaviour — the most natural and normal — has not been rewarded. Kharitonov belongs to the latter category. In 1974 he published a phantasmagoric novel about Gogol, *A Day in February*, and then for 20 years he was unable to publish anything making his living by translating from the German. He has not been a dissident but his writing deviates from the mainstream. He has many admirers but no name in the literary world. As a result, in the highly politicised atmosphere of perestroika, there was no demand for his refined apolitical work. For me Kharitonov is evidence of the existence of a rich and largely unexplored culture of the Brezhnev era — times in which a huge part of the cultural iceberg remained concealed from public eyes. Most of this iceberg remains frozen to this day. I am convinced that we have in store a number of highly interesting literary discoveries. Their authors failed to adapt to the Procrustean bed of official art under Brezhnev, but they never joined the dissident s — thus today there is no reason why the reader should be interested in them. The wave of fashion has rolled over them. Now that the Booker prize has lifted Kharitonov from obscurity, I hope more hitherto unknown names will be revealed to us.

Q. How exactly has the Booker Prize benefitted literature?

A. It has brought excitement into our drab literary life: for a whole month critics talked about nothing else. Any attention to contemporary literature is beneficial. But no matter how useful prizes are they can't save literature.

Q. What can?

A. Publishing initiative, selfless effort to carry on the literary tradition by publishing good non-profit books. Naturally, such publishers need support.

Apart from the main Booker prize, another anonymous prize was awarded to a publishing venture. It was shared by two small literary journals: *Solo* (Moscow) and *New Literature* almanac (St. Petersburg). These two journals specialize in contemporary literature, modern trends and experimental writing. As non-profit publishing ventures they have found themselves in a difficult financial situation after January 1992, when prices skyrocketed. Most publishers were stuck with camera-ready copy of books which they could no longer afford to produce. New Russian writing is certainly in need of special funding with a board of experts deciding which books to support. That would also be a kind of prize — a prize for a manuscript that will enable it to become a book. But at the moment it is hard to find the money in our devastated country. Non-profit publishing brings little benefit for the donor. At the same time if this situation — in which such books have no chance of publication — continues for much longer, literature will sustain irreparable damage.

Q. Many people believe that today's literature suffers from a lack of interest on the part of readers. The Russian public is no longer as literature-oriented as it used to be. Contemporary writers themselves are wary of the current role of literature in the modern world.

A. We are indeed witnessing a cultural crisis — not just in Russia but in other countries as well. This is not the first time that literature has proclaimed its own end. Zola and the Naturalists believed that literature would be dissolved in sociology, while the Russian futurists insisted that it would be replaced by hard facts. None of these predictions came true. Despite the somewhat faded interest in literature today it remains a significant part of our life and is likely to remain a major factor for many years to come. Here and there new talents continue to spring up. Literary continuity hasn't been interrupted. Any kind of support for nonprofit publishing ventures will contribute to future literary development.

The Editors of *Solo* and *New Literature* almanac express their deepest gratitude to the anonymous prize-giver. The prize will enable them to issue several more issues of their journals, which have been in camera-ready state for some time.

Solo: Alexander Mikhailov, Zufar Gareyev, Vladimir Zuev

New Literature: Mikhail Berg, Mikhail Sheinker

About the Authors

VICTOR PELEVIN (b. 1962) is one of the most acclaimed young writers of his generation. A graduate of a technical college, he has never had any difficulty in publishing his stories in periodicals. His first collection of stories appeared from Text Publishers in 1992 and sold out in a matter of days. Two further short novels are scheduled for publication this year. "He has a God-given talent for writing", says *Novoe Russkoe Slovo* (New York) about Pelevin.

"Few people, like Pelevin, are capable of creating wonderful new worlds. He is a true creator. These are fantastic worlds of dreams, talking sheds, philosophizing chickens, computer games, Soviet werewolves, drug addicts. He possesses enormous erudition which includes knowledge of Chinese philosophy, information science, mysticism, metaphysics, and much else. One can sense his pain and compassion for his unfortunate dislocated homeland." (From the introduction to Pelevin's book *The Blue Lantern*).

"If you see a glimmer of light in the darkness you must follow the light rather than wonder if it is going to take you anywhere," Pelevin writes in one of his stories. This simple idea reflects the tenor and sums up the message of his work.

The contemporary young generation has seen a cynical social situation crumble before their very eyes. They had no time to assimilate communist ideology or to work out their own counter ideology. Many have thus become disillusioned and uncaring. As a true artist Pelevin reflects the dominant moods of the times. His inimitable sense of humor enables him to bid farewell to Russia's communistic past with a final laugh. In this sense his manner can be called "satirical-philosophical fantasy."

All of Pelevin's stories and novels have fast-moving plots and a fluid, slightly narcotic quality. They embrace the reader right from the start and gently carry him towards an ending which is always unexpected and even dumbfounding. His best novel so far is *Omon Ra*, first published in *Znamya* Magazine and currently being translated into English. His work appears in English for the first time here.

ZUFAR GAREYEV. Born in 1955 in Bashkiria, Gareyev spent his childhood in a small provincial town. He worked at a timber factory before being drafted into the army. After national service he lived in Siberia for a few years working at an oil refinery and writing for local periodicals. In 1980, he enrolled in the Literary Institute in Moscow. Upon graduation he married and has settled in Moscow.

His stories have been published in the most prestigious literary monthlies, such as *Novy Mir*, *Volga*, *Solo*, *Golden Age* earning high acclaim from critics and readers alike. In his later works *Park*, *Multiprose* and *The Allergy of Alexander Petrovich*. (Stil Publ. 1992) — he has progressed further, combining elements of the grotesque and phantasmagoric with vividly depicted scenes from everyday life.

About the Authors

Together with Andrei Bitov and Evgeny Popov, Gareyev is currently working on the editorial board of *Solo*, a magazine of experimental writing.

Gareyev describes his manner as "game prose" — involving the reader in a round dance of Boschian characters, each slightly larger than life yet retaining veracity. Evgeny Popov has described him as "a brilliant stylist somewhat reminiscent of Kafka".

With his fertile imagination and outstanding literary talent Gareyev's stories are of a kind, that Gogol and Zoschenko might be writing if they were alive today. Their mood is that of a man trying to keep his balance on a breaking icefloe.

Gareyev is both delighted and disgusted with life, and optimism and despair rub shoulders in his stories. They feature common people struggling with everyday problems in an attempt to survive as best they can — a traditional theme for Russian literature.

He has been recognised as one of the most interesting and promising writers in Russia today. A German translation of his *Multiprose* is currently being prepared by Pipes Publishers. His story "When Other Birds Call" appeared in English in *Glas*, №1, 1991.

YEVGENY KHARITONOV. Born in 1941 in Novosibirsk, Yevgeny Kharitonov came to Moscow for the first time in the late 1950s to study at the Filmmakers' Institute. After graduation he taught acting and pantomime, defending his dissertation on the role of pantomime in teaching filmacting in 1972. Later he opened his own pantomime studio (remembered today especially for his production of the play "The Enchanted Island", staged with deaf-mute actors).

While this outward life was both successful and important, his real life existed on another, more hidden level. As he wrote in the preface to *Catalogue*, an almanac similar to the better-known *MetrOpol* which collected many of the same writers: "It does not matter what our qualifications say we are — we write and this is our life..."

Not a single line of his work was published during his lifetime, partly because of Kharitonov's subject matter — homosexuality, which to this day remains criminalized in Russia. Previously circulated in samizdat, it was preserved by his friends, miraculously surviving KGB searches of the late 1970s and early 1980s. He died in 1981.

Kharitonov worked in practically all literary genres, and even created his own. He gave a new image to the traditional Russian novel, story, poem and play and was the first Russian writer to use the stream of consciousness technique in the formless pieces of text stylized as diaries of which "Teardrops on the Flowers" is an example. His literary works are complex in form, style, language, and especially plot.

Their unifying subject is love. Uncommon, rare, different love — just as Kharitonov himself was a very different and exotic "flower". He never fitted easily into dissident culture either, despite the important and guiding role he played for many of his contemporaries.

In his own time, few were able to evaluate his work without prejudice — only those friends and intellectuals who did not shrink from the idea of homosexuality in Russian

About the Authors

literature. In most cases he and his works received the same treatment as homosexuality in Russia in general - at best regarded with irony, more often with hypocritical rejection.

He was Russia's first homosexual writer since Kuzmin and Dobychin — and the gap of more than 50 years between them meant that he developed a specific vocabulary not available to his predecessors. "He is the first writer to cover an openly homosexual subject matter," as Dmitry Prigov has noted.

But his importance goes beyond such narrow boundaries. The life of the homosexual in his work echoes the world of Dostoyevsky's *The Insulted and the Injured*, Gogol's "little man", and the other "marginal characters" of Russian literature.

Whether Kharitonov represents a special, unconventional and new aesthetics and subculture is an open question: quite possibly, he was one of its inventors. His work and personality stand above that "suffocated, rotten generation, which for two decades had trampled its own soul" in which he lived and died.

Kharitonov's work will be published in Russian this year by Moscow's Glagol Publishing House, edited by the author of this note Yaroslav Mogutin. As well as Kharitonov's own works, it will include critical and biographical pieces from many of his admirers, including Dmitri Prigov, Yevgeny Popov, Mikhail Aizenberg, Victor Yerofeev, Roman Viktyuk and Nina Sadur.

VLADIMIR MAKANIN was born in the Urals in 1937 and graduated in applied mathematics from Moscow University. Too late to be counted as a writer of the sixties, he is highly individual and obstinately refuses to be identified with any grouping. His first novel was published in 1965 but he became widely known with the publication in 1982 of his novella about a faith healer, *The Forebear*. His other works, many of which have been outstandingly successful in translation in Germany, France and elsewhere, include *Voices* (1977), *Antileader* (1980), *Blue and Red* (1981), *The Laggard* (1984). *Klyucharev and Alimushkin* is one of his stories of the mid-1970s which early heralded an entirely new climate in Russian literature preceding the collapse of the bogus official faith in a radiant future. Later he used the same protagonist in his other stories, including *Manhole*, which has been shortlisted for the Russian Booker Prise last year. He was described by Alla Marchenko as "a writer who digs out the truth from apparently unpromising soil."

FRIEDRICH GORENSTEIN was born in 1932 in Kiev, in the family of a professor of economics. In 1935 his father was arrested; he died later in one of the GULAG camps. Fearing arrest, his mother took Friedrich away to the provinces; she was imprisoned anyway. Friedrich lived in an orphanage for a while. Then he was taken in by relatives. He went to school in Berdichev. After school he worked in a coal-mine. He graduated from the Mining Institute in Krivoi Rog, and worked as a foreman on a construction site. In 1962, having already written *The House with the Turret*, he went

About the Authors

to Moscow to enrol as a student of scriptwriting. He and Andrei Tarkovsky tried to "force through" a film of *The House with the Turret*. They were stopped. He had nowhere to write. He wrote in the Nekrasov Library. The story "Winter '53" (about the lives of miners) was considered for a long time by *Novy Mir*. They rejected it. One liberal member of the editorial board remarked indignantly that the labour of free men was depicted as worse than a concentration camp. Certain kind and intelligent people once suggested to Gorenstein that he should take a pseudonym; they explained it would help get his work published. He thought about the idea and rejected it.

He became famous as the scriptwriter for the films "Solaris" and "Slave of Love". He has written 17 filmscripts in all.

He has written a lot. Several large novels: *Atonement* (1967), *Psalm* (1975), *No Place* (1976), *Fellow-Travellers* (1983). Three plays: "Discussing Dostoevsky" (1973), "Berdychev" (1976), "Childkiller" (1985). All three plays are in production in Moscow theatres.

"After the *Metropole* affair blew up, Gorenstein emigrated to West Berlin. Despairing of ever making it in his homeland of the USSR, Gorenstein became just one more of the countless victims of the "cultural" policy which impoverished Russian culture so triumphantly. It might seem that, not being a dissident, Gorenstein, an undisputed master of realist prose who learnt his trade from Bunin, could quite easily have found a place for himself in Soviet literature if he had wished. But he did not choose to find that place, remaining faithful to his existential themes, the tormented lives of his heroes, his intense religious preoccupations, and his own unpredictable personality. I remember him from Moscow: he had a Buninesquely wicked, but not malicious, sense of humour, he was simultaneously frivolous and intense, he was insanely egocentric and yet selflessly devoted to his ginger cat Christina, he took a sarcastic view of everything." — Victor Erofeev.

ZINOVY ZINIK was born in 1945 in Moscow and emigrated from the Soviet Union thirty years later. He became a British citizen in 1988, and has worked for some years as the producer and presenter of the BBC Russian Service's arts programme "West End". Since his arrival in the West, Zinik has written six novels and a number of short stories which have been translated into many European languages. His most famous novel *The Mushroom Picker* has been adapted for television by BBC2. His most recent novel *The Lord and the Game-keeper* is also available in English translation. The general theme of Zinik's novels and stories is the double life of Russian emigres abroad.

About the Authors

YURI MILOSLAVSKY was born in 1946 in Kharkov, Ukraine. He emigrated in 1973 and is at present a lecturer at Michigan University, Ann Arbor. He began writing in emigration and has been widely published in the Russian emigre press (*Kontinent, Echo, 22,* etc). A collection of his stories is available in English translation: *From the Noise of Horsemen and Bowmen*, Ardis, Ann Arbor, 1984; in French translation: *Romances de ville*, Actes Sud, 1990.

The main subject of his work is life back home — the Kharkov slums and hoodlums, the cruelty and the coarseness of the everyday life he observed in childhood and is now trying to expell from his system through his writing. His first novel, *Fortified Cities*, came out in 1980 and provoked controversy in the Russian emigre world. "The novel is disrespectful towards both dissidents and the law-abiding, towards emigres and the people back home, towards the Soviet bureaucracy and Israeli authorities, towards Soviet and anti-Soviet mythology. Miloslavsky's rich figurative prose, and his ability to depict the ugliness of everyday life both mercilessly and poetically makes him one of the foremost authors writing in Russian today. Miloslavsky insists that his novel is simply a love story, about a love that is crushed by the machine of state suppression. By moving to another country his characters acquire neither freedom nor happiness." — critic Alla Latynina, chairman of the Russian Booker Prize.

LEV RAZGON, born 1908 in Byelorus, is a noted critic and essayist. Graduate of the History Department of Moscow University he was active as a children's writer and critic before he was arrested in 1938 on a trumped-up charge, like millions of other innocent Russians in the 1930s and 40s. He was released in 1956, his spiritual fiber intact and immediately resumed his literary work writing fictionalized documentary novels about scientists and scholars as well as books for children.

His most famous book, *True Stories* (Kniga Publishers, 1989) is a collection of memoirs about fellow inmates from the labour camps. Despite the grim subject the book radiates love of life and a keen interest in people. It was reprinted several times in Russia and also published in France, Greece, and Germany. The story we offer you in this issue of Glas comes from this book.

About the Authors

MARINA TSVETAYEVA (1892-1941), a Moscow poet and prose writer is one the greatest Russian lyric poets of the 20th century. She wrote compulsively — poetry, letters, mytho-autobiography, verse plays and criticism. Her lyric poems fill ten volumes and are characterised by neologisms, onomatopoeia, and poliphony, all of which present a special challenge to translators but won her high praise from Akhmatova, Pasternak and other critics and readers of Russian verse.

Her fate was the most tragic of all the poets. Her husband, Sergei Efron, who she married in 1912, served during the Civil War in Russia as an officer in the White Army, but she was trapped in Moscow until 1922. One of her daughters died of starvation in an orphanage. From 1922 to 1925 she lived in Prague and then in Paris until 1939, always desperately poor. As a suspected agent of the GPU (the Soviet secret service) Efron was forced to flee France and went back to Moscow. Tsvetayeva followed him there only to find out that he had been executed on his return and that their daughter had been sent to a camp. When the war broke out Tsvetayeva was evacuated to the town of Elabuga in the Urals where she hanged herself in August 1941.

As woman poets of the same generation, Tsvetayeva and Akhmatova were often compared. The two reflected to a degree the contrasting characters of their cities. Akhmatova, the poet of the north, grand in her restraint and solemnity, Tsvetayeva, the Muscovite boiling over with intense emotion and highly charged poetic phrases, Tsvetayeva wrote a cycle of poems dedicated to Akhmatova in 1916 which Akhmatova carried in her purse until they disintegrated, but she nevertheless kept a certain distance. In 1940 the two poets met for the first time spending two days together in conversation. Temporarily overcoming their terrible circumstances "Tsvetayeva was sparkling. She was full of Paris and talked brilliantly." Isaiah Berlin quotes Akhmatova as saying: "Marina is a better poet than I am". — *Roberta Reeder* (from the notes to *Complete Poems of Anna Akhmatona*)

GLEB ARSENYEV is the pseudonym of Yuri Alexandrovich Sorokin, (b. 1936) poet, professor of Philology, a senior research fellow at the Institute of Linguistics. He specializes in psycholinguistics and the theory of communications, cultural studies, focusing on the problems of national specifics of speech and non-speech behavior, and ethnic conflictology. He has also published a popular science book *The Life and Death of Books* as well as translating poetry from the European languages and from Chinese. A sinologist by training, he has been a member of the underground literary group SMOG and a leader of the literary group known as "Russian Beatniks".

About the Authors

OLGA SEDAKOVA was born in 1949 in Moscow where she received her Ph.D. in Philology from the Slavic and Balkan Languages Institute, writing a dissertation on "Funeral Rites". She belongs to the "lost generation" of the 1970s writers, the generation led by Brodski, who were not published at home and thus remained little known to the reading public. Her first collection came out from YMCA Press in Paris. Her highly refined verse is apolitical and visionary, falling into the category of neo-traditionalism. Lately her verse has been widely published in literary periodicals and a collection of her poems appeared from Carte Blanche Publishers in Moscow in 1992.

ALLA LATYNINA is one of the most influential critics in Russia today. She does not belong to any literary grouping and is known for her independent mind, erudition and biting wit. Almost each article she writes inspires long and heated debates. Her extensive philological and philosophical background lends her articles a highly individual style and a wealth of varied information.

Alla Latynina graduated from the Department of Philology, Moscow University and later from the post-graduate department of the Faculty of Philosophy where she defended her thesis on "Existentialist Interpretation of Dostoyevsky." Her other interests embrace Apollon Grigoryev and Vsevolod Garshin.

Since 1980s, Alla Latynina has been mainly writing about contemporary literary developments, movements and trends. She has published more than 100 articles and essays in the country's leading periodicals. She also has three books to her credit: *Vsevolod Garshin:His life and Fate* (1986), *The Signs of the Times*, about literature of the early 1980s (1988), *Beyond the Open Barrier* (1991) about the literature of perestroika. She is a columnist on the *Literary Gazette* and was the first chairman of the Russian Booker Prize.

ELENA MUKHANOVA's papier-mache figures and panels, reproduced in this issue of *Glas*, are a beautiful woman's protest against the ugliness of the modern world and the wish to transform that ugliness into beauty by the sheer force of love. At the same time her figures convey an apocalyptic message from a sensitive artist witnessing the collapse of a habitual world. Elena herself claims that her style was largely inspired by Evgeny Zamyatin's *We*, which she had been illustrating. The theme of a breaking world conveyed in a language of exquisite beauty and original imagery — this is what Elena tries to capture in her work. She has had several one-man shows including one in Paris. She glorifies the fat woman as a natural woman, and this is another protest against an accepted norm.